ALL the BETTER to SEE YOU

GINA BLAXILL

SCHOLASTIC

Published in the UK by Scholastic, 2021
Euston House, 24 Eversholt Street, London, NW1 1DB
Scholastic Ireland, 89E Lagan Road, Dublin
Industrial Estate, Glasnevin, Dublin, D11 HP5F

ISBN 978 0702 31014 0

A CIP catalogue record for this book
is available from the British Library.

Printed by CPI Group (UK) Ltd, Croydon, CR0 4YY
Paper made from wood grown in sustainable forests
and other controlled sources.

1 3 5 7 9 10 8 6 4 2

This is a work of fiction. Names, characters, places, incidents and
dialogues are products of the author's imagination or are used
fictitiously. Any resemblance to actual people, living or dead,
events or locales is entirely coincidental.

www.scholastic.co.uk

To Guy, who I hope will always love reading

PROLOGUE

"Tell me a story." The child's voice was drowsy.

"I am a physician, not a storyteller." But the doctor took pity on the feverish boy and drew a stool up to the bed. The creaky bedroom was lit by a single candle positioned on the windowsill and, now the wind had died down, it felt warm and comforting. "I will tell you a short one. My favourite tale as a child was about a wolf, but it is hardly soothing. Have you heard of the wolf of Aramor?"

"My parents say the big bad wolf is just a legend."

"Not where I come from. It was real, very real. This wolf held the whole town prisoner, not just one long, bitter winter, but two. It dwelled in the deep, dark, ancient forest, only emerging at night. Then it would hunt for prey. Human prey."

The doctor paused, watching closely. The little boy looked more focused than he had a moment ago, even a touch less feverish. Perhaps this was the right story to tell, after all.

So the doctor resumed. "Growing up, we were taught to be vigilant. Be aware. Be safe. Never, ever go in the forest. If you have to, stick to the path. Other wolves made their home in Aramor's forest, but none like this one. Some believed it to be a phantom, conjured by a malevolent sorcerer. Those who saw it and lived – and there were very few – described it as an enormous, stinking beast with thick black fur. Eyes that were almost red, too. All the better for seeing you. Huge, pointed ears. All the better for hearing you. Most deadly and frightening of all, a set of big, sharp teeth. All the better to eat you with!"

The child shot into a sitting position, round-eyed. After a moment, he smiled and leaned into his pillow. The doctor smiled back.

"Am I frightening you? I liked to be frightened as a child, though others told me this made me strange."

"Who did it eat? What happened? Were you there?"

The doctor's eyes closed. Even years on, the winters of the wolf were painful to remember. Every attack – the scars, the blood, the panic – was etched deep in the minds of everyone in Aramor. Worst was the fear. Not knowing who to trust, or who to suspect.

Eventually the doctor said, "Yes. I was there. Although even now I do not know the full truth about what happened, I do know that it is not as people think. It is a rather dark tale and too long for tonight, but I suppose I can tell you a little. So." The doctor smiled again. "The big bad wolf, and Little Red Riding Hood."

"Who is she?"

"I will get to that. Now. Once upon a time, in the ancient forest of Aramor. . ."

The girl was back. Her hooded cape flashed in between the spindly tree trunks and naked branches. There was a spring in her step as she strode along the path that led deep into the forest, sometimes wandering across the muddied grass to inspect a shrub, or stopping to crane her neck at an owl's *twit-twoo*. Unlike the others who dared venture this far, she never seemed afraid, even in the dark.

The wolf bared its teeth and slunk deeper into the foliage, stalking the girl silently. Her delicious scent lingered in the air. The wolf's mouth watered as it remembered its last human prey. Saliva dripped from its jaws. If the wolf wished to, it would be easy to leap from the bushes, bowl her over and sink sharp teeth into her smooth, young skin. She would not have time to scream or struggle. A girl her size would provide food for days. Raw, firm flesh.

Hungry, so hungry. And so cold. The wolf whimpered. Frosty specks drifted from above and settled in the grooves of the hard mud. Winter days were difficult and empty and a struggle to survive.

The wolf needed to feed. Needed prey. Needed meat.

And soon.

RED

Deep behind her, something snapped. Red paused, shifting the package she was carrying from one arm to the other. Was someone there?

But all she could hear were the usual evening sounds of the forest: the soft hush of branches as they rocked one way to the other, and a muted bird's cheep. It was a shame, Red thought as she started walking again, that everyone else's fear prevented them from seeing the forest of Aramor as she did. Really, it was quite beautiful. Tall, elegant trees with silver flecks across the bark, leaves a lush green in summer, the little stream with a gentle trickle, and the many different birds who were really very tame, and would hop right up to Red's feet when she tossed them crumbs. In winter, the naked trees were somewhat foreboding, but there was still a certain beauty in the glimmer of ice on water and the clean, unspoiled whiteness of snow.

There was the wolf, of course, but Red heard scare stories about the wolf so constantly that she'd long ago stopped listening. It seemed silly for grown men and women to be so afraid of an animal who hadn't been seen for five years. Red only remembered what people still called "the winter of the wolf" in vague snatches. Several townsfolk, mostly woodsmen and traders who cut through the forest to more quickly reach the city road, had been dragged off and eaten. That winter, hiding at home with the door bolted and windows firmly shattered, had lasted an age.

Back then she'd been a child, free to spend her days wandering the forest picking flowers and dipping her toes in the stream. The big bad wolf was probably long dead. Certainly Red had never seen it, and she escaped to the forest whenever she could, much to the despair of her mother.

Red grinned; then, remembering what had happened earlier, her expression fell.

By the time the candle Granny placed in her cottage's front window every night came into view, it was entirely dark. Mother would not be pleased she was out so late. Red quickened her step and knocked smartly on the door.

"It's only me," she called. She had to wait some minutes before clicking told her Granny was unlatching the door.

"Is this a bad time?" she asked as the door swung open and Granny, bundled in a thick sheep's-wool shawl and straight-backed despite her age, appeared. Her smile made her chestnut-brown eyes twinkle.

"It's never a bad time to see my granddaughter." She sounded a touch out of breath as she adjusted her slightly lopsided coif. Normally Granny was not this dishevelled. "Look at your rosy cheeks! Come and get warm. I hope you stuck to the path like a good girl; don't you know how dangerous the forest is?"

Red giggled. "Mother's voice isn't anywhere near as high-pitched as that."

"Is this better?" Granny boomed, and Red giggled again.

"Worse! Are you all right, Granny? You seem a little..."

"Old and slow?" Granny laughed, and Red decided to leave it. She must have disturbed Granny napping.

"You never seem old to me, Granny. You are right, though."

She sighed. "Mother will tell me off when I get home, for sure. She doesn't want me visiting if it's getting dusky, but if I didn't then I would never see you at all. Most of the time I don't get out of the bakery in daylight, not now the days are so short."

Granny made a sympathetic noise, taking Red's cape and hanging it alongside her own. Even though Granny rarely lit a fire, preferring to draw warmth from many layers of clothing, her ramshackle cottage always felt welcoming to Red. It was tiny – one room which doubled as a bedroom and a parlour, separated by a tapestried curtain, and then a kitchen which was so cramped Red often bumped herself turning from the cupboard to the wonky wooden table where Granny prepared meals. Even though she had never lived here, it felt a lot more like home than the house Red shared with her mother.

"Talking of the bakery, are those by any chance honeyed buns?" Granny took Red's package and placed it on her knees as she eased down into her rocking chair. "Oh, dried fruit, wonderful. How is everything there?"

Red joined her, pulling up a stool. Granny pretended otherwise, but her eyesight wasn't what it had been even a year ago. "I still hate it. I suppose it's not the worst place I could work, but I am honestly so bad at everything. Kneading dough takes serious strength, and though my arms aren't as spindly as they used to be, it's hard work. I'm not very good at stewing fruit or meat for pies either – I always cut things wrong, or burn something. And I don't have Martha's eye for decoration, not that she'd let me help with her precious iced biscuits even if I did."

"Too much of a lady for the hard work, is she?"

"Something like that." Red played with the cuff of her gown, which was crusty with dried dough. "She's going to shout at me tomorrow because I got the bread orders muddled. Her parents have already warned me that if I make another mistake I'll have to find another job, but Martha will want to say her piece too, probably." She rubbed her temple. "It was my fault. I got distracted. Maybe I am useless."

"You are not useless, and you will not be made to feel so by vapid girls like Martha Baker." Granny's voice was sharp. "The bakery isn't the right place for your talents, that's all."

"Where would that be?" Red felt helpless. "We tried me working as a seamstress like Mother, but I get so restless squinting over a needle, and no one would employ me as a maid. I always say the wrong things, somehow."

Just one reason she had no friends, Red thought, but did not say so.

"My love." Granny grasped her shoulders, shrewd eyes kind. "I know life has not been easy. But there is nothing wrong with being different. However much other girls make you feel like it is. They feel threatened because you make them look at themselves, that is all."

Red couldn't imagine Martha Baker with her glossy auburn hair and pretty manners ever feeling threatened by her, and Martha wasn't even the worst one. Thank goodness Red saw less of Sabine Forrester these days. Her taunts burned Red's memory like a brand on skin. "The only thing they feel threatened by is the wolf."

"That old scare story?"

"People are talking about it again. The Millers' chicken coop was broken into. They found feathers trailing to the edge of the forest. And a couple of people say they've seen it." Red leaned forwards, taking her grandmother's hand. It felt bonier than it used to. Weaker, too. "Granny, will you really be safe out here? It worries me sometimes, you being so far from town, and alone."

Granny laughed. "I've not been eaten yet."

"Granny, I'm serious. Maybe you could stay with us for winter."

"If I had to share a house with your mother I would be driven mad, and that is much more frightening than an animal that may or may not exist. You're not scared, are you?"

Red hesitated. Was she? "Other people are, and that makes me think I should be too."

"I say you shouldn't be. The townsfolk are far too fixated by this one animal. There have always been packs of wolves in the forest. They are shy creatures, more afraid of us than we are of them." More softly, Granny said, "My beautiful granddaughter . . . a life of fear is not a life at all. Walk tall and do not doubt yourself. If you ask me, the town is the place that is really dangerous."

"What do you mean?"

"Never mind. What I am saying is, don't listen to other people. The only thing you should listen to is your heart."

She made it sound so simple. Even though Red wasn't sure Granny was right, she felt, just in that second, powerful. "I wish I was more like you."

"We're more alike than you know, Little Red Riding Hood. Let's try these buns and talk of happier things, shall we?"

Red smiled at her childhood pet name as she rose to fetch a knife. "As you wish, Granny. Who's afraid of the big bad wolf, anyway?"

ELLIS

There was no doubt about it, thought Ellis. The chicken coop had been ripped apart. The big question was who was responsible.

"It is envy, pure and simple," Ellis's father was saying for what felt like the hundredth time. Mr and Mistress Miller were inside the house, right next to the mill, but the front door was ajar and Ellis could hear the conversation even outside. "People resent us. They see our new shoes and warm cloaks and assume everything is easy. They want to see us suffer like they do."

"They did not have the opportunity we did." His mother's voice was cold and, Ellis thought, loaded. There was a shuffling noise. He imagined his father moving close, putting his arm around her.

"We did what we had to, my love. That was a long time ago. We needed to protect ourselves, our future."

Whatever his mother said next, Ellis didn't catch it. The next voice was his father's, clear and brisk.

"I had a nasty altercation in town earlier. Accused of overcharging for flour. Amos Baker got quite aggressive. And that woman was poking her nose into things that do not concern her again."

"Sometimes I think she knows. Or at least suspects."

What woman? Ellis hesitated, then edged closer to the door.

"You worry too much, Tamasin." And yet his father's voice was guarded. "No one knows."

"But what if someone does?"

A sudden gust of wind blew the door shut, making Ellis jump. He rubbed the side of his nose, feeling slightly grubby for eavesdropping. His parents sniping about their neighbours wasn't new, or even interesting, but lately there had been a lot of vague, ominous conversations between them that stopped the moment Ellis or his brothers appeared. Ellis could not imagine his upstanding parents doing anything that needed to be kept secret, or lying. All the same, he wondered. . .

Neither would tell him anything so there was no point asking. At almost fifteen they still treated him like a child. And he had better things to think about. Like the archery tournament he was planning with the other boys. He'd tell Martha about it when he delivered flour to the bakery tomorrow. She would definitely want to cheer him on. "One of the things I like about you is that you are better than the other boys at absolutely everything," she'd said the other day, and even though Ellis had laughed and protested that she was exaggerating, it was true that a lot of things did come easily to him. Maybe his parents would even come and watch this time.

Ellis inspected the coop again. It wouldn't be too tough to fix with the right tools and sturdy wood. Ellis had always been good at jobs like this, enjoyed them, too, though he'd left it a bit late to finish today. It was easy to forget how quickly darkness descended in winter.

Out of the corner of his eye he caught a flash of red.

Ellis frowned, wiping his grubby palms on his breeches. The forest wasn't far from the mill. Although he rarely had any time, what with helping his parents and chasing around after his younger brothers, sometimes on warm, light evenings he strolled to the trees and inhaled the peace and quiet and fresh, earthy smell. . . He never actually went in, of course. Not that stupid. Everything he cared about was in the town, anyway.

Red. . .

Of course. The girl from the bakery, the one Martha said was strange and clumsy. She always wore a red hooded cape. The way she stared when he delivered flour, as though he was some kind of exotic animal, was unsettling. Ellis couldn't remember her real name.

He should really jog over and shout at her to get out. She probably hadn't heard about the chickens. From what he saw she lived in a dream world. Or perhaps she was simple. Strange or not, he didn't want her mauled.

He sprinted across the field to where he'd caught that flash of red.

"Hey! Stop." Too slow – all he could see was darkness. Ellis raked sandy hair out of his eyes, debating what to do. He could chase after her, or shrug and turn back – he had lots to do, after all, and if she got eaten it was her fault for being stupid in the first place. He was fairly sure she hadn't stuck to the path, either. That looped south, and Red had been heading south-west.

He really should chase after her. It was the right thing to do, even if his friends would laugh at him for caring what happened to a girl like Red. He would be safe enough – he still had the axe in his hand, and you didn't work in a mill without building up serious upper-body strength.

For a moment, Ellis pictured himself running after Red, reaching her just at the moment the wolf slinked out of the trees ready to pounce... One well-timed blow, and it would be all over. Surely ridding Aramor of the big bad wolf would make his parents proud of him.

And now I am the stupid one, he thought, *because in the time I've spent imagining something that is never going to happen, she has well and truly gone.* His shoulders slumped. It was childish to picture himself as any kind of hero, the kind of daydream he ought to have grown out of. Feeling a bit guilty, he trailed back home.

Red would have to take her chances.

${SABINE}$

The bakery was always warm, even when closed, and Sabine had always liked how it smelled – so much more pleasant than her own home, where the air was thick with whatever dire dinner had been cobbled together out of nothing and angry shrieks from one child or another. Seven children and two adults in one cramped cottage did not a restful home make. Once upon a time, when woodcutting had been a more lucrative profession, it had been different. Never a day passed that she didn't count her blessings that she was out of there now. Compared to sharing a bed with a sister who snored and wriggled, kicking Sabine with ice-cold feet, her small attic bedroom in the manor house was heavenly.

"And then what happened?" Sabine tore a strip off an unsold yeast loaf. She was only half-listening to Martha's story about how she'd earlier snatched five minutes alone in the yard with Ellis Miller and he'd stroked her hair and told her it was the colour of a malted bun. As though malted buns were romantic! Sabine's hair was reddish brown, and she preferred it drawn tightly back so as to not distract her.

"That's it, the end of the story." Martha shot her a dirty look. "You weren't listening, were you?"

"All your Ellis stories are the same. Is it him you think is so special, or is it other girls being jealous you really like?"

Martha smiled and twirled one of her curls; it was the latter, then. "You're so unromantic. Why does everything have to have some other motive? He likes me, and I like him, and it is as simple as that."

"I'm sure."

"He does like me. He always lingers when he delivers the flour, asks me about myself and if we can walk together. It makes the day worth trudging through. Most people consider him very handsome, you know. His mother was the town beauty when she was our age. I think you're jealous."

"I'm tired of talking about him, that's all."

"Because you'd rather talk about the wolf?" Martha sneered, but Sabine smiled and popped the last strip of yeast loaf into her mouth.

"It's a million times more exciting than some gormless boy peddling unimpressive flattery."

"He is not gormless!" Martha snapped, and Sabine laughed.

"Don't get upset. I'm joking." She lowered her voice. "The last time the wolf menaced town that started with chickens, too... How long before it moves on to people? I have a feeling it is going to be a very long winter. Hiding in our houses after dark, jumping at every single creak or footstep, wondering who will be attacked next..."

"That was years ago. Ellis reckons one of the neighbours stole the chickens, anyway."

"That's what he would say. He doesn't want you to worry."

Uncertainty flickered in Martha's eyes. "Why do you think that?"

"He seems the kind of unimaginative boy who thinks he needs to protect people." Sabine leaned forwards, voice now a whisper. "Don't you think it was strange? A whole winter cowed in fear, then spring comes and the wolf vanishes, just like that. Almost... magic. No one has seen it since."

"Because it's dead. Wolves don't live more than a few years. Do they?"

"There have been stories about the wolf ever since our grandparents were little. . ."

"Not the same wolf," said Martha. "That's impossible."

"Is it? All the descriptions are the same. Matted black fur, almost unnaturally bright eyes . . . not an ordinary wolf. Certainly not one of the grey wolves woodsmen sometimes see running in packs, though there are far fewer now. Perhaps the big bad wolf has eaten them too."

"Sabine. Don't. It's just an animal. It's certainly not a being of . . . that."

"Witchcraft?"

"Stop it." Martha drew back, cheeks pink. She glanced over her shoulder. "We shouldn't even be talking about this. If someone heard. . ."

Sabine was always amazed by the power that word had over people. Witchcraft. It was pathetic, really, how afraid people were of what they couldn't explain. "All I'm saying is it isn't natural. I bet it is the same wolf. I hope so, anyway."

A floorboard creaked above. Both girls jumped. Martha slid off her stool.

"You'd better go. That stupid Red muddled orders today so tomorrow we'll need to make more bread. I wouldn't mind if she was decent company but most days she says nothing all day. Literally, nothing."

"Nothing she has to say would be worth listening to." Sabine's lip curled as she pictured abrupt, awkward Red, with her cumbersome arms and legs and perplexed eyes almost hidden under tangled dark hair which she never seemed to brush. It made Sabine laugh every time she remembered that Red's given name was Grace. How ill-suited! "Can't you find some way of getting rid of Red? There are only so many mistakes your parents will tolerate, surely?"

"I don't want to get into trouble."

Sabine rolled her eyes as she pulled the hood of her cape up. What Martha really meant was that Red was no competition for Ellis's attention, whereas another girl might be. She was so easy to read. Most people were.

Not Red, though.

Stupid, strange Red.

Outside, the chill made her pick up her pace. Sabine could do the short walk to the manor house blindfolded. Cut past the run of merchants' shops – the tailors, grocers, butchers. Cross the town square where once a week traders from nearby towns set up stalls with whatever was left from their most recent foray to the city. Trudge past the taller, richer dwellings to the track that crossed the river, curtsying if you encountered a guard on patrol. Ten minutes later the manor house would loom up, and Sabine would be swallowed into the comfortable lives of Lord Josiah and Lady Katherine. There were worse places to be employed, and a lady's maid was an unusually good position for a peasant girl, as her mother constantly reminded her, but most days Sabine swore she could feel her brain shrinking.

Fourteen years, and she had gone nowhere and done nothing.

Pathetic, really. The wolf had better be back, else she'd be dead of something much more frightening – boredom.

RED

By the time Red burst from the forest – face hot, and the toes of her boots dark with moisture from snow – she was out of breath. Why had she stayed so long with Granny? She'd intended to drop the buns off, share a bowl of soup, then be straight home, but, like always, she'd got distracted by Granny's stories, and then suddenly the outside world was black. Not dusky black, but proper black. The kind of black where something could creep up on you unseen...

The cottage front door swung open before Red reached it. Her mother stood there, skinny arms crossed.

"Where have you been?" she cried. "You finished at the bakery hours ago."

Red wetted her lips. "Only with Granny."

"And that makes worrying me better?"

"I'm sorry."

"Not an answer." Her mother stalked inside, and Red caught the door before it could slam. Inside, the cottage was the complete opposite of Granny's: spotlessly clean and tidy, piles of embroidery stacked and sorted, smelling only faintly of woodsmoke. "Grace, you have to stop doing this, please."

"Visiting Granny?"

"No! Going out after dark by yourself. It isn't safe. Especially now. Why is this so difficult for you to understand? None of the other girls go wandering through the forest."

Red's cheeks turned the colour of her hood. Those words again: none of the other girls. "Nothing bad has ever happened to me there."

"But it could. That is my point. You don't even stick to the paths, do you?"

Red wanted to say "the path doesn't always go where I want to go" but she had a feeling that would not be a good idea. "I'll try harder."

"You've said that before," her mother snapped, but now she sounded helpless as well as annoyed. She glanced round the room. Wondering why her daughter was the one thing that couldn't be neatly sorted into place, thought Red.

"I didn't want to upset you, Mother."

"Sometimes that isn't how it feels."

"Granny says I shouldn't be afraid."

"Granny should know better. It's all very well for her to do exactly as she pleases, she's had her time, but she shouldn't encourage you." Mother sighed, body sagging. Her forehead was lined in a way Red swore it had not been earlier in the year, hair further streaked with grey. "Oh, Grace. Why can't you be like everyone else? I've tried my best, but it's starting to feel like I have failed. . . All I want for you is to have a safe, easy life, but you make it so difficult. And you never listen."

"I do listen. And I do try to get along with people and do what I'm supposed to, even if you think otherwise. It's just. . . It's hard."

"No young man will ever be interested in you if you carry on in this way."

Red turned so her mother couldn't see how much the words stung. She thought of how Ellis Miller had looked this morning, standing at the back door of the bakery, with his easy, genuine smile, lively green eyes and broad shoulders, sack of flour under his arm like it weighed nothing. Boys like him did not want girls who said the wrong things and knew about plants and trees and birds. They liked girls like Martha, who knew how to keep them interested and make them feel important.

The humiliation burned. For once Red was glad the room was lit only by a single candle. She could just imagine how Sabine and Martha would laugh if they noticed the way she looked at Ellis. Sabine had sneered before that Red was destined to end up a sad outcast crone, being pelted with pebbles by small children whenever she dared to step out of her house. And Red feared she was right.

Mother locked the door, then moved round checking the windows were shuttered. Red closed her eyes, forcing herself to take deep, calming breaths. Being boxed in, without fresh air, always made her jittery.

"Can't we have a window open, just a touch?" she asked.

"No. It isn't safe."

She'd heard about the Millers' chickens too, then. "The wolf never comes this far into town. We should be fine."

"I am not taking that chance."

"Are we going to sit by candlelight in this room every evening, waiting for winter to pass, then?"

"If that is what it takes to get through it, yes."

Her mother stalked into the kitchen to where a pot was bubbling on the stove. Her hands shook as she picked up the ladle and sniffed. Red knew she ought to give her a hug and apologize, but it was starting to feel like all she ever said to her mother was "sorry" and it didn't change a thing. Whatever she did was never right, somehow. Maybe it was just her that was not "right".

So instead Red took off her cape – the red one which made Granny affectionately call her Little Red Riding Hood – and went to splash the day's grime off her face and prepare for another miserable evening of silence.

ELLIS

The next morning was the fresh, bright kind of day that made it easy to forget the bite in the air and clutches of frost over the fields. Ellis piled the mill cart high with sacks of flour, whistling to himself. Deliveries – which most days his parents were happy for him to take care of – were always something he enjoyed. Milling could be pretty monotonous, not to mention noisy.

"Off we go," he told Dorothy, his parents' sulky grey mare, and at a tug of the reins she set off. Ellis felt his spirits rise as they passed the farms on the edge of town. He called out cheery hellos to the labourers arriving at work, and stopped to chat to a couple of elderly weaver women who always made a fuss of Dorothy and asked after his family. His parents were wrong. Not everyone resented them, something they'd find out themselves if they came this way more.

At the edge of town he met Stephen, one of his friends, who mock saluted Ellis with his cap. He carried a bow and a quiver of arrows. Ellis grinned.

"Getting in plenty of practice? It is almost like you're worried you won't win."

"You are the one who should worry, Miller. Here. See the knobbly bit on the tree, under that branch? I bet you can't hit it."

"Can't I?" Ellis jumped down, taking Stephen's bow. He selected an arrow, drew back the string and released it. A second later it embedded itself in the trunk, right on target.

"You were saying?" Ellis executed a mock bow as he handed Stephen back his bow.

"It's so tempting to hate you sometimes. One day I will find out something you're bad at and make sure you never forget it. And the prettiest girl in Aramor only has eyes for you! Perhaps I do hate you after all."

"It breaks my heart to hear you say that, Stephen."

"Martha's probably sitting on the bakery doorstep pining for you right now." Stephen flickered his eyelashes and clutched at his chest, groaning Ellis's name. Ellis rolled his eyes as he climbed back into the cart.

"That is terrifying. Don't ever do that again, please."

Stephen immediately did, groaning even louder. He dodged the handful of flour Ellis tossed at him. They both laughed as they parted company. Stephen's cheer was the thing Ellis liked about him best. He was small for his age, often the butt of other boys' jibes, but he handled everything with good humour, even though Ellis knew that underneath the grin he did not feel at all secure.

Deciding to start deliveries on the far side of town, then work his way backwards, Ellis spurred Dorothy on, crossing the market square. At the water pump on the other side was Mistress Forrester. Spotting that she was struggling, he halted the cart.

"Can I help you?"

Mistress Forrester smiled, tucking stray hair under her coif. The coif was probably clean but looked grubby; washed and repaired several times, no doubt. Ellis swung himself down. He was expecting the pump to be stiff, but to his surprise it moved without so much as a squeak. Funny. He was aware of her eyes on him as water sloshed into the bucket. Like her daughter Sabine, Mistress

Forrester was none too tall, with the same pointed nose and chin and sharp cheekbones. Although he towered over her, somehow she always made him feel small.

"How is everything at the mill, Ellis?" Her tone was pleasant, conversational. "I hear from the tailor that you're all getting thick new clothes for the winter. Very nice if you can afford them. Your parents must be doing well. But then you're beginning to supply flour to other towns too now, aren't you?"

Wonderful – gossip. Ellis made a non-committal noise and concentrated on the pump. Mistress Forrester leaned close. He felt her breath on his cheek.

"Lord Josiah's been very supportive to your parents, I hear. Not everyone would be happy to lease extra land like he has, or allow the mill to expand. He's not often one to be kind, according to my Sabine. And did I hear he actually visits every few weeks to speak to your parents?"

She clearly knew, so why she was bothering to ask him, Ellis had no idea. He wished he'd pretended he hadn't seen her.

"Not very chatty this morning?" she asked. "Nothing wrong, I hope? If you ever need any ... motherly advice, I'll always be happy to lend a listening ear. Your parents... Well. I know they aren't the warmest people."

This time, Ellis couldn't help but flinch. "Everything is fine."

"Are you sure?" Her eyes swam with sympathy. Almost too much sympathy. Ellis suddenly wondered why Mistress Forrester was at this pump, when there was another much closer to her home.

"I have work to do," he said, and doffed his cap at her. Mistress Forrester watched him clamber into the cart, in no hurry to move. Then she chuckled.

"It's funny."

"What is?"

"You, being so fair still. Your brothers are all dark. It always used to make me smile seeing your mother walk about town with you as a little one. It was almost as if she'd picked the wrong child up."

Ellis narrowed his eyes. She met them. There was something calculated in her gaze that he didn't like. It was the same look Sabine often wore. As though she was summing you up. Then Mistress Forrester turned and hefted up the bucket as though it weighed nothing.

She had definitely been pretending to struggle.

He set off again. Dorothy's hooves clip-clopped on the cobbled paths. A couple of passers-by waved, but Ellis didn't respond. He was frowning, going over the last five minutes.

That comment about his hair . . . it had been pointed. And from what he heard of Mistress Forrester, she never did anything by accident. Ellis rubbed his chin, then wished he hadn't – his fingers were grubby from the pump. He'd have to find somewhere to splash his face before stopping by to say hello to Martha, else she'd wrinkle her nose and complain.

Was Mistress Forrester playing some kind of game? She was a well-known gossip, but he'd never thought her anything more than that. And women with seven children didn't have time to play games, surely? Ellis knew he didn't look much like the rest of his family. Apparently he resembled his mother's father, who'd died before he was born. As far as he was aware, his mother and Mistress Forrester had never been friends.

And that smile.

There was something wolfish in that smile.

RED

"Anything to say?" demanded Martha. Red pressed her fingers to her temples. Were they throbbing? She smacked dough on to the table. It splattered outwards. Too wet. She couldn't even get a basic mix right.

"I've said I'm sorry I made a mistake yesterday."

"Not what I asked."

Red felt weary, and that wasn't just from a patchy night's sleep. She'd already been scolded by Martha's parents. She knew she was as good as useless. What more did Martha want? An apology for existing? Meanwhile there were yeast rolls waiting to be rationed and shaped, and a batch of hardy black loaves to cool.

Last night's argument with Mother kept bouncing around her head. Red had felt so sure of herself when she was speaking to Granny. Now she was having doubts. Maybe her mother was right and Granny was wrong. After all, Granny didn't need to live in the town, did she? And Granny wasn't fourteen, with a whole lifetime to pave and navigate.

Keep quiet, she thought. *Don't be strange. Then maybe everyone will let you be.* "No, nothing, Martha."

Martha looked taken aback at Red's meek tone. She opened her mouth, then instead turned her attention to arranging baskets of small cheese loaves to go in the shop window. A lock of hair escaped from her braid. It gleamed rich auburn in the light. Red felt a stab of envy. If only she was pretty and dainty, then life would be so much easier.

The girls worked in silence for the next ten minutes, interrupted only by Mistress Baker coming in to check the oven. *I hate bread,* thought Red, and with every smack of dough against the table, she thought it louder and louder. *Hate bread. Hate bread. Hate bread.*

"I hate bread."

"Excuse me?" Martha's eyes swelled. Had Red said that out loud? Help, she had. At that moment, there was a smart rap at the door. A second later Ellis poked his head round it. Red let out a breath. What good timing!

"Two sacks of the freshest and finest flour," Ellis announced. He was smiling as usual, but it didn't meet his eyes. Had something happened? "Where would you like them?"

"Where do you think?" Martha purred, and Red scowled, knowing full well what that meant. She still cringed when she remembered the time she had gone to see if Ellis and Martha needed help in the storeroom after they had been gone a suspiciously long time. They'd broken apart before she appeared at the door, but the pinkness in Martha's cheeks and the tousle of Ellis's hair were etched into her brain. She felt a naive fool for not realizing they'd be kissing – and how much it bothered her.

"Of course." Red hated the way Ellis looked at Martha, like she was one of the malted buns he was so fond of. Martha wetted her lips, glancing at Red. "Come and get me if my parents shout."

Red smacked dough against the table in response. Martha snaked her hand round Ellis's waist. Ellis, however, was looking at Red.

"What made you go into the forest last night? I saw you from the mill. Thought maybe you'd wandered in by mistake. By the time I was close enough to warn you, you'd gone."

Her heart did a strange skippy thing and for a moment stopped. Ellis Miller had noticed her?

"My granny lives there."

"Oh! I didn't realize you were related. Why does she live all the way out there? Doesn't it get lonely?"

"She says not."

"I see." Ellis sounded doubtful. Probably he couldn't even imagine being alone himself – people flocked to him like bees to honey. "I am glad nothing bad happened, anyway. Maybe not the best idea, going in there by yourself at the moment."

Was he saying this because he cared? Or because he was the kind of person who liked to be friendly to everyone?

"Red does plenty of stupid things," said Martha, impatiently. "She just said she hated bread."

Ellis laughed. But it wasn't a nasty laugh. And then he leaned forwards – towards Red. "Sometimes I think I hate flour," he whispered. "But don't tell my parents that. If they ask, I love it more than life itself. I dream about it. Wonderful, lovely flour."

Red giggled, and Ellis grinned.

"Your name isn't really Red, is it?"

"It's Grace. But my granny made me a red cape as a child and everyone started calling me Little Red Riding Hood. The nickname stuck."

"And you're still wearing red capes. Not the same one, I assume."

"It would be a bit small by now."

"Most things are too small for you, aren't they, Red?" Martha cut in, and Red was immediately ashamed of her big hands and feet with their specially made boots that didn't look a dissimilar size to Ellis's. Before she could reply there was a bellow from the front of the bakery. Martha grabbed the baskets she'd been arranging, scowling. Red opened the door to the passageway that led out front, closing it behind her. Ellis heaved the sacks of flour into the storeroom. He paced up and down. Red tried to pretend he wasn't there. Minutes passed. Then Ellis sighed.

"Better get on. I can't wait for Martha. Time is money, my parents say."

"Is everything all right?"

Ellis looked startled, and Red wished she hadn't spoken. Now he knew she'd been looking. "Why wouldn't it be?"

"You seem different, that's all. Is it the chickens?"

He hesitated. "Sort of. Not the chickens themselves – we have new ones arriving today – but . . . well. My parents seem convinced someone means them ill. The way they have been talking, it's like. . ."

"Go on."

"There is some kind of secret. Something they've done. And maybe that is why people dislike them. . ." He gave a short laugh. "I don't know why I'm telling you this. I'm probably imagining it. Everyone is unsettled, that's all. Including, apparently, me."

And his usual smile returned. Red wasn't fooled. Unsettled. That was a good way of describing the mood right now. Red thought back to her walk to the bakery. On the face of it, everything was normal – shops opening their doors, small children tossing sticks for dogs, early-rising housewives throwing buckets of waste into the drains. Yet there had been an undercurrent of something else: shuttered windows, hushed conversations, deep creases between eyebrows. . .

"Why does everyone care so much about the wolf?" she burst out. "It ate a few people five years ago. That was horrible, of course it was, but it's one animal. It could be hunted down if people were really afraid. It must be old by now. I don't believe the stories that it's been around for decades and is somehow unnatural."

Ellis flinched, and Red stopped. "Ignore me. I forget myself sometimes. I'm sorry you're worried about your parents."

"I just want a simple life," said Ellis, eventually. "I don't want— Never mind."

He moved to the door at the same time as Red. Their arms brushed. Red shivered – but not in a good way. A sudden sense of something ominous rose up in her. . .

She opened her mouth to call "wait". Then she closed it. *Do not act strange.* Instead she watched Ellis step up into the cart. Seconds later she heard the clip-clop of hooves.

Unsettled. It wasn't just that people were worried, Red thought. They were waiting for something to happen, whether they fully realized it or not.

Something bad.

ELLIS

A high-pitched squeal tore Ellis from sleep. He rocketed to a sitting position, disorientated and breathing rapidly. In his dreams, he had been sliding over ice trying and failing to draw his bow. His parents were shouting at him to herd chickens like a sheepdog, but Ellis had lost control of his limbs and couldn't stop spiralling, round and round.

Inside his room it was black apart from moonlight shining through a gap in the shutters. He must have been asleep a couple of hours. Had he imagined the noise? Or was it just the disturbing dream? He'd returned from town to find the chicken coop restocked. His parents had talked of little else all afternoon and evening, so perhaps—

There was a dull thud. Squealing. Clucking. More thudding. Ellis launched out of bed, pulling on hose, doublet and boots, grabbing his cloak from the back of his door, and hastening down the wooden staircase to the back door. There he grabbed the axe he used for chopping firewood. Whoever had stolen the first lot of chickens was going to regret returning! How dare they do this to his family?

Outside ice crunched softly underfoot as Ellis crept round the side of the cottage towards the coop. The chickens were frenzied now, flapping round squawking. Then there was a low ripping sound. The coop, being torn open. The thief wasn't trying to hide what they were doing.

Ellis counted to three, then stepped out into the moonlight, clutching the axe.

"Don't you dare—"

The next second his back smacked against the side of the house, knocking him breathless. The axe thumped on to the grass. A shape tore into him. Savage pain erupted from his shoulder. Ellis yelled in agony. Bright eyes flashed above him. Everything was claws, and teeth, and blood.

SABINE

Sabine squatted, holding her candle over the herb garden and doing her best to ignore the chill of the night air. Her breath escaped in wispy tendrils. There it was – chamomile. Balancing the candle on the grass, she tore a bundle of the white flowered plant and slipped it into her muslin pouch. Sabine could not remember when she had first discovered that chamomile eased her sleep, or even when she had first started experimenting with grinding and mixing herbs. Combined with the nameless green root that grew by the river south of the village, chamomile was even more potent.

Sabine knew what people would say if they saw her collection of herbs. How absurd it was that they would be considered dangerous. No one batted an eyelash when Lord Josiah and Lady Katherine's physician prescribed poultices or potions, but then he was a man of fine standing with years of practice and education.

She had better be quick. Visiting the herb garden openly was risky. Confident that no one had seen or heard her slip out, Sabine gathered up the candle and her skirts and prepared to slip through the side door.

Then there was a shout.

She whipped round, poised to bolt behind the closest tree. A small figure was pelting up the path from town, arms windmilling. Sabine squinted. A child? She glanced over her shoulder. If she couldn't see him properly, then he couldn't see her. Should she slip back inside? Getting involved with other people's troubles made her wary.

The child shouted again. And Sabine could make out the word. *Help.*

Sabine cursed under her breath. Martha might joke that she was cold, but she wasn't *that* cold. By the time she reached the gate the child was doubled over and panting. It was one of the younger Miller boys. Sabine crouched by his side.

"What is wrong?"

The child wheezed, gasping for breath. Sabine could not make out all the words. But two jumped out at her.

Doctor. And *wolf.*

Lord Josiah's physician went from asleep to alert within seconds when Sabine knocked on his door in the south wing of the manor. Immediately he gathered various implements and bottles from the cupboard at one end of his room. For an old man Doctor Ambrose was surprisingly nimble. Sabine watched, knowing she should retreat to her room but secretly intrigued.

"Mauled, you say?" Ambrose demanded. "And the lad can't move his arm or shoulder?"

"Something like that. His brother's still outside. He'll have caught his breath by now."

"No matter." The doctor swept most of the middle shelf into his sturdy cloth bag, ramming a pair of thick glasses on to his nose. "I will need assistance either way. Grab warmer clothes. Quick, now."

"Me?"

"I don't see anyone else, do you? My assistant is sick. You are here."

Sabine opened her mouth, then closed it and sped to her room, taking the stairs two at a time. A little thrill danced through her.

A sleepy-looking groom was bringing a horse and cart round to the gate when Sabine emerged. The Miller boy's teeth chattered as he hugged himself. He looked ready to keel over, though his wool cloak looked thick and new. How long would it take to run here from the mill, twenty minutes? The apothecary in town was far closer.

Sabine climbed into the cart, instructing the boy to sit beside her.

"I hope your duties with her ladyship aren't pressing ones tomorrow." Doctor Ambrose joined them, giving the reins a firm tug. "We'll be gone some time."

This was far more exciting than listening to Lady Katherine ruminate about whichever tedious book she was studying, or strolling round the garden, but Sabine kept that to herself. Even the track from the manor felt different speeding along in the dead of night, with the hush of wind through trees and the barest sliver of moonlight guiding their way.

"Is it really a wolf attack?" she asked.

"The boy describes deep, bleeding gashes," said Ambrose. "Probably claws rather than teeth. I suspect a broken arm or shoulder too, possibly both. Ellis mumbled something about being flung against a wall."

Only yesterday Sabine and Martha had been talking about Ellis having everything. *Not any more,* Sabine thought. "Did his family interrupt the attack?"

"No. Ellis woke them up shouting. It's likely he was knocked unconscious for a while."

"Then it can't be the wolf. It wouldn't have left a perfectly good meal simply lying there."

"So Ellis Miller is a meal?" The doctor arched a bushy eyebrow. Sabine raised hers back.

"To the wolf he is."

"It is a good point. Here is something else for you to mull over: yet again, the coop is empty of chickens."

So the wolf – assuming it was the big bad wolf, rather than one of the shyer grey ones – feasted on the chickens instead? Sabine pulled a face to herself. That made no sense.

"What do you need my help for?"

"You'll find out."

Mr Miller ran out of the mill the moment the cart drew up outside.

"Come," he said, tersely. Ambrose climbed out, holding his hat against the breeze, and Sabine followed. The main door opened on to a kitchen with a wide hearth and an exposed stone wall covered with shelving containing pots, pans, tankards and tools. Ellis's twelve-year-old brother fanned the fledgling fire. Mistress Miller crouched by Ellis, who was sprawled in one of the dining chairs. He mumbled and twitched, eyes closed. Blood coated the shoulder and chest of his doublet. Sabine knew at a glance that there was something wrong with the way his right arm hung loosely to one side. Ambrose bustled forwards, ordering Mistress Miller to step back so he could examine his patient.

"Candle," Ambrose said. Sabine picked up the first she saw and held it close. Ambrose felt around Ellis's shoulder, then loosened the doublet and peeled it away. Sabine sucked in a breath. Claw marks! Angry, red and unmistakable, they crossed Ellis's shoulder, stopping halfway down his chest.

"Look worse than they are," said Ambrose. Sabine marvelled at how he could tell that from one speedy glance. "No stitches needed. This, though. Not good." His thumb grazed a lump protruding from the front of Ellis's shoulder. Sabine peered closer.

"Is that bone?"

"Yes. The shoulder is dislocated. Looks square, too – another telltale sign. And this—" Ambrose inspected Ellis's arm. "Broken. Possibly in more than one place. Ellis?"

Ellis's eyes flickered but did not open. His mother leaned over.

"Wake up, my love. The doctor is here."

There was no response. Ambrose pushed his glasses further up the bridge of his nose. "Sabine, lay out bandages and cloths and get a pitcher of water. Pour some in the bowl, the larger the better."

"Can you pop his arm back in?" asked Sabine, remembering a similar injury she had once heard her father talk of. Ambrose nodded.

"Exactly that. I am sorry, young man. This will hurt."

He took hold of Ellis's arm and deftly snapped it backwards. Ellis released a yell that even startled Sabine, then went limp. The jutting bone disappeared. Sabine felt herself smile.

"Impressive."

"I am glad I have your approval, Miss Forrester," the doctor said. "Must have been painful; he's passed out. Probably for the best."

Sabine busied herself emptying the doctor's bag, laying everything neatly on the kitchen table, then collected water from the pump Ellis's brother showed her to. She wetted cloths for Ambrose to dab at the claw marks, then washed them clean in the bowl. It didn't occur to her to be repulsed or feel sick. To be focusing on something like this, something important, made her feel clever and bold, especially when Ambrose asked her to unstopper a bottle containing a dark liquid that Sabine could smell contained cloves and feverfew. So they dulled pain. She would have to remember that.

And only yesterday she had worried about dying from boredom!

Thank you, wolf, thought Sabine, as she filled the second pitcher. Life, suddenly, was interesting again. Mysterious, too.

Why hadn't the wolf killed Ellis?

ELLIS

All boys got into fights, some more serious than others. Ellis had never been much of a brawler. Popular boys didn't need to thump people to get their voices heard. The one time he had been pummelled – years ago, by two older boys, for a reason Ellis couldn't remember – it had felt like he was dragging his bruised body around for days.

He felt far, far worse now.

The first thing he was aware of was his right arm. It was strapped to his chest, immovable. And his shoulder felt like it had been thumped repeatedly with a hammer, then twisted out of its socket. Ellis groaned. A voice he did not recognize said, "Ah. He's coming to properly. Cloth, please."

Something cool and wet pressed against his forehead. Ellis's eyelids felt weighted. He fought them open. He was in his room, propped up in bed under a blanket. The lined face of Lord Josiah's physician swam into view.

"Good morning, Ellis. What do you remember?"

Snatches of last night came back to him. Squeals and clucks. Fury. The axe. Being catapulted backwards. Teeth, claws. Pain. *Wolf?* "What have you done with my arm?"

"Grateful lad, aren't you? I, young man, have done everything I can for your arm. The question is more what the wolf did to it."

Behind Doctor Ambrose stood his mother, skin ashy and lips pressed into a thin line. Also present – Ellis squinted, wondering if this was a dream – was Sabine, hair knotted on top of her head and sleeves rolled to her elbows. Her gown was speckled with blood. His blood.

Fear balled in his belly. "Why can't I move my arm? It's not broken, is it?"

"Very much so," said Ambrose. "I have done what I can; you will need to keep it strapped up for at least six weeks, maybe more, but I cannot predict at this stage how it will heal. There is plenty of bruising around your shoulder too and also muscle damage. You'll be left with some beautiful scars from where you were clawed, but I dare say the girls will consider them dashing. Now sit back and rest."

Panic shot through him. "What do you mean, how it will heal? I need my arm."

"So do most people," remarked Sabine dryly. Ellis scowled.

"I'm talking about the mill. I can't hoist sacks from the loft or lift quernstones one-armed. And there is an archery tournament—"

"You cannot do anything right now. Let's worry about the future later." Ellis blanked out as the doctor talked through the poultice and bottles he was leaving to tend to Ellis's injuries, and how frequently to change his bandages. Ellis felt hot and cold at the same time, not entirely as though he was there. All the things he suddenly couldn't do raced through his mind.

"But it will heal?" he blurted.

The doctor paused tying up his cloak. "Are you talking about the arm or the claw marks?"

"The arm. I don't care about scars."

"Then yes. You'll get better. But your arm may not ever be as strong as it was before, even once you start using it properly again." His voice softened. "I cannot say for certain at this stage."

Ellis stared at him. Archery. Axe throwing. Wrestling. All lost to him. Not for ever. But he certainly wouldn't be the best any more. "No. That can't happen."

"It may well not. I am merely warning you it's a possibility. Try not to dwell on it. I'll be back to check up on you soon." The doctor looked at Ellis's mother. "Don't hesitate to call for me if he gets worse. I am..." He coughed delicately. "Aware of the situation."

What situation? Ellis's mother did not meet Ambrose's eyes as her head bobbed in assent. He gave her a look that to Ellis came across as searching, then left, followed by Sabine. Through the side of the shutters Ellis saw that the light was still murky, but rapidly lightening. So it was dawn. Ellis closed his eyes. Normally, he would be grabbing breakfast around now – bread and cheese, with an apple if there were any – and heading to the loft to assess their stock, then sweeping the mill floor clean in preparation for a hard day's work.

He wouldn't be there today, or be making deliveries, or clambering up and down ladders, or unloading carts of corn and grain, or even operating the pulley that stretched from loft to cellar.

Everything he knew as normal, gone in a moment.

His parents could employ another mill hand. But whoever they found wouldn't know as much as Ellis did. Work would be slow.

Money lost. His parents would resent that, and no doubt blame him.

And what happened if six weeks passed and his arm still wasn't right?

The mattress dipped as his mother perched next to him. The expression in her eyes told him she was angry and trying to hide it, but the way she pushed his hair from his forehead felt unusually tender.

"You have been passing in and out of consciousness ever since it happened," she said. "It was a real job to get you here from the kitchen. Ellis, do you understand how lucky you have been? No one has ever been attacked by the wolf and survived. No one."

Ellis didn't feel very lucky. "I did take an axe," he mumbled. "I thought I could handle whoever was there. I didn't expect for a moment it was the wolf. You and Father were so sure it was the neighbours, and I was angry."

"Even so, you should not have been so foolhardy!"

"I'm sorry. I only wanted. . ."

The words *you and Father to be proud of me* stuck in Ellis's throat. They seemed so silly and childish. It was hardly as though his parents were harsh or unkind. Why proving that he was worthwhile still mattered so much. . . He should have grown out of caring years ago.

Ellis sniffed, feeling suddenly very much like a child. His mother sat watching him. Her eyes were sad and weary.

"Perhaps you should know—" She stopped herself. "Never mind. Now is not the right time. Just rest."

She left. Ellis attempted to raise his bound arm. Pain shot from his shoulder down his side.

Tears gathered in his eyes. He wanted to wipe them away but it felt so strange using his left hand that it only made him cry harder. At least there was no one here to laugh.

He had been stupid and hot-headed and he had let his family down.

And the fabled, feared wolf of legend was back.

RED

She was running, faster than she ever had before. Naked branches tore past as she plunged into the depths of the forest. There were no paths and no flowers, just endless trees. Tears streamed down her cheeks. Her throat roared with thirst.

Pursuing her, hot on her heels, was darkness. An inky black cloud. Run as fast as she could, Red could not outpace it. A tendril clutched her leg, another her arm. She crashed to the forest floor. When she attempted to crawl, an unseen force held her back. And still the choking blackness came. . .

"Red. Red." It was her mother. Red launched upright, gasping for breath.

"I can't escape—"

"Shush. You are having a nightmare."

It took Red a moment to realize that she was in her bed. First light was teasing its way through the shutters. She put her hand to her forehead.

"What?"

"It really must have been a bad dream. You've scratched yourself again."

So she had, across her lower arms. At least she could hide it under her gown. Red wondered if it was normal to have such vivid dreams, and always of the forest. Even in her sleep, it seemed, she was strange.

Quickly Red changed into her under-gown and heavy winter tunic, and rammed her feet into tough leather boots. These had been specially made by a cordwainer in the city for her large feet, an expense that at the time had been a real stretch. It was one of only three times Red had ventured properly out of Aramor. The bustle of the city, with its fast pace and surging crowds and colour, had overwhelmed her. Being invisible for a change felt freeing, but the whole experience had been so . . . loud. She decided she wasn't cut out for city life – or maybe even town life. Perhaps Granny had it right, living in soothing solitude.

But there was no time to daydream now. Red tied back her thick, dark hair, grabbed her cloak and stepped outside.

Perhaps it was her imagination – it usually was her imagination – but the familiar lanes felt different this morning. No longer unsettled – it was more than that. Tension hung in the air as heavy as early morning mist. As though the world had changed overnight. A farmhand Red saw most days scurried past without making eye contact. Red watched him vanish into the mist. His torch picked out a woman standing at the bottom of the lane, long cape blowing gently around her ankles. Red frowned. Wasn't that Sabine's mother? It was a funny hour for someone like her to be out.

Nothing to do with me, thought Red, and pulled her own cape tighter.

Martha was pacing about the kitchen when Red let herself into the bakery, hair loose and hugging herself. Her face was pinched and eyes bloodshot.

"The wolf attacked Ellis."

Red's first thought was that this had to be a joke. It wouldn't be the first time. She knew the other girls thought her gullible. But

Martha was not much of an actress and crying at will was taking things far even for her. And she had no idea how Red felt about Ellis.

So therefore it was true. Coldness crept over Red. She wasn't sure what to do or say. Martha wouldn't want her sympathy. And she couldn't risk appearing too interested. "What happened?"

"That is the question. He doesn't remember." Red jumped. Sabine was sitting on a stool by the blazing oven, boots flecked with mud and gown filthy. She had a pale complexion at the best of times but today she looked positively wan. Dark rings hung under her eyes but they danced in a way Red mistrusted. "There are claw marks that I can't see being done by anything else."

"Is he all right?"

"Do you care?"

Red hesitated, not sure if this was a trick question. Luckily Martha spoke up. "I care. We need to go and see him. I can't believe you actually enjoyed assisting Doctor Ambrose! All that blood."

Sabine shrugged. "Blood is natural enough. I found it fascinating seeing the doctor work. What is also fascinating is why he was at the mill at all."

"What do you mean?" asked Red.

Sabine smiled. "Doctor Ambrose doesn't normally attend to us lowly peasants. It would be much more natural for the Millers to send for the apothecary. Cheaper, and closer."

"But less skilled."

"Indeed. I wonder if the Millers will pay Doctor Ambrose or not? My mother says... Never mind." Sabine turned to Red. "You are in the forest all the time. Have you ever caught a glimpse of the wolf?"

Red struggled to remember the last time Sabine had been this ... well, not friendly, exactly, but not unfriendly. "Once I thought I did, a few months ago. I spotted something slinking through the trees. It had dark fur, so it couldn't have been one of the wolves that hunt in packs. They're grey. And they seem to be dying off. It's not uncommon to see their carcasses."

"Never mind the grey wolves. What happened?"

"It attacked something. I don't know what – maybe a snake? There are lots of them in autumn – they're nasty things, poisonous. Anyway, there was a colossal snarling, and I – well, I ran off."

"And that didn't scare you off returning?"

Had Sabine blinked? She was certainly listening intently. And people called Red strange. "No. Animals do attack each other, don't they? I didn't feel threatened myself." Red paused. "It's really not a frightening place. The forest is quiet, mostly. It wasn't a few years back when my granny first moved there. There were more birds, and rabbits, even deer. The last few years... I don't know. The animals seem to have vanished."

"Huh," said Sabine. "Maybe that's why the big bad wolf has returned. There's nothing else to eat..."

There was a clang from the table. Martha banged down a heavy-bottomed bowl, glaring at them.

"I don't care about the wretched wolf and I wish you'd stop going on about it! Sometimes I think you want it to be stalking about, gnawing on arms and legs and mauling people. What I care about is Ellis. He nearly died."

"No, he didn't," said Sabine. "And that's what's most interesting of all." She glanced at Red, a tiny smile playing round her lips. Realizing her meaning, Red stiffened.

"Oh."

Their eyes locked a moment, pale blue-green on earthy hazel. Then a knock at the back door made them both jump. Two girls Red often saw laughing with Martha and Sabine peeped round, faces flushed.

"Is it true?"

Sabine told her story again. When she mentioned that Red had actually seen the wolf, the girls' eyes went big and wide.

They looked repulsed, but also eager, so Red described what she'd witnessed.

"I would have been terrified," whispered the first girl. "You are brave to even set foot in there, Red."

Was that an insult? But all Red saw in the girl's eyes was admiration. Something unusual swelled in her chest: pride. Martha offered the girls some fresh rock cakes. The five of them sat round the hearth, chewing and chatting. No one told Red to leave, or that she didn't belong. Red felt warm inside. Then she thought of Ellis with his arm in tatters and felt bad.

They were broken up by Mistress Baker, who told them smartly that bread wasn't going to bake itself. She did, however, give Martha permission to leave early that afternoon to visit Ellis.

"Take him something nice," she said. Mistress Baker was a willowy woman, with hair that had turned white early and never seemed to grow far past her shoulders. "His parents I have no time for, but Ellis is a nice lad." She lowered her voice. "Don't let your father know I said that, though, Martha. And take Red with you."

Martha's eyes popped. Red was just as surprised.

"I don't—" she started to say, but Mistress Baker held up her hand.

"It is safer if there are two of you. Or three. I assume you are going, Sabine? I'm sure your mother will be dying to hear all the details." Sabine tilted her head, but didn't respond. "The mill is hardly remote, but it is still outside town. Come back before dark, please."

When the door closed behind her mother, Martha said, "She can't really be afraid the wolf might pounce on us walking there, can she? Even five years ago it barely ventured out of the forest, and only ever at night."

"And that means it will do the same now?"

Sabine's question went unanswered.

ᴥSABINE

Sabine did not feel tired, even after having been up all night, but if she stayed at the bakery much longer she would be expected to help. Sabine had always hated the clingy texture of dough, especially under her nails, and how crusty it was when it dried. And she had her own duties to attend to, even though Doctor Ambrose had assured her that he would let Lady Katherine know she needed to rest after the long night. As Sabine walked back to the manor house she felt a curious buzz. Merchants kept their heads bowed as they set up market stalls. Mothers held their children's hands tightly as they hurried along. Everyone, it seemed, had heard. No one stopped Sabine. Her own role must have gone unremarked on. It gave her a thrill to overhear snatches of gossip, knowing she knew more than any of the townsfolk did.

Back in the manor house she headed to Lady Katherine's chambers. Her ladyship was pacing up and down her sitting room, books unopened on the table by the window and embroidery abandoned in her comfortable chair. Her quilted gown – grey today, which suited her blonde hair and pale, freckled skin – made a soft swishing noise as it brushed the rug. Her ladyship's dogs – two bloodhounds, the third a large sable creature with coarse fur and intelligent almond-shaped eyes – stood by the fire watching their mistress, ears cocked. For once Lady Katherine paid the dogs no attention. Ordinarily she treated them like children, perhaps because she had none of her own, and, nearing forty, was unlikely to ever have. It was a shame – Katherine was just the kind of woman Sabine could imagine in deep conversation with daughters on strolls through the beautifully tended garden, or patiently teaching young sons to play chess.

Lady Katherine shook her head when Sabine asked if she needed anything.

"I will take care of myself. You'll keel over with tiredness before too long. Doctor Ambrose is used to interrupted nights, but young people need their sleep. Why were you outside so late? He tells me you were in the garden."

Sabine had prepared an answer already. "I was unable to sleep, your ladyship. I find a walk calms my mind."

"Go and rest now, then." Lady Katherine laid a slender hand on Sabine's shoulder, giving it a squeeze. Sabine stared at the smooth, unchipped nails, and for a moment instead saw her mother's hand, with hard skin under the fingers, and dry knuckles.

"Thank you." It was difficult to resent Lady Katherine for her wealth and comfortable lifestyle when she was this kind. Her lady-ship let go, giving her a gentle push. Sabine climbed the creaking staircase that led to her attic bedroom. As soon as Sabine entered her chambers and saw her unmade bed, a wave of weariness hit her, and undressing was all she could manage before clambering under the covers.

She was woken by a servant at lunchtime. The meal was only rye bread and a light lamb stew that Sabine was not overfond of, but today every mouthful tasted full of flavour. Lady Katherine did not appear, so Sabine decided to assume that she wasn't needed and left quietly from a side door. If her mother discovered that Sabine was sneaking out she would be absolutely furious. Mistress Forrester was proud of herself for securing Sabine such a prestigious position, a cut above the servant she could have been. How her mother had managed it was a mystery, even to Sabine. Whenever she asked, Mistress Forrester had just smiled and tapped the side of her nose in that irritating way she had.

"I expect you to make the most of this, Sabine, my love," she had said. "It offers not only you prospects, but the rest of the family, too. If you are clever, and win her ladyship's like and trust, then she may be generous, and perhaps then we can even move on from this sorry excuse for a house. Your father cannot be relied upon any more so it is up to us."

There had been malice in that last part. Another reason to be glad she no longer lived at home. Sabine's father was not useless – Sabine fiercely resented him being called so – and his work as a woodcutter was steady, if not terribly well paid. It was true that he spent much of his time sitting at home in a kind of melancholy, but there were good reasons for that. Perhaps, Sabine thought, she might be able to ask Doctor Ambrose if he could prescribe anything to lift her father's spirits. She didn't dare try to present her father with any of her own herb mixes.

Martha and Red were waiting for her at the town square by the water pump. Martha clutched a basket and had changed into the pretty blue gown that matched her eyes, as though that was going to magically make Ellis feel better. Red was chewing her lip, shoulders slouched. She often chewed her lip when she was nervous and something about it maddened Sabine. She narrowed her eyes, contemplating sending Red packing, then decided it was easiest to leave it.

The girls did not talk much as they left the town behind and slogged along the dirt track to the mill. Sabine could see the grooves from the wheels of the Millers' cart in the mud, as well as the footprints of farm labourers. The track hadn't felt this peaceful last night. She closed her eyes a second, and she was back in the cart with Doctor Ambrose, jolting up and down as they clattered through the darkness, and nerves tingling. Even the memory of it was a thrill. Nothing that exciting had ever happened to her before.

The mill looked the same as it always did, bar the empty coop. The large waterwheel secured to the side of the tall cobbled building circled, the splash and heave from the river so deafening they were forced to raise their voices. It almost concealed the constant, heavy grind of the millstone. Sabine wondered how the Millers could stand it.

"Hello?" Sabine tapped the door to the cottage next to the mill where the family lived. No one answered. It wasn't locked so the girls stepped inside, loosening their hoods. Suddenly it felt very quiet, the only sound their heels tapping on the coarse stone floor.

"Should we be doing this?" whispered Martha. "They might not like us coming in without asking."

"I thought Ellis was your beau and you were desperate to see him?" said Sabine.

Martha hesitated. Her fingers pressed so tightly to the basket that her knuckles turned white. "All I meant was that we are intruding."

Sabine tossed her head. "Stay here, then. Red and I will go. Won't we, Red?"

Red's eyes went big. Pink tinged her cheeks as she nodded. *Pathetic*, thought Sabine. *She actually believes we're friends now. She really is simple.*

Sabine led the way up the narrow, somewhat uneven staircase to the room she remembered from last night. Ellis was sitting propped up in bed wearing a loose undershirt, looking rather grey. When he saw the girls, he went even greyer. It was difficult to make out in the gloom – the thin window would let in very little light, even in summer – but Sabine thought his forehead was sweaty, even though it wasn't at all warm. Doctor Ambrose had warned a fever might set in.

There was a funny, awkward silence. Then Martha thrust the basket forwards.

"We've brought you biscuits. I iced them myself. Are you in a lot of pain?"

"It aches, mostly." Ellis's voice sounded gravelly. "I did try to get up but I felt dizzy. I am happy you came, though. Really happy. Though I wish you did not need to see me like this."

Martha said nothing. Ellis gestured to the chair next to his bed with his good hand, eyes never leaving her. When Martha didn't move, Sabine gave her shin a sharp kick. Rather unwillingly, her friend perched on the very edge of the chair. Ellis reached for her hand. Martha let it hang before reluctantly taking it.

"I feel so useless lying here," he murmured. "I should be working, or training for that tournament. . . It is so dull." He waited, but no one said anything. "I suppose I'd better get used to it. As you are here . . . do you mind helping me change the bandage? I can't do it myself."

He looked at Martha. She swallowed.

"I wouldn't know what to do."

"Please?"

Patience snapping, Sabine opened her mouth to say she'd do it, if Martha was too delicate to get her hands dirty. Then she caught sight of Red. The way Red was gazing at Ellis and Martha, eyes wistful, hanging back so as to not draw attention to herself. . .

That was interesting.

Sabine hesitated. Then she said, "Red will do it if it's too much for you, Martha. Won't you, Red?"

RED

A jolt went through Red's body. "What? Me?"

Martha and Ellis blinked at her. She wasn't sure he'd even realized she was in the room up until now. Sabine was smiling, in an open, friendly way Red immediately knew wasn't genuine. She gave Red's arm a little tug.

"Martha doesn't like blood, it seems. I'm sure you don't have that problem. Your beloved granny used to be a midwife, didn't she? So many skills run in families."

"That doesn't mean I know anything," Panic rose inside Red. "I don't want to. I—"

"Someone's got to change those bandages. You heard Ellis, he can't do it himself. And I imagine his parents are busy. I could, of course, but I thought you might like to."

Red started to sweat. How could Sabine know how she felt about Ellis? Red had told no one, not even Granny, and she was always careful not to change her behaviour around him. No, Sabine couldn't know, she was just doing that thing she always did, nudging and needling people until they danced like puppets. It was easiest to do as she said – even if it meant drawing Ellis's attention.

She moved to the bed, avoiding meeting his eyes. "I will do my best. Please tell me if I hurt you."

Gingerly, she rolled up the sleeve of his undershirt, then realized it would not go high enough. From behind, Sabine said, "I think you'll have to take it off, Red."

She sounded like she was holding back laughter. Ellis noticed Red's discomfort.

"I shouldn't have asked," he said. "Leave it. My mother will come and check soon enough."

Ellis being kind made it even worse. She could feel her cheeks blazing now.

"No, I'll do it."

The wound smelled fusty this close up. It definitely needed washing. Red could not recall much of what Granny had said about her time as a midwife, which had included basic nursing, but she did remember the time her mother had sliced the tip of her finger off cooking. Granny had walked to the cottage every day to bathe and re-bandage the wound, ignoring Red's mother's protests.

Doing her best to block out Sabine and Martha – and to silence her mind screaming that she was touching a boy and basically undressing him – Red helped Ellis out of the shirt, then peeled back the binding covering his shoulder and upper arm. She sucked in a breath. Suddenly she was not in Ellis's bedroom any more but outside, a crescent moon above. She saw a coop, heard the door bang as Ellis strode out of the house, angry and righteous. Then his body hurtled backwards, hitting the wall hard, and there was claws and snarling. . .

Red shuddered and pulled herself back to the present. Now was not the time for her imagination to run wild. She focused on the claw marks. They weren't anywhere near as severe as Red had been expecting. And like Sabine had said, that was odd. Had the wolf held back for some reason? It hadn't been interrupted by Ellis's family. Or had someone else disturbed it? But then why would anyone other than the Millers be outside the mill in the middle of the night?

Using one of the cloths on the windowsill and the pitcher of water next to them, Red dabbed the wound. There was a sharp intake of breath from Ellis.

"Stings?" she asked.

"A bit."

It probably stung quite a lot, only Ellis didn't want to embarrass himself. Red hunted round for the salve the doctor had left.

"It's that one, I think," said Ellis. "The blue bottle."

Red undid the stopper. Pungent-smelling liquid wetted the cloth.

"The wound isn't very nice, is it," said Ellis, as she pressed it to his skin. Red made a non-committal noise, concentrating on what she was doing.

"What happened to you isn't very nice. Don't worry, it doesn't bother me."

"You're showing Martha up, Red," said Sabine. "So did you see the wolf, Ellis? You weren't making much sense last night."

"I don't know," said Ellis. "My memory isn't clear. I thought I did, but. . ."

"Are the rumours true?" pressed Sabine. "The red eyes and

black fur? Is it really the same wolf as five years ago? That's what everyone wants to know."

No, it is what you want to know, thought Red, but kept her mouth shut. She felt Ellis tense.

"What are they saying in town?"

"Just gossip. Is it, then?"

"It was strong. The force with which is flung me against the wall. . . I didn't even get a chance to raise the axe, let alone swing it."

"I am sure you were very brave." Martha's voice trembled. She was still in the room, then.

"I wasn't, though. I didn't do anything. Ouch."

"All done." Red wiped her hands, then bound Ellis up again with a fresh bandage. "Sorry if this is messy."

"That doesn't matter. Thank you, Red."

He'd said her name. For the first time ever. Her name, on his lips. Despite cringing inside, Red felt a small, happy glow.

"You should sleep now," Martha said. "We need to be getting on."

"I've done nothing but sleep," said Ellis. "Can you stay and talk to me, Martha?"

Red's happy glow vanished. Ellis didn't care about her. He only had eyes for Martha, even though she was barely able to look at him.

Anger at how unfair it was bubbled inside her. "We don't need to be getting on, actually."

Immediately she knew that was a mistake. Martha's face contorted. Suddenly she didn't look at all pretty.

"Yes, we do. My mother wants us walking together, remember?"

Red picked up on the veiled threat. Not looking at the other girls, she helped Ellis back into his nightshirt, then turned and left without a word.

Outside, Sabine broke the silence first.

"Well. Wasn't that interesting."

"It was disgusting," Martha snapped. "Those wounds stank. And Red's disgusting for touching them. Not that we didn't know that already." Red flinched. "Those scars, ugh! He didn't even get hurt fighting it."

Don't say anything, Red thought. But the words came out anyway. "Why would that have made a difference?"

"Fighting it would have been impressive. Brave. Worth breaking an arm for. He'd always be the boy who fought the wolf. That's who I thought he was. Now, well. I don't know what he is." She wrinkled her nose. "It didn't hurt him that badly. Maybe there's something wrong with him, and it sensed that. . ."

Sabine burst out laughing. "Are you suggesting Ellis Miller is some kind of witch?"

"I told you, don't say that word!" Martha hissed. Red was shocked, too – Sabine dropped *witch* into conversation so casually, almost as though it amused her. "And no, I'm not. I am only saying it's strange and I don't like it."

"You're speaking like you'd prefer him to be dead," said Red.

"People will say things. I can't see him striding round town joking with everyone any more, or teaching their sons how to fire bows, or even taking flour into their houses. If they know he's courting me..."

"And what everyone else thinks matters so much?" Red could hardly believe what she was hearing. "I thought you cared about him."

Martha narrowed her eyes. "Oh, be quiet, Red. You don't understand."

"If this is how you feel, then you won't mind if he starts courting Red." Sabine's voice dripped honey. She nudged Red. "That would make you happy, yes? Tell me I'm right, Red. I saw you making eyes at Ellis. You clearly enjoyed getting your hands all over him..."

Red's stomach gave a scary flip-flop. "Leave me alone."

"I was trying to help."

"No, you were making fun of me." Red surprised herself by snapping back. "You like causing trouble, just like your mother. It's not as though you are so very respectable and normal yourself, talking about the wolf all the time. What's more, I've seen you sneaking about at the forest edge, picking plants—"

Sabine flew at Red, pinning her to the closest tree. Red gasped as breath thumped out of her.

"Go away, Red. I'm tired of you tagging along with us. I bet you are secretly glad this has happened to Ellis. It is easier being shunned when you have company. Worked out very well for you, hasn't it? I would be careful if I were you. People are unkind when they are afraid."

Up close, Sabine's eyes were cold and hard. The fight left Red. How had she forgotten the power this girl had to hurt her? From now on there weren't only going to be jibes about Red's awkwardness, or tangled hair. She and Sabine had crossed a line into something much more serious.

Sabine let Red go, turning her back.

"Come on, Martha. Leave Red. I wouldn't worry about the wolf eating her." Underneath the scorn there was a note of satisfaction in Sabine's voice. A note that said she enjoyed putting Red in her place. "Probably even it thinks there's something funny about Red. Shame. It would be easier for everyone if she was gobbled up. Her mother might actually start smiling instead of looking so woebegone all the time."

Red sank down against the tree trunk, hands over her face. She heard the crunch of boots grow quieter as Sabine and Martha left. She was stupid, so stupid. For a few moments, standing up to Sabine had felt good. Granny would have been proud. But all that had led to was Sabine fighting back, meaner and harder than she had before. How did Sabine know the rows Red had with her mother, how very hard Red tried to please her, and how she always, always, failed, and how much that hurt? Mother looked pretty when she smiled – she wasn't so old, and Red had noticed how the widowed tailor found excuses to come to the cottage, and lingered chatting. Maybe it really would be better if Red was gone. Mother could remarry and quietly forget she ever had such an embarrassment of a daughter. . .

With shaky legs Red stood, brushing moss and leaves off her cloak. She hovered where she was. Dusk was creeping in. She should go home. But instead she turned back towards the mill. Ready to run the second she heard footsteps, Red searched for and soon found the coop. Its wooden top had been ripped open.

Red frowned. She couldn't decide whether this was an improbable thing for a four-legged animal to do or not, unless it really did have supernatural strength. A human, on the other hand...

The claw marks on Ellis definitely looked animal, though.

Voices sounded nearby. Red dived into the closest hiding place – an evergreen bush. Cursing her bright red cloak, Red wriggled as far as she could into the ferns, hoping the poor light would help obscure her. Just as she was settling down, a pair of boots appeared, and someone squatted down beside her, breathing heavily. It was Caleb, Ellis's twelve-year-old brother. He looked as surprised to see Red as she was him. Red raised a finger to her lips. Caleb mimicked her, nodding.

"...trying to draw us out." The voice was Mr Miller's. "We should have seen this coming. We did very well to hide the truth all this time."

"No one said anything when you went into town?" asked Mistress Miller. "Bridget Forrester?"

"You fret about that woman too much. I didn't see her. All anyone is talking about is the wolf."

"They all believe it has returned?"

"You know what Aramor is like. Everyone loves to get hysterical. All I care about is our safety. What possessed Ellis to go outside like that? If he'd been worse hurt, even killed. . . He is so close to turning fifteen and this all being over."

"Ellis is not a thing to 'be over'," Mistress Miller snapped. Her husband sighed.

"Those were the wrong words. I apologize. This is not easy for me either, Tamasin."

"You betrayed me."

"I was trying to do what was best."

The Millers' voices faded. Red was now certain they'd gone inside. She glanced at Caleb. He was frowning, as though concentrating intensely.

"I wasn't here," she whispered.

"Neither was I," he whispered back. Trying not to catch her clothes on the bush, Red crawled out, and ran as fast as she could away from the mill. Her ears were tingling.

So Ellis's parents had a secret. One they seemed to be afraid Sabine's mother knew. Red should probably forget all about it. All the same, Red wondered. Secrets – and what people did to protect them – made her afraid. The coldness in Sabine's eyes just minutes ago told her that much.

ELLIS

After a day, Ellis managed to drag himself out of bed. After two days, he was pacing, unable to sit still or concentrate on anything other than how maddening this was. He hated the way his arm hung dull and heavy and useless. It felt like it was dragging the rest of his body down with it. He missed the healthy ache across his shoulders from a hard day's work, and the tired feet, and being busy. After three days, he had succeeded in climbing the ladder to the top of the mill, and had swept the floor, which at least made him feel like he'd done something. But seeing the mill hands steadily getting on with work had been too difficult to watch.

Most of all his missed packing the cart and setting off to town just as the sun was rising, birds cheeping and wheels trundling. He closed his eyes, picturing the smiles and waves of townsfolk, the friendly questions and "how are yous", the way little children would beg to be given a ride, knowing Ellis always caved and let them. There was no better feeling in the world than the comfort of knowing exactly who you were. And who even was he, now?

Ellis stood in front of the cart, sizing up the sacks of flour waiting to be loaded. It was early morning, five days after the attack, and he had had enough of this nothing. Ellis squared his jaw. He was going to fight. Surprise everyone. Get his old life back, exactly as it had been. He'd never met a challenge he couldn't overcome, not if he tried hard enough.

One of the sacks waiting to be loaded appeared less full than the others. Ellis grasped the top with his good hand but couldn't even heave it off the ground. Instead he squatted down, wrapping his arm round the sack and clutching it against his body. His legs wobbled as he straightened, muscles straining. . .

Snap. Ellis's arm gave way. Flour exploded across the cobbles in a snowy cloud. When it cleared, the sack was lying on its side, half empty. Ellis cursed as he squatted down and tried to brush flour back in before realizing there was no way they could sell this.

"Ellis! What are you doing?" Of course it was his father. Ellis shuffled his feet.

"I was trying to. . . I want to help."

There was an exasperated sigh. "The most helpful thing you can do is to stay out of everyone's way."

"I could take the cart. Dorothy's placid. I am sure I could direct her one-handed."

"How is the flour going to get from the cart into people's store cupboards?"

"People could. . ."

"Carry it themselves? No, Ellis. I cannot ask customers to do that. And it would only make you uncomfortable."

Ellis pictured Martha heaving an enormous sack into the bakery while he held the door open for her, and his shoulders slumped. His father was right.

But he was not about to give up yet. "How about I take Caleb? He can manage the lifting. It might be helpful for him to see how the deliveries work."

Mr Miller sighed, rubbing his forehead. "No."

"It's either that or you go again," pressed Ellis. "I know how you dislike town."

"I said no. Sorry, Ellis. But playing hero was a foolish thing to do and you only have yourself to blame."

Play hero, like his youngest two brothers did, pretending their sticks were axes and swords. Ellis bristled. He almost wished his parents would shout at him. All the frustration and annoyance remaining unsaid was worse, somehow. But then that had always been his parents' way. None of his family ever spoke about anything that mattered.

Mr Miller marched inside, as though the matter was settled. Ellis drew a circle in the flour he had ruined with his toe, fuming. He glanced at the horse, saddled and ready to go. Dorothy made a "hmmphing" sound, as though to say, *What are you waiting for? We'll be late.* Ellis scratched her behind the ears. Then he strode inside to find Caleb.

Driving the cart was not too bad. Caleb sat next to Ellis, ready to take the reins if necessary, but Dorothy plodded steadily towards town without any encouragement. Halfway there it started to drizzle, and they had to halt so they could pull sacking over their cargo. Mr Miller would have discovered the cart was gone by now.

He'd know exactly who'd taken it. Ellis wondered if he'd be angry. *If so, good,* he thought. Striving to please his parents clearly went unnoticed. Maybe disobedience would get a reaction.

Caleb peered at him from under his thick dark fringe. At twelve he was naturally slighter than Ellis, though since starting to work in the mill a year ago he had already become a lot stronger. Their looks were not their only difference – Caleb was uninterested in anything sporting, and preferred his own company to that of others. Ellis often thought it surprising they were close.

"We're not supposed to be doing this, are we?" Caleb asked. "Mother and Father agreed it was better for you to stay away from town for a while."

"How do you know that – eavesdropping again?"

"And you don't do it yourself?"

"Not on purpose."

"Then you should." Caleb glanced over his shoulder. "Something is going on, Ellis. They're scared. And I don't think it is of the wolf."

"What else could it be?"

"That's what I want to know."

A jittery feeling settled in Ellis's stomach as they neared the edges of town. Maybe it was just that it was a dull, overcast day, but it felt as though the town was shrouded and silent. Was this such a good idea? People would react when they saw him, naturally, but he'd imagined well-meaning sympathy, perhaps a few questions. Everyone liked him, didn't they?

He took a deep breath. "We'll head to our furthest point first, then work our way through the outskirts. We'll. . ."

Two children Ellis recognized ran out into the road. Both stared, eyes big, mouths closed. Ellis smiled at them.

"Fancy a ride to the market square?"

The girl shrank back, crossing her fingers as though to ward off evil. Her brother skipped down the street, shouting excitedly. Shutter after shutter shot down. Ellis's mouth dropped. A woman hanging washing ripped the shirts and shifts back into her basket and vanished. Someone else crossed their fingers before ducking into an alley.

"What are they—"

"I think this might have been the reason Father didn't want you to go to town," mumbled Caleb. Ellis passed him the reins.

"Hey!" he called to the little girl. "Don't be afraid. It's me. Nothing has changed, apart from this." He gestured to his arm. The girl backed against the wall, chanting the same word, over and over.

Wolf.

Ellis's head shot round. A crowd swelled behind the cart. Men, women, children, even boys he'd considered friends, all watching with tight expressions and tensed shoulders.

There was silence. Then suddenly they were all yelling at once.

"Why didn't it kill you, Ellis?"

"Did you make a bargain with it, to save your life? Or did your parents?"

"Perhaps that's why Lord Josiah favours them so. They've a hold over him, too."

"Of course not!" cried Ellis. "Listen to yourselves. This is foolish talk. We are all scared, I know that, but I haven't done anything."

"You don't remember what it was like five winters ago." The voice was an old woman's. "Good men being savaged trying to do their jobs, cowering at home fearing your son, or your friend would be next. I always said that wolf was too powerful to be earthly. The other wolves don't have the same savage thirst for blood! It's a being of wickedness. I say of witchcraft!"

The crowd recoiled. A snatch of red appeared in the corner of Ellis's eye. A girl stood by the entrance to the bakery yard four houses away, waving: Red.

"Everyone needs flour, wolf or no wolf." Ellis was horrified to hear his voice shaking. "Please let us through."

At first the crowd did not budge. Then, grumbling and cursing, they slunk back, several crossing their fingers. Ellis was sweating as he guided the cart into the yard. Red shut the gates behind them.

"You should stay here a while," she said. "Let them cool off."

"I don't understand it." His head was spinning. "I know those people – the boys are friends. I thought they'd be pleased to see I was all right. Not making out that—"

The wolf is an unnatural beast, and that I am somehow in league with it because I am alive. He couldn't say the words. He knew people were superstitious, but to go this far, entirely baselessly. . .

"They've lost their minds. They have completely lost their minds. Does everyone think this way?"

Red shuffled her feet. "I wouldn't know. Do you need any help? With the flour, I mean."

"We can manage," Ellis snapped, and felt bad when Red flinched. "Sorry. That was unkind. I am just—"

"I understand. You feel scared yourself when people turn on you like that. I don't think people like things they don't understand. And I should know."

Vague memories of his friends laughing about Red came to Ellis. Stuff about her talking to birds in the forest, and the practical jokes she fell for, every time. Ellis hadn't really listened, but neither had he told them to be quiet. For the first time, he felt ashamed of that.

"But everyone likes me." He knew he was being insensitive, but it was so baffling. "For them to turn so quickly . . . it is like they're the ones possessed."

"People might change their minds," said Red, in a tone that suggested they wouldn't. Ellis looked at Caleb.

"I am sorry I dragged you out here."

Caleb rubbed the side of his nose, still looking rattled. "I thought they might attack us, hound us out of town."

"There's nowhere else nearby to get flour from. They know that as well as we do." Their trade would offer Ellis and his family some safety – or at least he hoped it would.

It had gone quiet outside. Too quiet. Had the angry townsfolk gone home to cool off? Or were they waiting? Ellis clambered down, directing Caleb as to which sacks to deliver. His brother stumbled into the bakery hugging the largest sack, face scrunched up with the effort. Ellis could have carried double that without a second thought.

Ellis turned away. "Is Martha here?"

"Where else would she be?" muttered Red.

Seeing Martha would feel normal, at least. To her he could still be someone strong. Ellis started towards the door, then spun round again. "Did I thank you? I didn't, did I? That was a decent thing you did, just now. So thank you, Red."

She smiled. Her mouth was wide, with a gap between the front teeth. It brought a liveliness to her hazel eyes he liked.

"Was it you who changed my bandage the other day too?" he asked. "I don't remember that very well."

She nodded, but she coloured too. Deciding to pretend he hadn't noticed, he strode inside. Martha was bent over the table, icing gingerbread.

"Shut the door, Red," she called without looking up. Ellis went over and looped his arm round her waist, kissing the top of her head. Martha flinched. A biscuit bounced on the floor and broke in two. Ellis backed off, holding up his good hand to show he meant no harm.

"Sorry for sneaking in. You just looked so pretty there I couldn't resist."

He waited for her giggle, or to pretend to go all haughty and tell him he could do better than "pretty". Instead, she folded her arms.

"You are up, then."

He smiled. "I wanted to see you."

She put a few steps between them. "I don't think my parents will be happy if they find you in here, Ellis."

"Come outside for a few minutes, then. It's not that cold. Tell me what's been going on. Better still, let's meet somewhere later, the river, maybe. If it's still iced over we can skate. I'll make sure you get back safely. I still have two working legs."

He'd hoped that would make her laugh, but Martha didn't even react. "I really think you should go."

Ellis frowned. "Martha, what is this? If you are embarrassed about not liking the sight of blood the other day, don't be. Aramor feels a strange place today, but that doesn't have to change anything with us. You don't care about what people are saying, do you?"

Martha's murmur was inaudible. Before Ellis could ask her to repeat it the door crashed open. Red appeared with a sack of rye flour.

"Do we need this today, Martha? I thought your mother—"

"On the table." Martha looked straight past Ellis. She had not made eye contact once, he realized. "Thanks, Red."

Red looked a little floored, as though she was not used to courtesy. "Oh. Yes. Um, Ellis, your brother checked outside. Everyone has gone, so— Not that I want you to leave or anything. . ."

She trailed off. Even someone without any observational skill whatsoever would have picked up on the atmosphere. Ellis cleared his throat.

"We should go. Everything will take longer today." He waited for Martha to say something, but she was silent. "Goodbye, then."

A cold wind hit him as he closed the door. Caleb was hunched on the cart, arms wrapped round himself. He looked miserable too. Probably fretting about what their father was going to say when they got home, and if he was going to be punished. Yet another mistake Ellis had made.

Ellis kicked his heel against the ground, hard. It hurt, but nowhere near as much as he did inside.

ϖSABINE

It's not as though you are so very respectable and normal yourself. Sneaking about at the forest edge, picking plants.

Even a day on, Sabine was fuming. How dare Red talk about her like that! She half-wished she'd gone harder on putting Red down, but it was too late now.

I am perfectly respectable and normal, Sabine thought, balancing the wooden tray in one hand as she positioned a brimming tankard on the table next to the chair where Lady Katherine always sat. *Red is just bitter and jealous.*

"Is there anything else I can bring you, my lady?"

"No, thank you, Sabine." Lady Katherine was frowning over a parchment she had idly picked up from the desk where her husband was reading. "Josiah, is this a report from the captain of the guard? There used to be twice this number of guardsmen patrolling Aramor, were there not?"

"That is none of your concern." Lord Josiah turned a page. "Take your dogs out if you have nothing else to do."

"I have already enjoyed a lengthy walk. And Aramor's governance *is* my concern. Do we not have the coffers for such a guard? Or indeed the repair work on the south gate? That wall crumbled quite some time ago now. If we are in need of coin, could we not lease the fields Farmer Warner used to plough?"

"Aramor's finances are perfectly healthy. Recruiting more guards takes time and effort, that is all, as does organizing repair work."

"Then allow me to help. I have plenty of time."

Lord Josiah stuck his nose deeper into his book. Lady Katherine put her hands on her hips. Sensing an argument, Sabine gathered a pile of books from her ladyship's table that she had earlier been asked to return to Doctor Ambrose and took her leave. She flicked through the top one as she walked. This book had illustrations of the body, and people afflicted with various ailments, and herbs that Sabine guessed were suggested as treatment. Was that St John's wort? And chamomile? This orange root she had never seen before, but the picture indicated it was helpful in lowering fever—

If only she could read! And if only people were not so narrow-minded she could do something with the knowledge she already had. Not for the first time, Sabine felt frustrated. No one she knew who could read would spare the time to teach her; she had already tried. To most, the idea of a peasant girl learning such things was laughable. Not even Martha had any sympathy, telling Sabine sharply that boys wouldn't care for a girl who knew things they didn't. Sabine hated the idea that she was some kind of joke.

Doctor Ambrose did not answer her knock. However, his room was unlocked, so Sabine strode in and dumped the books on the large wooden table in the centre. Deciding that Lady Katherine wouldn't appreciate her reappearing quite yet, Sabine leafed through the other books. Two were also medical but the last, bound in black and half falling apart, was quite different. On the opening page was a lurid print of some kind of demon, bright red, with a pointed tail and grotesque, startling yellow eyes. On either side of it two hounds stood on their hind legs, snapping jaws that dripped blood.

Sabine's eyebrows shot up. On another page was a winged cockerel-headed reptile she recognized as a basilisk, then a vicious werewolf, a hideous gargoyle and various ghouls. Was owning a book of supernatural beasts heresy? Sabine supposed it was no worse than frightening and thrilling children with such tales after dark, which everyone did.

Although... Close to the back was a picture of a wizened old woman stood under a tree, with what Sabine guessed were charms at her feet. A ghostly demon lurked behind her. Witchcraft again. *Because of course people believe ugly old women can conjure phantoms*, thought Sabine.

Knowing it would be unwise to be caught here, she slammed it shut and left.

As she closed the door, there was a low growl.

Mere feet away was a four-legged creature, teeth bared, ears cocked. *Wolf.* Sabine's hand flew to her chest before she realized it was Lady Katherine's large sable dog.

"You scared me," she snapped.

The dog growled again. Funny – he was not ordinarily unfriendly. *Maybe he knows I was snooping*, thought Sabine, and almost laughed. Even such a well-trained dog was not that clever.

What was funnier was that Lady Katherine had even been looking at such a book. What possible interest could she have in such things?

RED

Early morning darkness was different to night darkness, Red thought as she slipped out of Granny's cottage. It was rare for her to stay the night, but since the attack on Ellis she had been feeling unsettled and in need of comfort. Granny was still asleep, tucked under her quilt, bed cap low over her head.

"My sleep is patchy these days," she'd told Red last night. "Don't be surprised if you hear me shuffling around in the night. I may even go for a night walk."

Red herself felt weary. Her entire left side ached. She must have fallen out of bed again – the pallet she slept on at Granny's was narrower than her bed at home, and she always struggled to get comfy. But at least in the cottage she'd been able to forget about everything for an evening.

Yet another long day stretched ahead of her. But for once, Red was thinking of something other than how badly she missed long summer days, when she could escape into the trees the second the bakery closed and stay for hours before night crept in. And that something was Ellis. Not that Red didn't think about Ellis a lot – perhaps an embarrassing amount – but this was different. *He* was different. Yesterday, when she'd closed the bakery gates on the hostile crowd, he had shown another side, a spikier, less confident one, and she wanted to know more. Was it the first time he'd questioned the people around him, even encountered any hardship? It was funny to feel sorry for a boy so popular, with the ability to excel at most activities, but she couldn't not.

It was hard when your world changed. Red knew that herself. She had been too young to remember her father's death, and as a sailor he had not often been home anyway, but she had seen the effect it had on her mother and Granny. None of them had been quite the same again.

Not that Ellis would care for her sympathy. He still wanted

Martha, Red could tell, even though Martha had done nothing but pull away since he'd been attacked, for reasons Red considered silly. It had got under her skin yesterday and it needled her today. It wasn't fair. Why did he even like Martha so much in the first place? Or were all boys shallow?

By the time Red approached the bakery, dawn was breaking. She stomped the mud off her boots and rubbed her soles on the grate in the yard. The friendly tabby cat that sometimes sat on the wall watching the world go by jumped down and rubbed itself against her legs, purring.

"I'll bring you out something to eat," Red said, petting him behind the ears. "Stay there."

She opened the door – and immediately forgot the cat.

Someone was crying. These weren't normal sobs, either, Red could tell at once.

They were the tears of someone who had lost everything.

Red's skin goose-pimpled. Suddenly all her senses were alive. It smelled wrong. Something sharp, almost metallic, cut through the soft warmth. The air was cold, as though a door had been left open too long. And when she stepped inside, she gasped. The huge table where she and Martha unloaded loaves and decorated biscuits was on its side. A chair was broken. Knives and rolling pins and other tools were scattered everywhere. And what the sharpness was became apparent.

Blood.

Crimson smeared the white-painted wall by the door. Some of the marks looked like handprints. Red's breathing went shallow. Her hands closed around the closest weapon – a knife, resting on the cobbles by her toe. She edged to the door that led to the front of the bakery, and into the house.

"Hello?"

Crash. Red jumped, almost dropping the knife. The noise came from above. If whoever had done this was still here she should go. And yet her feet moved to the stairs, and carried her up them. Blood pounded in her ears.

"Hello?"

Martha's father appeared in the hallway, face full of fury. He barrelled past Red as though she wasn't there. Bewildered, Red opened her mouth to call after him, then changed her mind and inched to the room he'd left. The sobbing was louder now.

She took a deep breath and peeped through the gap in the door.

The person crying was Mistress Baker, shoulders slumped, as though she was broken. She clutched her daughter's hand. Martha lay in bed, twitching and moaning. Her mother blocked Red from seeing much of her.

"What happened?" Red whispered before she could stop herself.

Mistress Baker whipped round, eyes bloodshot. Red barely noticed. Her eyes went straight to Martha. And her jaw dropped.

"Oh. *Oh.*"

Bandages were strapped across the entire right-hand side of Martha's face, over one eye, and around her neck. On the small table by the bed were towels in a shallow pitcher, soaked with blood. Martha's hands were criss-crossed with scratches.

As though she'd flung them up to defend herself.

Red went cold. "Is it. . ."

Mistress Baker howled. As though those simple two words were keys to a floodgate of pain. Red moved to put her arms round her but the woman reeled away.

"Get back!" she screamed. "I don't want anyone here."

Realizing she still held the knife, Red dropped it. "Is there anything I can. . . Should I get the apothecary?"

"He's been. Not that he could help!"

"But she's. . . Martha. . . She'll be all right? She's not badly injured. . ."

"Easy for you to say." Mistress Baker rose to her feet. Her hands were fists. "Why couldn't it have been you? You're not even pretty. My girl, my beautiful Martha, with her perfect face and everything in front of her . . . savaged. By that animal. Here, too!"

Red's head spun. The wolf slinking in the bakery, right in the centre of town? Mauling Martha while her parents slept upstairs? "Are you sure?"

"Of course I'm sure! Martha saw it. The wolf is attacking people in their own homes now. No one is safe any more. No one!"

ELLIS

"Martha's been attacked?" Ellis stared at his friend Stephen, who had hailed the cart halfway between the mill and town. "It's not. . ."

Stephen mopped his brow, leaning over and resting his palms on his thighs as he gulped breath. "It's the wolf all right. It slunk into the bakery in the night, went for her. Ate her face off."

"What? Is she all right?"

"She's alive," said Stephen, after a long pause. "I don't know more than that."

"When you say ate her face, you. . ."

"I'm only repeating what I heard. But she's not going to be the town beauty any more, that's for sure. Might want to move on, El."

Before he knew what he was doing Ellis leapt from the cart and shoved Stephen with his good hand, catapulting him into the mud.

"Shut up!" he shouted. "Shut up."

Stephen's hands flew to shield his face. "Calm down! I said the wrong thing. I didn't mean to make fun."

"Sounded like it. Don't you dare speak about her like that."

"I won't, I won't! I was coming to warn you, you know. I didn't want you to hear about this from the wrong person."

The red mist in Ellis's head cleared. He helped Stephen to his feet.

"Thanks, Stephen."

Stephen brushed himself down, but he sounded a little off. "I didn't realize you liked her that much. It's not as though she's been there for you."

Ellis grunted. He climbed back on the cart. He and Caleb shuffled up to make space for Stephen. They started off towards town. Ellis fixed his gaze on the road ahead. The track faded, then vanished. Instead he saw teeth, and claws, and spittle, and... No. He squeezed his eyes shut.

Martha. He saw her in the back room, preparing dough for the morning, flour coating her lower arms, hair pinned up into a coif. The door, creaking open. . . Nails scuttling on the cold stone floor. A low growl. Martha's head jerking upwards. A black shape hurling into her in an explosion of ruby red. . .

"Ellis?" Caleb's face swam into view. "Are you all right? You've gone very pale."

Ellis couldn't speak. Ate her face. What did that mean? Quite literally that it had eaten her face? In that case she would be dead, or close to it. Had she merely been scratched? That must be it – Martha's parents heard the commotion, and the wolf had run off before it had the chance to rip off an arm, or a leg. . .

He thought of his bandages, the scars he was going to live with for ever. The brand of the wolf. Now they were healing he didn't feel bothered by them. But then people didn't look at his shoulder every day. Not like eyes were drawn to Martha's face, with its high cheekbones, and smooth skin, and light dusting of freckles, and the full, pink lips he spent far too much time thinking about. . .

"Can you handle the deliveries by yourself?" he asked his brother. "I will tell you what needs to be done."

Caleb bit his lip, eyes flitting back at the full cart. "All this?"

"I have to see her, Caleb. She'll be in pain, confused, and she'll hate everyone talking about her. I need her to know I understand. Please, Caleb. You can do this, I know you can. It's simple."

"What if. . ." Caleb stopped. He tilted his chin up, attempting to square his shoulders. "It's fine. I can do it. Of course I can."

Of course he couldn't. This was only his third time out. Even Dorothy was looking at Caleb with mild contempt in her eyes, making no effort to walk on even though Caleb had tugged the reins. Stephen couldn't help – he had gone out of his way for Ellis already, and judging by how silent he had fallen, he already wished he hadn't. No, Ellis would have to be the dutiful son, as usual, because time was money and family was everything. . .

Or not. He had defied his parents once and he could do it again. "The deliveries can wait," he said. "If people get their flour an hour late it doesn't matter. Come on."

The front of the bakery was shuttered when they arrived, but the gate to the yard was open. As Ellis guided Dorothy inside he noticed that the small bakery cart rested under the shelter, rather than safely stowed in the shed next to where the Bakers' horse was stabled. *Funny*, Ellis thought. The Bakers had only bought the cart a year ago, and were normally very careful with it.

Ellis left Caleb to bring in the flour and ventured inside. It felt cold, with none of the usual bustle and enticing smells. The oven had not been lit. Red was on her hands and knees, scrubbing the wall methodically. Ellis crouched down behind her.

"Hey, Red? I heard what happened."

Red didn't look up. "Do you know what I'm cleaning?"

"No. . ."

"Martha's blood."

A chill crept up Ellis's spine. "Oh. Do you need help?"

Red went still. Then she shook her head. "You should see her."

"Are you all right? You weren't there when it happened?"

Water sloshed over the side of the bucket as Red plunged in the cloth. The water was dirty pink with blood and grime. "No," she said shortly, and carried on scrubbing. Ellis looked at her a second, then decided to leave her be.

Bracing himself, he climbed upstairs. He would be calm and comforting. Tell Martha he understood. And those were not empty words to make her feel better. Perhaps this would bring them closer together, in the way only big things did. There had always been something a bit elusive about Martha, as though she held her real self back. Some days he was not sure if she even liked him very much.

One door on the landing was open. Through it he could see Martha almost hidden under a heap of blankets.

"Martha?" He didn't know why he was whispering. "Can I come in?"

Martha mumbled something, eyes closed. Ellis tiptoed in and perched on the chair by her bed. He took one of her hands, stroking the scratches gently with his thumb. Martha thought he had ugly thumbs. "Why are they so broad and flat?" she'd once asked. Ellis had explained it was something that happened when you worked in a mill, from repeatedly rubbing grain between thumb and forefinger to check for quality and texture. He was quite proud of his miller's thumbs, viewing them as a sign of belonging. His father's were the same.

"I heard what happened." Ellis wasn't sure if Martha was even awake, but the silence was making him uneasy. "I wanted to tell you it's all right, and I'll still like you. People will stare and say things, and maybe you will lose friends ... but it will be all right. This gives us something in common. Both the only people to ever have survived a wolf attack. Maybe one day we'll be proud of that, who knows?"

What else could he say? The bandage across Martha's face was bloody. He would change it. Doctor Ambrose had been very strict about Ellis keeping his bandages clean. It might give him something to joke about later, in a gentle way, of course – something about how it was a good thing not everyone was afraid of blood.

Perhaps next time Ellis visited he could bring some of the salve Doctor Ambrose had supplied. No doubt it would be more soothing than whatever was in the bottles from the apothecary.

For the first time, it occurred to Ellis to wonder why his parents had sent for Doctor Ambrose. As far as Ellis was aware, the doctor had never treated townsfolk. Ellis's mother disliked the apothecary, but she'd still summoned him when one of his younger brothers had been sick last year.

Strange, he thought. Very gently, Ellis peeled the bandage away. The fusty smell reminded him of uncooked meat. Which, to the wolf, of course, was exactly what he and Martha were...

Martha's eyes flew open. They were wild and unfocused. Ellis froze.

Her scream was almost impossibly loud. "Get away from me!"

Ellis jumped up, sending the chair tumbling. The bandage fell away. Gashes stretched from Martha's forehead to chin, and across her neck. They were far broader than the slashes on his chest had been, gaping and oozing. Ellis's stomach leapt, and not in a nice way. Martha burst into tears.

"Don't look at me! I can't stand it."

"It's all right." He tried to sound reassuring. "I know how you are feeling."

She ignored him. "People are whispering that I am tainted, that I've sold my soul to the wolf. If they block me out too— I don't know what I'll do. It's too much."

"Martha, I don't care about that—"

"Of course you do. I'll never be beautiful ever again. The teeth and claws – tearing at me, all over, like it was going to rip my whole body into shreds. Crazed eyes and hulking black and trees, trees everywhere! That place is cursed. It's a monster. A beast of evil! It's not natural."

Someone grasped Ellis's shoulders, hauling him back. The next second Mr Baker's round, bearded face was pressed close to his, forehead vein pulsing. "Leave my daughter alone. How dare you. Go on, out, before I send you packing."

Ellis pulled free. "That wound needs washing and re-bandaging. I could see if Doctor Ambrose—"

"He wouldn't lower himself to come here."

"He treated me—"

"Because your parents have Lord Josiah in their pockets! Now get away!"

Martha was screaming again now, clawing at her hair. Mistress Baker had run in and was struggling to lay her back down. Ellis backed away.

"I'll bring round some of the salve I was given."

"We don't want you here!" Mr Baker roared. Realizing Martha's father was about to lose his infamous temper, Ellis retreated. At the bottom of the stairs was Red, hovering as though poised to either flee or run to help. She said something, held out a hand, but Ellis shook his head, stumbling into the yard, on to the cart, and away.

"Perhaps they will realize you meant well," said Ellis's mother, later that afternoon. She sounded disapproving, though Ellis couldn't tell whether that was levelled at him or the Bakers. It should feel comforting to be back home, the whirr from the mill and the smell of chicken and vegetable stew, but Ellis was finding it hard to shake off a feeling of being on edge. The townsfolk had not mobbed the mill cart today, but they had gone silent when he passed, and someone had hurled a large stone after him. Would they treat Martha with the same disgust? How long before they refused to buy flour? When would this stifling suspicion end – spring, when maybe the wolf might back off? Ellis did not feel confident. Winter was only beginning. And this year the wolf was far bolder. . .

"What if Martha won't see me any more?" he asked.

"Give her time. This is raw and difficult. I might have reacted the same way at her age. Beauty is sometimes a curse." Mistress

Miller heaved a sigh, looking for a moment sad. Ellis pulled a face. He didn't want to imagine his mother being courted by anyone other than his father. "But if Martha pushes you away, then she's a sillier girl than I thought."

"You think she is silly?"

"I think Martha is not worth you feeling bad over. Aramor has many other girls with kinder hearts."

Ellis felt he ought to defend Martha, but something about the word *kind* hit home. Perhaps his mother had a point. "Please don't tell Father about today," he said. "He was angry enough about me taking Caleb and the cart before."

Mistress Miller pursed her lips. "It would serve Amos Baker right if we stopped supplying him flour. The bakery wouldn't last very long without us. He's a troublemaker, and his wife is empty-headed and gullible. Now they know how it feels to have a child suffer."

The vicious note in her voice took Ellis aback. Had he underestimated the bad blood between his family and others? He watched his mother go to the stove, inspecting the contents of the pot. "Mother ... isn't now the time we ought to be putting aside all these arguments and grudges? If everyone worked together we would stand a better chance of dealing with this wolf. Instead all anyone's doing is accusing other people of being in league with it, or witching it up."

His mother half-smiled. "You are very sweet, my love. If only life was like that."

"Why can't it be? Everyone banded together five years ago."

"Aramor was different then."

Better governed and more prosperous, she meant. Ellis had memories of guards on the streets, and swift repairs to broken water pumps and the leaky church roof, and the summer festival a flurry of colour and song and dance and laughter. Aramor felt much more austere now.

"I did not mean to talk down to you." The pot clanged as Mistress Miller replaced the lid. "All I meant was that you see the good in everyone. That is nice. But it is also naive. The world can be a dark place, Ellis. Full of envy. Never underestimate people's maliciousness."

"Not everyone is like that."

"No. But most of us are trying to get by."

And that made people malicious? Ellis remembered what Caleb had said about his parents being scared. He joined her at the stove, winding his arm round her like he had as a child.

"Mother. Whatever is upsetting you. . . I could help, if you let me. Even if it's only listening."

She sighed. "Oh, Ellis. You can't. I wish you could."

So there was something, then. "You could at least tell me."

"You will find out soon enough."

"Is it to do with money? Martha's father said you have Lord Josiah in your pockets."

Had she tensed? "I don't have time for this, Ellis."

"But I'm asking."

"And I'm busy. Amos Baker only says these things because he's resentful. If Bridget Forrester mentions anything to you, ignore her too. She's worse than he is."

Ellis scowled. "I'll leave then."

She caught his good shoulder. Her eyes had softened. "Ellis. I didn't mean to snap. I'm sorry. We're all on edge."

She didn't need to remind him.

$\mathcal{S}$ABINE

The bakery had been cleaned up by the time Sabine arrived. She had been desperate to get away sooner, but Lady Katherine had been unusually talkative, to the point that Sabine had been seriously thinking she might have to sneak off and risk dismissal.

I need to speak to Martha, Sabine thought. Hidden in the pouch that hung from her belt was a herbal mix she'd concocted that she was almost certain was the same as the one she had seen in the book she had returned to Doctor Ambrose. If Martha's parents gave them a moment alone, perhaps she could persuade Martha to take some.

Her palms were clammy as she knocked on Martha's door. Mistress Baker looked up.

"Oh. Sabine. Come in. I thought for a moment you were the Miller boy again."

Her stomach somersaulted. "He was here?"

She nodded. "I don't know for how long. I was asleep. So was Martha, until she woke up screaming."

"Did she say anything to him?"

Mistress Miller looked surprised at the sharpness of Sabine's tone. Sabine silently cursed. She *had* to keep a cool head. "About. . .?"

"The attack."

"I don't know. My husband chased him out."

"Has she said much to you yet?"

"No. Whenever we ask. . ." A tear rolled down her cheek. "I don't understand why Martha was even downstairs in the middle of the night!"

So far, so good, then. Sabine drew a deep breath, and stepped closer. She knew what to expect but even she was shocked to see Martha's face. There was no way those gashes were healing completely, however proficient the doctor. A strange feeling tightened Sabine's chest. It was the same curious one she had experienced the other night, racing through the darkness to treat Ellis: a thrill. It hadn't troubled her then. Ellis was not someone she cared about. But Martha...

Martha ought to be different. They'd been born within a month of each other, friends their whole lives, arguing often but never quite falling out. Sabine knew all Martha's embarrassments and hopes, and Martha knew ... well, Martha didn't truly know what Sabine wanted, because even as a small girl Sabine had been wary of trusting, but that didn't stop them being close.

So why did Sabine feel so ... detached? Was she protecting herself, because what had happened – really happened – hurt too much to properly face? Sabine's mother had always impressed on her that emotions were messy, and best ignored. Or did she not, ultimately, really care very much about Martha? *That cannot be right*, thought Sabine, and the tightness got worse. Maybe she wasn't always very kind, but she wasn't heartless. Was she?

With great effort, Sabine shut the doubts down. She took Martha's cold hand. "Martha."

"Sabine." Martha's hollow eyes bored into her. Sabine couldn't work out if she was angry or not.

"I can't believe this has happened," murmured Mistress Baker. "Why us. Why the bakery. So deep within town... We should have been safe. It never ventured far from the woods five years ago. The attacks were all on merchants, or woodsmen."

"I know. My father lost friends." *And himself*, she thought.

"I understood the wolf before. It was winter, and it was hungry. But this . . . maiming. . ." Martha's mother's voice became a whisper. "It makes no sense."

Perhaps not to you, thought Sabine. The attack on Ellis was the one that bothered her. It was almost as though the wolf had chosen not to eat him. Sabine remembered her conversation with Doctor Ambrose. Could she contrive another meeting, and steer the conversation to the wolf? It boiled her blood that she couldn't just walk into his room and ask him, even after assisting him the other night, because that wasn't what girls like her were supposed to do.

"Martha was in the wrong place at the wrong time." Sabine glanced at her friend. Martha said nothing. She had closed her eyes. The ball of tension that had knotted Sabine's stomach ever since she'd left the manor unwound a touch. If only they could speak alone. Sabine offered to sit with Martha while her mother rested, but Mistress Baker looked nervous and said she didn't think that was a good idea, and maybe it would be best if Sabine left.

Reluctantly, Sabine followed Mistress Baker into the hallway. Martha's mother paused at the top of the stairs.

"Why did the wolf come here?" she burst out. "That is another thing I do not understand. It couldn't have smelled meat from the pies, not at night. Everyone cooks meat in their homes anyway." She lowered her voice. "Martha describes it so vividly. A beast of evil. I am so afraid..." She seemed to be struggling with the words. "Perhaps it only looks like a wolf. Perhaps it really is ... a phantom. And if it has been summoned ... someone is controlling it."

"No one has any reason to think that," Sabine said in her firmest voice. "Martha is shocked and in pain and saying things."

But Mistress Baker was shaking her head. "How else could the wolf get through a solid, locked door? It was not damaged. We always bolt it when we close the kitchen. My husband worries about thieves."

"Perhaps it wasn't last night."

"No. It certainly was."

A bead of sweat rolled down Sabine's forehead. Curse Martha's mother! She was never normally this sure of herself. "Whose job is it to lock the door?"

"Martha's. She wouldn't forget. She's always so careful. It must be witchcraft. There cannot be another explanation. Oh, I don't know what to do, or who to tell! Why us?"

Sabine hesitated. Hesitated a long moment. "There is another explanation."

"What?"

"Maybe someone who isn't Martha or you or your husband left the door open."

For a long moment Mistress Baker looked perplexed. Then her entire face went tight and she went downstairs without a word. Sabine wiped her brow and waited. Then came the shriek.

"Red! Come here, now!"

RED

The sound of her name sent foreboding shooting through every inch of Red's body. She skirted a glance at the back door, but before she could vanish outside, Mistress Baker crashed in, eyes feverish and breathing shallow.

"You left the back door open when you went home last night. How could you? How could you!"

Red's stomach dived. Had she? "I. . ."

"Because of your carelessness, Martha was attacked. I've overlooked so many mistakes, but this!"

Red's head swam. "But I didn't – at least, I don't think I did—"

"But you are not sure," a new voice said, and Red's blood froze. Sabine stepped in behind Martha's mother. If anything she looked even more tired than the other day, with deeper grey circles round her eyes. "You've forgotten to lock up before. I know you have. Martha told me so."

"Only once, and I learned my lesson." Red raked through yesterday's memories for something definite and drew a blank. "I've been trying hard—"

"Not hard enough." Sabine stepped right up to Red. How was she so composed? "You've wrecked Martha's life. No one will want a girl with a ruined face."

Behind them, Mistress Baker gasped. Red knew she had to defend herself, or this was going to spiral. "I did not leave the door open." She tried her best to sound assertive. "I might sometimes forget to take loaves out of the oven or confuse an order, but I've been careful whenever Martha has asked me to lock up. How do we know Martha didn't leave it open herself?"

"Because she never has before and you have?"

"That does not mean it was me! I remember closing it properly now, I—"

"And that means it was Martha? After her beau was horribly

mauled and Martha's done nothing but worry about staying safe ever since? I don't think so."

"No. I didn't."

"No one believes you, Red." Sabine took a step closer. "No one will believe a single thing you say from now on either." The menace in the words sent a chill tingling down Red's spine. "What happened *is* your fault."

"You can't prove anything."

"I don't need proof. There is no other way this could have happened."

"Isn't there?" Red was lashing out, knowing she was losing, but to her surprise, Sabine flinched. For a second, her composure slipped, and Red saw something else in those icy eyes. Fear. The next moment they were iron-hard again. And angry.

"Are you going to accuse Mr or Mistress Baker of leaving it open?"

"Of course not!"

"Then it has to be you. I understand why you mightn't have realized quite how dangerous the wolf is, as you so enjoy cavorting about in the forest yourself, but—"

"I don't cavort. I visit my grandmother. And I never said I wasn't afraid of the wolf. I think you're jealous."

"Of what? You?" Sabine laughed.

"Yes, me. I think you'd like to cavort in the forest yourself, but you're too scared, so you spend all your time gazing into it instead. You certainly got upset enough about this last time."

Sabine raised her hand. But instead of smacking Red she grasped her shoulder, fingers digging in.

"No, Red. The townsfolk won't believe a thing you say, remember? So think twice before you throw baseless accusations around. No one likes a liar."

"And no one likes being accused of something they didn't do." Red clenched her teeth. "You're a cold person. Are you even upset about Martha? You don't look it."

Sabine turned her back on Red. Martha's mother was watching the girls, mouth hanging slightly open. "You're not going to continue to let her work here, are you, Mistress Baker? It would be an insult to Martha."

Red's defiance shattered into tiny pieces. "No! Please, Mistress Baker. I swear it wasn't me. I don't know why the door was open, but I am begging you, believe me. I cannot lose this job, for my mother's sake." Mistress Baker sniffed and looked away. Grasping for something that might save her, Red said, "If Martha is unable to work, you'll need someone who knows how the bakery works. I know I'm not perfect but I'll do the very best for you, I promise."

Mistress Baker looked overwhelmed. She was shaking her head, mumbling about her husband being angry. Sabine looped her arm around Martha's mother, patting her arm, as though it was them against Red. Red clenched her teeth.

"I've done nothing to you, Sabine. Why can't you let me be?"

"Because you left the bakery door open and my best friend was attacked."

"No. You've always hated me. Why?"

The front door slammed.

"I think that's Martha's father," said Sabine. "I would get away before he hears what you did if I were you."

"I'll be back tomorrow," Red said to Mistress Baker, but the woman had her hands over her face and Red wasn't sure she'd heard. Red grabbed her cloak and slipped out. Only now did she realize she was shaking. Would she still have a job after this? Mother's disappointment would destroy Red. She'd been so pleased to finally have found Red a position she stood a chance of keeping, after failed attempts as a seamstress and at a farm.

You left the bakery door open and my best friend was attacked.

The way Sabine spoke the words, it was as though they were

fact. And the more she said them, the more they'd be believed by everyone else. For the briefest moment Red herself had almost believed her. Sabine was so . . . mesmerizing, somehow. How did a fourteen-year-old girl – a low-born girl without education or influence – have such power?

The townsfolk would believe her. Before too long it would not matter whether Red really had left that door open or not. As for where that left her, with the mounting anger and fear she sensed every time she stepped outside, especially now there were whispers that the wolf had been witched up...

"I am in so much trouble," Red whispered to herself.

SABINE

She listened to the Bakers raging at each other in the hallway outside Martha's bedroom, all the time holding her friend's hand.

"I simply will not have her here any more!" Mr Baker was hoarse from shouting. "Her carelessness has cost Martha everything. Us everything, if people decide we are cursed! That's what they are murmuring. I heard it."

"We need her." His wife's tone was pleading. "For now, anyway. We won't cope otherwise. And we do owe her family. If it wasn't for her grandmother's skills, I mightn't have survived childbirth."

"Damn her grandmother! She is not normal. No one else lives by themselves in the forest. She should be chased out and we would all be better for it." *Crash.* Had he kicked over a chair?

"Amos, calm down, please! I'm frightened. If that animal really can slink through the streets undetected, it can do anything. What if it comes back?"

"If it is really the wolf, it will be old and weak by now. We should hunt it down once and for all."

"That was not a success last time. Whatever Sabine's father saw that day. . . He will never be the man he was."

Sabine felt as though she had been smacked. She squeezed her eyes shut. Suddenly she was nine again, flinging her arms round her father as he and four other woodsmen prepared to venture into the forest and hunt the wolf.

"You'll come back, won't you, Father?" she had asked, and he'd hugged her in return, thick beard tickling her cheek.

"I promise, Sabby."

And she had believed him. Later she lay in bed hugging herself and remembering how proud she had felt earlier that day when her father had vaulted on to the fountain in the market square, announcing the hunt.

"We won't return until it's dead." he had boomed. "Soon Aramor will be free again!"

The cheers had been deafening. Her father's axe had caught the rare winter sunlight, and glowed. Sabine had almost burst with pride. He looked so strong and powerful. A hero bigger and better than those in stories. There had even been tears in her mother's eyes.

"No one will forget this," Mistress Forrester had said. "Only a humble woodcutter, and he has everyone cheering his name! This, Sabine, is how people change their luck. Life will be different from now on."

When dusk fell the men had strode off, townsfolk lining the streets to clap them on their way. Sabine's father had looked over his shoulder as he vanished into the trees and smiled straight at her.

She would give anything to see her father smile like that again.

After the hunt had left, Aramor had been unnaturally quiet. Sabine had sat in bed, determined to wait for her father, but the heaviness of her eyelids had overpowered her. Next she knew, it was morning.

The men had not returned.

The townsfolk went to wait. There had been murmurings of sending a search party but no one was willing to volunteer. A rumour circulated that howling had been heard in the night.

At midday, Sabine's father emerged from the forest – alone.

What exactly had happened no one knew, even years on. But the other men were dead, set upon by the wolf. Sabine's father would not talk of how he had survived, even to his wife.

No one ever blamed him for the hunt's failure, or ostracized him for returning when others had not. The Woodcutter – for some reason, that was what everyone called Sabine's father, even though he was one of many woodsmen and foresters – was not regarded as a hero, exactly, but there was an unspoken appreciation of what he had tried to do, and he had everyone's respect.

But he would rather still have his friends alive, Sabine thought. She opened her eyes. They felt wet. Sometimes she almost wished her father had not returned. He had closed in on himself ever since, a man going through the motions of life rather than living it. Sabine clung on to hope that the father she had so adored was still there somewhere. One day, she was determined, she would get him back.

Sabine wiped her eyes. Tears would have been useful earlier, when Red had dared imply Sabine didn't care about Martha. She looked down at her sleeping friend. The wounds really were unsightly. Would Martha be tough enough to endure the stares and jeers? It mightn't have been so bad if she hadn't made such a big thing of her looks. Maybe she'd become a recluse, a strange old lady like Red's precious grandmother. Sabine sometimes thought that mightn't be the worst life. At least if she lived in the forest she could do as she wanted, and get away from her mother.

The floorboards outside creaked. Martha's mother slipped inside.

"Sabine, you should go. There's nothing else you can do here."

"Are you sure?"

The woman tried to smile. "Martha's going to need good friends more than ever now. You won't abandon her, will you?"

"Of course not." And Sabine meant it, whatever Red might imply. Mistress Baker caught her arm in the doorway.

"Will you be safe, walking back? I would never forgive myself..."

"I'll go to my parents, and then my father can escort me to the manor."

"Good. Be quick. And stay alert."

After being cooped in Martha's bedroom the air smelled sweet. Sabine stood a moment, enjoying its cleansing bite. Two women with baskets scurried past, picking up their pace when they passed the bakery. As though the wolf was still lurking. Sabine fought the sudden urge to laugh.

She strolled to the market square before doubling back home.

A few merchants were packing up their wares. They moved hastily, as though suddenly aware the darkness was near and they'd dallied too long. The other stalls were empty, if they'd even been filled at all. The wind bounced a small basket across the cobbles.

By the water pump a wooden horse lay discarded, as though its owner had been whisked away. It was a little chipped, and crudely carved, perhaps by some parent in the candlelight. Sabine's father had whittled her animals out of wood when she had been small. Her favourite – which felt darkly funny now – had been a wolf. She kept it under her mattress in the manor along with her herbs. In softer moments she sat stroking it, remembering how she had once raced through meadows making the wolf leap through the air, and how her father had joked about a vicious beast being a little girl's toy.

Sabine picked the wooden horse up. Perhaps one of her smaller siblings would like it. Whittling wood was one of the many things her father no longer did. She trudged homewards.

As it always did these days, her mood sank at first sight of the ramshackle cottage that until recently had been home.

"Sabine! How nice." Her mother opened the door and enveloped her in a hug. Over her shoulder was the usual chaos. Children everywhere, some screaming, another crying, her father with his eyes closed on the rocking chair with her eldest sister's baby asleep on his chest. The fire in the hearth was pathetic, bringing next to no warmth. No wonder someone was always sniffling.

"I will eat at the manor." Sabine didn't take off her cloak. "I've been with Martha."

"I thought you might have been." Mistress Forrester's eyes gleamed. She steered Sabine over to the doorway that led to the bedrooms, lowering her voice. "So what exactly happened?"

"Red left the bakery door open and Martha was unlucky enough to be downstairs when the wolf crept in." Sabine kept her voice bland. Her mother pursed her lips.

"So it really has been prowling the streets in the night."

"It appears so."

"The butcher's wife heard scratching at their back door last night. And one of your father's friends swears something frightened his dogs."

Sabine's lips curled. People's stupidity really shouldn't surprise her any more. "I'm sure."

"What is the reaction at the manor?"

"I don't know. I've barely been there much today."

"I didn't mean the attack on Martha. The Miller boy. How did they react to what happened to him?"

Sabine shrugged. Her mother grasped her shoulders, grip pinching.

"Sabine. You know I need to know these things."

"Mother, I didn't notice. I hardly see Lord Josiah anyway."

"Lady Katherine?"

Sabine shrugged again. Her mother let go.

"Watch more carefully in future." Mistress Forrester gave her a long, steady look. "You are a very lucky girl to work for Lady Katherine. I got you that position. Remember that if you're ever tempted to turn your back on me. I don't think you would like scrubbing floors instead, would you, my love?"

Sabine said nothing. From the main room, one of her brothers shouted. Won his game, probably. Sometimes it felt as though she was a piece on a game board, with her mother as games mistress.

"So how is Martha?" asked her mother, as though everything was normal again.

"Why are you asking? You already know. Maimed."

"Pity. One less pretty girl for competition, at least."

Competition for what? The pick of Aramor's young men? Sabine had no interest in being courted by any of them. She made a non-committal noise.

"You don't seem too heartbroken," said Mistress Forrester.

"You've schooled me well." Sabine meant it as an insult, but her mother only smiled.

"I'm not cruel, my love. I am doing the best for myself and my family, same as anyone. If you have nothing useful to tell me, I will get your father to walk you to the manor." She tapped her lightly on the back. "Don't want the wolf to gobble you up, do we?"

Back in her bedroom at the manor, Sabine hunched under the covers, not even trying to go to sleep. She didn't want to surrender herself to nightmares, to lose control. Even stroking the wooden wolf in her palm offered little comfort.

I hate this place, she thought. *I hate the people, everything.*

She thought of Martha, lying under her own blanket. Ellis would be slumbering too, over the other side of the town. Was Red awake? Or had she slipped into the forest, quiet as a ghost? Sabine had seen her emerge with bunches of pretty wild flowers before, leaves in her dark hair. Other times she ambled out with an expression of serenity on her face that made Sabine feel fierce and hot. It didn't seem fair that Red had a place she could vanish into and forget herself. Sabine did not have that luxury.

Especially after what had really happened last night.

RED

The next morning Red edged the door to her cottage open and glanced up and down the lane. No one was about. Perhaps she could get to the bakery without being spotted. She hadn't heard word from the Bakers that she was not needed any more, so she would chance going in. Her insides were jittery. Word about what she had supposedly done must have spread. She'd half been expecting someone to bang on the door last night, shouting abuse at her, yet it had been eerily quiet ever since sundown. Her mother, who'd been very busy yesterday and had not left the house, was none the wiser, but Red knew that would not last. At least cooking dinner had distracted her from imagining claws tearing at Martha's face. Picturing the attack on Ellis was bad enough.

She took a deep breath, then another. Then she stepped out and trotted off, keeping her head down. If she could just—

A pair of sturdy boots appaeared in her path. Red leapt back, narrowly avoiding colliding with the boots' owner. She recognized him as Bart, Martha's cousin. He worked at the butcher's, occasionally stopping by the bakery when he wanted something to eat without paying for it.

"Oh!" she said. "Sorry. I didn't see you."

Slowly and deliberately, Bart leaned in and spat in Red's face.

"I wonder what made that noise," he sneered. "I don't see anything. Do you?"

"Nothing worth looking at." said another voice, and Red realized Bart had a friend with him. "Just dirt."

Red wiped the spittle with her sleeve and dodged around them before it could happen again. As she fled, Bart called, "You deserve to pay for what you did! Leave town, go on. You're not welcome any more."

Red didn't stop running until she was safely inside the bakery, back door and gate closed behind her. It felt empty without Martha there. Red closed her eyes as her breath slowed.

She should be used to this by now, she really should. Not spit. That was new, as was animosity from Bart and bigger boys who considered themselves too important to pay the likes of her any attention, but it wasn't the first time she'd been told to disappear. Anger surged through her. This wasn't even her fault! Bart and his friend had just blindly believed a rumour. She should go back and put them right. Stand her ground. Sabine hadn't liked it when Red talked back yesterday, had she?

Red's hand was on the latch before she realized that Bart would be long gone by now. And was it really wise to pick fights when she was only clinging on to her job because there was no one else and Martha's mother had an old debt of gratitude to Granny? She'd always thought Bart self-important and big-headed, but this morning he had displayed a nasty side, too. He wouldn't listen to her and neither would anyone else. They'd expect Red to deny everything.

She suddenly yearned for Granny. Granny always made Red feel like her worries were less important than they seemed, or laughed at them in a way that made Red want to laugh too. There was no way she'd find anything funny in this, but Red ached for someone to be on her side, to listen.

I'll see her whenever I'm done here, she decided, dangerous or not.

Red wound apron strings round her waist, and got started on the first batch of bread. Soon she was too busy to think. A tap on the door made her jump. It was Ellis.

"Hello? Flour."

On automatic Red pushed hair from her sweaty forehead, then too late remembered her hand was coated with sticky dough. *What does it matter,* she thought, as Ellis disappeared to the cart. *He thinks I'm strange already, like everyone else. And once he finds out about the door, he'll hate me too.*

Caleb teetered in clutching a sack almost as big as he was. He stumbled on the step. If Red hadn't been there to catch him he'd have been on the floor.

"Here. Let me help," she said, and slid her hands under the sacking, shifting some of the weight from Caleb. He looked a little nervous but didn't shy away. Together, they shelved it, then returned to the cart for the three other sacks. Ellis stood scratching the horse behind the ears, pretending not to watch.

"You shouldn't have to do that," he said, when Red came out for the last time.

"Well, I did." She folded her arms, conscious of her perspiring face and grubby apron. "Are you going in to see her, then?"

"Only if she wants me. Could you. . .?"

Why was he bothering after yesterday? Stubbornness? Red didn't think Ellis was one of those arrogant boys who pushed themselves places they weren't wanted. She banged back inside and up the stairs to Martha's room. She was alone, her mother front of shop, and her father at the market.

"Ellis wants to see you," announced Red.

"Tell him to go away."

"Tell him yourself."

Martha hunched forwards. A tear trickled from the eye Red could see. "I don't want to speak to him ever again."

"What if he wants to speak to you?"

"He doesn't, even if he thinks he does. I don't know what to say to him anyway."

"Talk about what happened. Or talk about whatever you talked about before."

"Before. All I have now is after. Go away, Red." Martha turned to the wall. *No one can say I didn't try*, Red thought, and left. Ellis pushed off from where he was leaning against the wall when he saw her.

"So?"

"She wants you to go away and says she doesn't want to speak to you ever again." Immediately Red regretted being honest. Ellis's face crumpled.

"Does she mean that? Or is she delirious? Yesterday—"

"She means it. Sorry."

He looked at his feet, scuffing his heel in the dirt. Then he heaved a big sigh.

"Maybe it isn't a surprise. She could barely look at me when you all came to the mill. I told myself she was scared of blood, but I was making an excuse, wasn't I?" Ellis was looking at her now. "Martha only really liked me when I was popular, and other girls would see us out together."

Red tucked her hair behind her ears, not sure what he wanted her to say. Despite everything, her heart was singing. He had finally realized! "Martha likes nice things. I suppose you were a nice thing too."

"It makes me so angry." He dug his hands into his pockets. "In one moment, everything I knew as normal, gone! Sometimes I think it would've been better if the wolf had eaten me."

"Don't say that. A lot of people care about you."

"Then they have a funny way of showing it. Do you know something? I've spoken more to you about this than anyone outside my family. My friends would rather point and whisper and avoid me. Sorry, I don't mean to make you awkward. I'll go. I know you have work to do."

Red didn't want him to leave yet. "How's it healing?"

"I don't know," said Ellis after a pause. "Based on what the doctor said it ought to be more comfortable by now, but it isn't." He glanced at Caleb, who was over the other side of the yard playing with the friendly tabby cat. "If there is a problem, a lot of work is going to fall on Caleb. My other brothers are too young. I worry he isn't suited for the mill. I've always thought he should go to the city and study. He's smarter than I am."

Maybe too smart for his own good, thought Red, remembering how Caleb had crept into the bush to eavesdrop on his parents' conversation. What else did he know about that he shouldn't? There was something imploring in the way Ellis was looking at her, as though he thought she had answers. He had such nice, kind eyes – a soft kind of green, like moss. And before she knew what she was doing, Red said, "My granny might be able to help you."

A line appeared between Ellis's eyebrows. "Your granny in the forest?"

"She knows a little about medicine. Normal medicine, I mean. She's not a witch, if that's what you were thinking."

He flinched, and Red wished she hadn't said that word. "I wasn't thinking anything."

"You were. I know what people say."

"Thanks for trying to help. But I shouldn't."

"Do what? See Granny?"

His cheeks coloured. "People are on edge around me already. If they hear I've been in the forest—"

"No one need know. I don't have anyone to tell even if I wanted to."

Ellis rubbed his arm. Red could hardly believe how outspoken she was being – only a few days ago she couldn't look at Ellis directly for fear she'd blush. "Does your granny ever come to town?"

"The forest isn't scary, Ellis, really," said Red, more softly this time. "I know the way. If we set off in daylight, we'll be safe. We'll stick to the paths. The wolf only ever attacks at night. Sunday, maybe? If we can both avoid church, we could set off early and make the most of daylight."

Ellis fidgeted. Then he tried a smile. It came out looking wrong.

"Sunday, then. But it'll need to be secret."

ELLIS

Every time Ellis thought about walking into the forest he felt twitchy and ill at ease. Vulnerable, even. This was a new feeling for Ellis, and he didn't like it. When he remembered how he'd strode outside that fateful night, axe in hand, completely confident, it felt like a different person.

Sunday came. Ellis's heart started thumping the moment he opened his eyes. At breakfast – Sunday was the one morning when the Millers sat down together – he felt sure he was going to give himself away.

"Ellis?" asked his mother. "Do you feel unwell? You look a little grey."

"Didn't sleep well, and my head aches." That was not a lie, at least.

"Is it too bad to go to church?"

Ellis nodded, hoping this would be easy. His mother looked sympathetic, but his father spoke before she could. "I expect you to come today however unwell you feel, Ellis."

"Why?"

"We are not having a discussion. Fresh air will do you good."

"Then Ellis can go for a walk," his mother snapped. "I will not force him to attend church just because—"

Mr Miller's knife clanged on the plate as he got up and left without a word. Ellis blinked after him. Even his little brothers were staring, mouths hanging open.

"Ignore your father." Mistress Miller rose. "You better go back to bed, Ellis."

Ellis did as she said, not sure whether to be more surprised that his mother had taken his side or that his father – who grumbled about church – was so insistent he go. Was something special about today? Guilt started to needle away at him. He could have met Red after church – there would be plenty of light left then. If people saw them together, did it really matter? Being jeered at for walking off with her couldn't be worse than what he'd endured already.

Ellis lay back, listening to his family getting ready to leave. Instead of the forest, he thought about Red. Now he'd spent time with her, he didn't think she was anywhere near as strange as everyone said. A bit abrupt and awkward, maybe, but she had been kinder to him than anyone else. Including Martha. And kindness was something that suddenly mattered a lot to him.

The front door slammed. His family's voices died away. Ellis waited ten minutes, then slipped out.

As soon as Ellis stepped under the trees, every part of his being screamed at him to run. Even without leaves the branches formed a thick canopy over his head, blocking out daylight. The forest was even more untamed than he remembered from the few times he'd walked to the edge – brambles springing up either side of the path, nettles and weeds winding across tree stumps, the path uneven and muddy.

Red strode ahead, humming to herself. She wasn't small or slight but she was still a girl who as far as he knew had never swung an axe or shot an arrow. How could she be so unafraid when his breath was rasping, every muscle tensed? Ellis felt deep, grimy shame. *I am supposed to be strong and fearless*, he thought. The axe in his left hand felt three times its weight and only made him feel the slightest bit safer.

Red stopped, waiting. In the town, she shuffled, head kept down, but outside, her tread was light and back straight. He was very conscious of how her red cape leapt out among the mossy greens and dirty browns. Were wolves attracted by colour? Dogs and horses weren't, so maybe not, but the bright crimson still set Ellis on edge.

He joined Red, bracing himself for her to tease him, or worse, jeer. If Martha were here she would have laughed, probably not kindly. He remembered one time they'd been in the storeroom and an especially large spider had scuttled over his boot. Ellis had jumped, and quickly moved away. Martha's face had worn an expression of surprise and disgust.

"A big boy like you, afraid of spiders?" She had sounded incredulous.

"I'm not scared," he had said. "I just don't like the way they move."

"They are harmless. Aren't you supposed to be brave?"

Red waved her hand in his face, and Ellis snapped back.

"Are you all right?" she asked. "Sorry, I forgot about you a moment. It's been a few days since I was in the forest and I've missed it. Every time I am here I feel ... at ease, somehow. Like I am exactly where I'm supposed to be. It seems so beautiful to me, even in the winter."

Ellis concentrated on the path ahead as they started walking again. "How far is your granny's house?"

"Not far. She's not mad enough to live right in the centre. She's not mad at all, anyway. She's wonderful and clever and fearless. But you'll see that for yourself." She smiled. "In summer there are the most beautiful flowers, just past that bush – big, drooping petals, usually yellow but sometimes white. I've thought of finding out what they are, or naming them myself, but it feels nicer for them to be mysterious somehow. Who needs to know everything? There is a beauty in very simple things, I think."

Ellis glanced over his shoulder. "If we do get attacked, Red, you should run. I'll do my best to protect you."

She laughed, actually laughed. Ellis scowled.

"That wasn't a joke."

"Oh, I wasn't laughing at you. Just, you don't need to protect me."

"I don't see you holding a weapon."

"Because I don't need one. Nothing will happen to us. I promise. You really do not need to be afraid."

"I'm not afraid. I'd just feel better if I had my right arm. This one is nowhere near as strong."

"Do you want to give me the axe?"

"No!" Ellis snapped. Then, feeling bad, he added, "I'm sorry. It's ... I don't feel much like me at the moment."

Red laughed again. "There's more to you than doing strong boy stuff though, isn't there?"

"Strong boy stuff?" He pulled a face.

"You know what I mean. It isn't like you've suddenly become nothing, even if other people act that way."

Had she always been this wise? Suddenly he found it hard to meet her eyes. "That's not how it feels."

"Well, maybe it should." The pink of her cheeks deepened, and Ellis felt his face colour too. "You're kind. You care about doing the right thing. And you clearly really hate letting people down."

Ellis rubbed his jaw. "Well. I am not sure, but thank you."

"Maybe you should be more sure, Ellis Miller. Look, Granny's house!"

Through the trees was a stone cottage, all crooked and funny looking, with windows of different sizes and a chimney so wonky he was surprised it stayed upright. Ellis couldn't believe he hadn't spotted it already. Suddenly feeling ridiculous for how tightly he was clutching the axe, he let out a shaky laugh.

"Was that conversation a plot to distract me?"

She grinned. "Worked, didn't it?"

Red's granny had an unexpected vivacity despite her age, and reminded Ellis a lot of Red. If she was surprised to have another visitor she did not show it. She brewed them tea while Red gave the main room a quick dust. The liquid in the cup smelled pungent. Ellis hesitated before sipping, waiting for Red and Granny to drink first. Granny's eyes danced.

"Nothing funny in there, just nettles."

Red laughed. "Ellis thinks you are a witch."

Granny groaned. "Oh, how unimaginative."

"I already said I didn't!" Ellis could feel his face had coloured, again.

"It makes little difference to me whether you think I am a witch or not, young man, but we will get on a lot better if you can forget the scare stories." Granny put down her drink. "I assume you're here because you would like me to look at your arm."

His cheeks burned hotter. "Red said you could maybe help. Um, Grace, I mean. Or Red. I don't know which you call her."

"And now he's really flustered." Granny grinned. For an old woman she had surprisingly good teeth, with the same gap between the front two as Red. "Let's have a look."

She untied the sling, resting Ellis's arm on the cushion she placed on his lap. He peeled off his jerkin. "Do you need, um. . ."

"I can feel everything perfectly well through your undershirt." Granny's fingers pressed around his shoulder, then moved down to his elbow. "Hmm. Can you move the arm at all?"

He shook his head.

"Flex your fingers?"

"I can, but it hurts."

"Well, Doctor Ambrose was right, it is a bad break." She spoke with calm authority. "You are lucky he was able to pop your shoulder back in. There will be hidden damage around the joint, but time and rest are great healers. In a few weeks, try flexing your arm. Slowly build strength through movement, rather than rushing to do everything at once and damaging it again. Come back in a few weeks and I'll show you what to do. I've seen breaks as bad as this heal right, with care. No witchcraft, just experience and observation."

She smiled, and this time Ellis smiled back. "Thank you. I'm sorry if it came across like I was suspicious of you at first."

"What nice manners. You can definitely return." And this time, they all laughed. Red, Ellis noticed, was beaming at Granny with a glow to her eyes that reminded him of the way his mother had watched his brothers when they were little. From the way Granny linked her arm through Red's, he could tell she felt the same.

They chatted a while about other things, ranging from how to stop Red scratching her wrists during nightmares to Red's suspicions that the tailor was sweet on her mother.

"A second marriage wouldn't be the worst thing," said Granny. "He is a good man who will make her happy. She is a skilful seamstress, too. I expect she would enjoy working alongside him in his shop." She drained the last of her tea. "What other new horrors are unwinding in town? I hope you don't believe that malicious fabrication that Sabine has been spreading, young man."

Ellis admitted he'd been so wrapped up in himself that he hadn't given it much thought. "We are a little stuck out at the mill. I heard what people were saying, but... Has it been really bad?"

Red shrugged, face clouding over.

"Red. How bad has it been?"

"Some boys spat in my face. One of your old friends tripped me up, and I fell in a puddle, and had to change, so then I was late. Almost everyone pretends I am not there. Even adults. Could be worse, I suppose."

"They can't treat you like that." He slammed down his tea. "Which boy pushed you? I'll tell them all to—"

"Because they'll listen to you?"

They would have a few weeks ago. He met her eyes. "We should stand up for ourselves. If we can work out what really happened in the bakery, then maybe everyone will leave us alone."

"What do you mean, what really happened?" Red sounded guarded. Granny, Ellis noticed, was watching him closely, though she said nothing. He switched his attention to Red.

"Do you really believe Martha went into the kitchen during the night because she heard a noise, leaving her nice warm bed? That's not her at all. She'd shout for her father."

"Another reason, then? Like ... she was meeting someone? That might explain why she opened the door – she didn't want whoever was there to knock and risk waking her parents?"

"I don't know, Red. Martha loves her sleep. I have, uh, asked to meet her late before and she always said no." Something was bothering Ellis – something he'd spotted around the bakery the day after the attack, maybe – but he could not quite put his finger on what.

"I bet Sabine would know," muttered Red. "Sometimes it feels like she knows everything."

He lowered his voice. "Do you really believe someone could have conjured the wolf up?"

"To attack you and then Martha? Why would anyone want that?"

"To hurt our families? Both my father and Martha's rub people the wrong way."

Red shook her head. "I think it's just the wolf again, Ellis." She paused. "People are only talking of witches because if the wolf is responsible they can't do anything with their anger other than try to hunt it again. Feelings that big . . . they need to go somewhere."

Granny cleared her throat. "Do you know why I live out here?"

Ellis wasn't sure who that was a question for. "Because you don't like the town?"

"Town is nice enough. It's the people I keep my distance from. Can you guess why?"

Ellis thought of his parents' mistrust of their neighbours. The Bakers and their resentment. The anger of Martha's father, and the nastiness of the other teenaged boys. Lord Josiah, rarely seen, apparently preferring to read rather than govern. Mistress Forrester, always appearing where she shouldn't, asking probing questions, and her silent husband. Sabine, who didn't seem to care about anyone or anything.

"I don't know."

"Oh, I think you do, even though I suspect you're a lad who likes to believe the best of everyone. People –" Granny leaned forwards – "have an endless capacity for darkness. The wolf, now, the wolf acts on instinct. It maims and kills to survive. It bears no one ill feeling. The same cannot be said of the townsfolk."

She paused, but Red and Ellis were both silent. Ellis was thinking of his mother, and how she had said something similar.

"I think that we are the real wolves," Granny continued. "People are scared and want someone to blame. That's why the two of you need to be very careful – in the very place you should feel safest."

$\mathcal{S}$ABINE

Morning light streamed through the window into Lady Katherine's bedchamber. In the mirror, Sabine could see that her ladyship's brow was furrowed, lips slightly pursed.

"You look tired, my dear."

Sabine continued brushing Lady Katherine's hair. "I am quite all right. I sleep poorly sometimes, that is all."

"Any reason?"

"No, my lady."

"You seem to have enough energy. Doctor Ambrose may be

able to provide something to help. I will ask when we return from church."

"I could go and see him myself. With your permission, of course."

Lady Katherine smiled. "You are interested in his work, aren't you? He told me you were a very competent assistant the other night."

Deny everything, Sabine thought. But curiosity got the better of her. "He said that?"

Her ladyship nodded. "There is no need to pretend you aren't because such interests are supposedly unmaidenly. I happen to think it is perfectly healthy for girls to occupy their brains with more than domestic affairs. Although you are making fine work with my hair."

She smiled, and, cautiously, Sabine returned it. She finished securing Katherine's hair into a sleek updo and stepped back. Lady Katherine turned, arm over the back of her dressing table chair. "You must have had lots of practice doing your sisters' hair. You have three, haven't you? Or is it four?"

"Three, though the older two do not like me much."

Sabine had not intended to be so blunt, but Lady Katherine laughed.

"Perhaps my idea of what having a sister is like is too idyllic. Dogs are clearly superior. Aren't you?"

One of the dogs on the rug raised a shaggy head. Katherine went over and stroked him. She seemed in a good mood this morning. "I hope you know you can talk to me, Sabine. It's very easy to feel isolated living here, and I like to know about others' lives. Especially young people. I know you are friends with poor Martha Baker. It must be distressing. If you ever wanted to talk about it, I would listen."

Sabine's eyebrows shot into her fringe. Surely most grand ladies were not this informal or friendly? Perhaps Katherine was seeking distraction. Or perhaps like Sabine's mother she enjoyed watching people. There were only so many long walks she could take with the dogs, and Josiah did not seem keen to allow her to assist him.

"It is distressing," Sabine allowed. *Not entirely for the reasons you would no doubt assume*, she thought. "I was planning to call on Martha after church, with your permission."

"You must. Good friends are hard to find and even harder to keep. And you must tell me how she is afterwards."

The door banged open and Lord Josiah appeared. He reminded Sabine of a duck – short legs and feet that turned outwards, giving the impression of a waddle. He was half a head shorter than his wife and at least fifteen years older.

"We need to leave," he announced. "I will not be late to church today, not with the town in such a furore."

Lady Katherine rose obediently. A few minutes later the lord and lady, Sabine, a couple of other servants and Josiah's personal guard, Vincent, were in the carriage, clopping towards church, two footmen marching briskly alongside them. Sabine always thought these monthly church visits were a joke – hardly enough to convince the townsfolk that Lord Josiah really cared about them. According to her father, Lord Josiah had once been a fair and conscientious governor, but Sabine saw little of that energy now.

Families trudging the puddled lanes stepped on to the grass to let the carriage pass. At church, a building with an unusual round tower which Sabine had always thought austere, Josiah climbed down, holding out a hand for Katherine with a courtesy he rarely showed her at home. Sabine noticed his eyes raking the crowd, as though looking for someone. She wondered who. Normally the townsfolk stood back, allowing Josiah and Katherine to sweep in first. Today, groups hunched around talking, paying little attention. As the group from the manor passed, Sabine heard a fisherman mutter, "He should be the one getting up and preaching, not the priest. Our children are being attacked, and he does nothing."

Inside, Sabine passed her family. They occupied a pew at the back, looking shabby although the clothes were their best. Her father leaned forwards in silent prayer. Sabine tried to catch his eye but instead caught her mother's. There was a gleam in them Sabine didn't like and she quickly looked away.

"Excuse me, Lady Katherine. This is yours." The speaker was Mr Miller, smartly dressed with what looked like a new doublet. The rest of the family were equally well turned out, though Ellis, Sabine noticed, was missing.

"Oh! Thank you." Lady Katherine took the glove he handed her. Sabine's eyebrows drew together. It was freezing here. Why had Katherine even taken off her gloves? Mr Miller executed a bow. He looked at Katherine directly, not keeping his eyes low like the other townsfolk would have done. In an undertone he said, "There is an ugly mood this morning. It might be for the best if. . ."

"I took to the pulpit and gave a rousing speech?" Lord Josiah had heard. "People need to calm themselves. The wolf isn't dragging bloodied bodies into the forest just yet."

Mr Miller's mouth twitched. "With respect, your lordship, it has done plenty of damage already. As you are well aware."

"I don't care for your tone," snapped Lord Josiah. Mistress Miller took her husband's shoulder, trying to pull him back. Mr

Miller shook her off. His hands balled into fists. Sabine glanced between the two men, eyes big. They were not going to fight, surely? Then an almighty crash rang out from the back of the church, echoing loudly. A heavy ornamental candleholder lay on its side, candle snuffed out. Standing over it was Martha's father.

"What are you going to do, your lordship?" he bellowed. "Let more children be maimed and mauled? Call yourself a leader?"

He kicked the candleholder. It clattered against a pew. No one moved. Somewhere a baby bawled. Sabine looked at Lord Josiah. Anger flamed in his eyes. Stiffly, he said, "This is a place of worship. If any of you have concerns, pray express them outside, or consult the priest—"

"Faith alone cannot protect us!" shouted Mr Baker. "My daughter has seen it. And it is a phantom! Someone here controls it!"

Murmuring rippled through the church. Lord Josiah looked taken aback – and, for the first time, afraid.

"This has gone too far." The priest's voice rang out. "See that your uncle gets home."

This was directed at Bart, who was leaning against the wall a few feet away, watching proceedings with a tiny smile playing round his lips. He did not move. Mr Baker marched up to the priest and gave him a shove. The priest overbalanced into a pew. Someone behind Mr Baker threw a punch, and Mr Baker went down like a skittle.

Then the crowd erupted. Suddenly everything was arms and legs and shouting. A tapestry tore off the walls. Something shattered. Two men barrelled past Sabine, and her back bumped the wall. She badly wanted to stay, but Vincent was hurrying Katherine and Josiah through the door to the vestry. Sabine knew she must follow.

She caught them up outside, piling into the carriage. The footmen had their weapons drawn, circling the carriage protectively to keep the crowds streaming out of the church back.

"We cannot leave yet!" Katherine sounded frenzied. "I need to check he's safe—"

Sabine missed Josiah's reply. She squeezed into the carriage. Vincent leapt on the back, and they clattered off. Sabine craned her neck to watch the church. The shouts were so loud! It was like a battlefield. Were those flames?

"We cannot run away, Josiah." Lady Katherine's face was snow white but her voice was strong. "We need to summon guards and restore order. It's only going to get worse. If you will not do it then I will. And we must do something about this wolf, whether it is beast or phantom—"

"The wolf is not the problem," snapped Lord Josiah. "They are."

"People are afraid! The wolf is breaking into their homes."

"No it is not. A stupid girl left a door open. And phantoms do not exist."

"They can be summoned. I have seen it depicted in books."

"Katherine! Do not interfere."

Without thinking Sabine grasped Lady Katherine's hand. Her ladyship leaned back. She looked sick. Sabine felt a little sick herself. Things had escalated so quickly! It was as though the townsfolk wanted to rip into each other, neighbour swiping at neighbour, all the rivalries and annoyances of years past dredged up again. She wanted to jump from the carriage and run back and shout that they were fighting over a lie.

Her lie.

RED

By the time Red and Ellis bid goodbye to Granny the promising sunshine had faded. Clouds hung low in the sky, darkening every time Red glanced upwards. Normally she enjoyed the drama of the forest before a storm, but Granny's ominous words bounced around in her head.

You need to be careful.

Red glanced at Ellis. His eyes were moving from the treetops down to the trickling stream and across to the wild bushes where berries grew. A bird twittered.

"Maybe I'll come back in spring," he said, and Red felt herself smile.

"Not afraid any more?"

"I wasn't afraid," said Ellis, but he smiled back in a way that made it feel like a shared joke. Their boots crunched dry mud and twigs as they set off along the path. Ellis still had his axe, but she could tell he wasn't poised to use it any second. He broke the comfortable silence first.

"I like your granny. I feel a bit bad."

"About what?"

"The things I've heard the other boys saying when none of us even knew her. I am ashamed I never challenged them. It's easy to be unkind without thinking." He paused. "My friends used to say things about you, too."

"I know."

"It must hurt. You say you are used to it, but you shouldn't have to be."

He said it like it was simple. Maybe to him it was. She shrugged. "I've never felt like I belonged."

He hesitated. And then he said, "I don't always feel like I belong either."

"Since you were attacked?"

"Since for ever."

Red shot him a disbelieving look. "How can you? Whenever I see you – saw, I mean – you were always surrounded by people. The way you always have something to say to everyone, and you remember little things they tell you – like asking the butcher's wife about her bad feet, or the ginger boy who runs errands about his imaginary dog. . . You couldn't belong more."

The tops of his ears coloured. Red wished she hadn't spoken. It wasn't fair to assume, even if she had been surprised. Her intuition told her to wait, let Ellis gather the confidence to explain. As they neared the edge of the forest, he said, "My parents don't treat me the same as my brothers. It's difficult to explain. Little things – I wasn't allowed to dive in the deepest part of the stream when I was little. Whenever I got sick, my mother would fret, really fret. And I have been taught things that a miller's son has no use for."

"What things?"

"Well." He adjusted the sling. "I can read and write."

"Oh! Do you need that to run a mill? You'll be in charge some-day, won't you?"

"I suppose so. We never talk about it. I always thought it was my parents being ambitious. But they didn't engage a tutor for Caleb, and he is the clever one."

"So you feel an outsider in your own family?"

"A little. And despite all this I can't shake off the feeling my parents don't like me as much as my brothers. However hard I try."

Red was starting to understand. "Is that why you pushed yourself to do so well at everything?"

"Maybe. I've always wanted to please them." In a hurry, he added, "I know it's stupid. I don't know why I am even telling you about it."

"It's not stupid." Red reached to brush his shoulder, then stopped herself. "I don't have answers, but I understand. Things are not always easy with my mother. Granny says even the love that should be the simplest can be complicated."

His smile was a shy one – as though relieved to have got it off his chest. They broke from the trees. Red had taken them towards Aramor, rather than the longer route that would bring them up closest to the mill.

"Thank you for today," said Ellis. He tilted his head, and Red's heart skipped a beat. "You're different, Red. And I don't mean that in the way Martha and Sabine do."

Red held eye contact, even though her heart was hammering away. She wanted to ask how she was different, maybe even dare to hint how much she had always liked him. But something distracted her. She sniffed. "Can you smell that?"

"Smell what?"

"The air's all heavy. Bitter. Almost . . . I don't know. Unclean."

"Seems normal to me. You must have a very sharp sense of smell."

"Maybe, I— Oh." Red grasped Ellis's arm. She had placed it. "Something is on fire."

ELLIS

Together they raced into town. As they crossed under the main gate, the ashy air intensified. Ellis could see smoke too now, foul grey tendrils curling into the air. The houses they passed were shuttered, the streets empty.

"The breeze is heading east," Red cried. "The fire must be this way."

"The church." Ellis's stomach went tight. "That's where everyone is. Or was. My family are there!"

His chest was heaving from the run to town, but there was

173

no time to rest. He tore down the lanes, hearing Red follow. The smoke grew thicker. All he could think about were his family, and how he'd lied to them. If they were hurt, or worse, his last memory would be of deceiving them—

He skidded to a halt at the end of the road, mouth forming a big O. The church still stood, though a putrid cloud funnelled upwards. Townsfolk – mainly men and boys – were passing buckets of water from the nearest pump in a human chain. Their faces were filthy and exhausted. But the fire appeared to be under control. Several feet away the apothecary's shop was open. A number of people sat outside looking dazed, though none seemed to be badly hurt. One of them was Stephen. Ellis darted over.

"Are you hurt?"

Stephen shook his head. "Someone hit me by accident and everything is a bit blurry. I'll be all right. Where were you?"

"Doing something. Have you seen my family? Are they—"

"They're fine. Probably back at the mill by now."

Ellis felt his shoulders slump in relief. "I'll get home as soon as I can. Is anyone badly hurt? What happened?"

"A fight broke out. I'm not sure who started it – I was outside. But Bart says Lord Josiah was rude to your father, and then Martha's father got up and started shouting about the wolf, and everyone started scrapping. Candles were knocked over and set fire to a pew. That broke things up. I don't think the damage is that bad. And no one is really hurt."

Ellis exchanged a glance with Red, who had joined him. Was she thinking back to what Granny had said about the townsfolk being the real wolves? "I can't imagine people we've known all our lives fighting like that," he said. "In church, too!"

"Five years ago I remember the wolf drawing people together, not apart," said Red.

Ellis glanced at the water pump. "At least they're working together now."

Stephen pressed a cloth soaked in something strong-smelling to his head. "Bart sounded like he enjoyed it. Angry about Martha, I suppose. It's not like Lord Josiah is doing much about it."

That was no surprise to Ellis. Many boys from Aramor, including Bart, had grown up wanting to travel to the city and train as soldiers. But times now were peaceful, so that was no longer an option. Being apprentice to a butcher must bore Bart rigid. Ellis could understand the frustration.

"Last time it was Sabine's father who took control," said Red. "He organized a night watch rota, and got the houses closest to town to strengthen their doors and shutters."

That was right – it was coming back to Ellis now. The Woodcutter had been a real tower of strength. "I can't see him doing the same this time. He seems..."

"Broken," Red finished the sentence, and they went quiet. Then Ellis caught a woman with a split lip glaring at Red and that brought him back to the moment. He placed his hand on her back. In an undertone, he said, "Red, you ought to go. People blame you. I don't want anyone to throw a punch your way."

Red looked like she wanted to argue, but she nodded. Ellis didn't feel right leaving her, so he offered to walk with her. Stephen caught his arm before he could go. He lowered his voice.

"El, the other boys..."

"The other boys what?"

"They've been saying things about cutting you out. They don't trust you. I spoke up for you, but then they threatened to cut me out too, and..." Stephen stopped, swallowed. He didn't meet Ellis's eyes. "I thought you should know."

Ellis stared at his friend, barely able to believe what he was hearing. "All because I was attacked?"

Stephen nodded.

"Are you going to side with them?"

Stephen did not reply. But his miserable face said everything.

Ellis opened his mouth to argue, then found he did not have the energy. Instead he walked off with Red. Their route took them past the inn. Normally on Sundays it was closed, but today the innkeeper had rebelled and it was teeming, patrons spilling out on to the street. Despite the ale flowing, everyone looked very far from merry. Ellis and Red hurried past.

At Red's cottage they said goodbye. It was hard to believe that not long ago they had been in the forest, feeling light and hopeful. Red looked pensive. Ellis wanted to say something to make her feel better but he couldn't think what. She knew as well as he did how serious things were.

$\mathcal{S}$ABINE

Sabine's eyes fluttered open. The light spilling through the shutters of her manor bedroom was murky, the very first hint of dawn. She sat up, rubbing sleep from her eyes. Had she been having a nightmare? Something about Martha... For once she'd dropped unconscious the second her head hit the pillow. Lady Katherine had forbidden her from going into town after they had returned to the manor, and part of Sabine was secretly grateful.

Voices, down below. Perhaps they had woken her. Sabine's skin goose-pimpled. Had there been another attack? Not here, surely?

Suddenly she was completely awake. Quickly she dressed, pausing only to splash water across her face. Outside, the corridor was still. Sabine crept down the staircase, following the voices. As she neared Doctor Ambrose's room, someone cried out, followed by the doctor's commanding, "Calm, now."

The door was ajar. Through the gap Doctor Ambrose leaned over someone stretched out on his large wooden table. A man. His mud-splattered boots jerked as the doctor pressed a cloth against a gash on his leg. Another groan. Then Ambrose said, "Come in, Sabine."

Sabine drew in a breath. "How did you—"

"I can see you in the mirror."

Of course. She almost laughed – this talk of witchcraft was getting to her.

"Fill that pitcher with fresh water," said Ambrose. "If you're spying you may as well be a useful spy."

She didn't like the way he said that word, but she was not going to turn down the invitation. Sabine took the empty pitcher to the water pump outside the kitchens. When she returned Ambrose dipped a fresh cloth into it and pressed it to his patient's chest. For a moment Sabine did not recognize Vincent without his smart guard's regalia. He was whimpering, his forehead shiny with sweat. Either he was drunk, drugged, or very good at handling pain, because blood oozed from criss-cross gashes across his chest, with more wounds on his leg. *Claw marks again*, thought Sabine. From the way his head was bandaged she guessed he was either missing an ear, or one had been badly damaged. His hand was bound, but in a vial on the other end of the table was what looked like the top of a finger.

"What do you need me to do next?" she asked.

"Bring bandages from the cupboard. Then apply pressure, if you can. Especially where the finger was. I did have help, but the silly man fainted. Someone with a stronger stomach is supposed to be arriving from town, but without any speed, it seems."

Sabine grabbed the bandages, then unravelled what had been tied over the gap where Vincent's finger had been. Blood pumped out. Swiftly she re-bound it, then held it tight.

"You should have called for me," she said.

"Should I?" Ambrose arched an eyebrow. Sabine had the feeling she had given herself away – or perhaps Lady Katherine had had a word – but she held her head up high.

"I helped you last time. I returned to visit Ellis, and I've tended to Martha."

"Tell me, then, Sabine. How do you think our friend Vincent came by his injuries?"

"I couldn't possibly guess," Sabine said dryly. That made Ambrose chuckle. He took a threaded needle, holding the tip in the flame of his candle. Then he plunged it into Vincent's flesh, sewing a gash on his leg as though it was a jerkin or tunic.

"Our friend here is blind drunk, though I've also drugged him a little too," he explained. "At least this makes him an easy patient."

"Where was he attacked?"

"Believe it or not, the forest. Excessive consumption of ale, it seems, leads people to do clever things like go hunting for deadly wolves by themselves. No doubt he was encouraged by his equally drunk friends, but it was spectacularly foolish nonetheless."

Vincent mumbled something. His face was drained of colour.

"How much blood can someone lose before they die?" asked Sabine.

"You would be surprised. He'll live. Thoughts on that?"

Sabine knew she shouldn't let Ambrose draw her into speculating again, not after the scene at the church. She was on thin ice as it was. Listen lots, speak little – that was another of her mother's sayings. But it was so refreshing to be treated as though her opinion meant something that holding back was impossible.

"I think the wolf had a golden opportunity for a lovely meal which, again, it passed up. Was it disturbed, by any chance?"

"Correct. Men from the inn where Vincent had been drinking came to find him. They didn't see the wolf, but they did hear something disappearing into the trees."

Sabine frowned. Five years ago the wolf had been bold, not fearful. "Why isn't it killing people? Three times this has happened now. It must be hungry. What has changed?"

"Something certainly has."

"But it's an animal. It doesn't attack for fun, or play games. It was once so ... efficient. Teeth to the throat, a quick death. It decimated an entire hunting party!"

"Wash this." Ambrose cut the thread with a knife, handing Sabine the needle. "One explanation is that it keeps getting disturbed. That is what happened when it attacked your friend Martha, is that not correct?"

Panic shot through Sabine before clearing. There was no way Ambrose knew the truth. He was clever, but not that clever. "Yes, by her parents."

"Therefore, we have an explanation for why Martha and Vincent didn't die. Perhaps not a very satisfying one, but an explanation nonetheless. What I find more curious is what happened with young Ellis. But we have reflected on this before."

Sabine screwed up her face, thinking. "Last time didn't the

wolf sometimes drag people into the forest and hide their bodies to eat later? My father found a sort of den when they investigated the forest. One of the bodies there was almost untouched. There were a couple of legs, too."

"Well-remembered. Not squeamish, are you?"

She wasn't sure if he meant it as a compliment or not. "Why didn't the wolf drag Ellis off if it was full up on chickens? The forest isn't far from the mill."

"I'd say we're dealing with a very strange wolf, wouldn't you? Some would say supernatural..."

"I don't believe whatever everyone else says," snapped Sabine. "Do you?"

Ambrose rubbed his eyes. Suddenly he looked old. "I think it wiser not to have an opinion, after what happened at church. But if you are asking whether I think it is a mere animal? No. I do not."

Sabine and Ambrose worked in silence after that. Ten minutes later assistance came in the form of the apothecary's yawning assistant. Ambrose turned him away without even looking up.

"I have all the help I need."

Sabine felt proud. She didn't care that her dress was stained deep red or that the room stank like a butchery. As Ambrose turned to stitch the last cut, she said, "Can I do it?"

The doctor's bushy eyebrows shot up. "Excuse me?"

Too much interest, thought Sabine, and silently cursed herself. "Sorry."

"I don't think our friend Vincent here would take kindly to you experimenting on him. Sealing a wound is not the same as embroidery. However. . ." The needle sank into flesh once more. "When I have a patient with a less severe injury that we can take time over, I will show you how it is done, and perhaps, when you've observed me at work several times, then we will see about you having a go. Enter."

Sabine jumped. She hadn't heard the knock. To her surprise, it was her father, face ashen, clutching his cap in both hands.

"Apologies for interrupting, Doctor. But how is he?"

"Alive. You found him, is that correct?"

The Woodcutter nodded. He was a big man, towering over Ambrose, and had to bend forwards to avoid hitting his head on the door frame. "Vincent likes a drink. He started bragging that he was going to kill the wolf. We didn't think much when he lurched out. But later we started to wonder." He closed his eyes a moment. "I have lost too many friends to that creature. I will not lose more – oh."

He spotted Sabine. He blinked several times. Sabine folded her hands in front of her, demurely.

"Hello, Father."

"I thought you worked for her ladyship," he said.

"She does," said Ambrose. "But somehow, your daughter and I keep bumping into each other at fortuitous moments."

"I see." The Woodcutter's tone said he really didn't. "Well. If that is all, I should go. His lordship asked to speak to me."

"Don't tell Mother you saw me here," Sabine blurted as he turned round. "She wouldn't be very happy if she knew about this."

"You know I tell your mother everything."

Because if he didn't she'd find out anyway. "Please, Father. For me."

But he backed out, shaking his head. Sabine felt a sinking sensation. She could just imagine her mother's response to this. *You're in his lordship's house to improve your family's lot, and that does not include playing doctor! You must never be seen to involve yourself in things that aren't your business, even if you are.*

Sabine glanced at Doctor Ambrose. "If you don't need me any longer I should go."

The doctor nodded. He sighed. "You're an intelligent girl with a strong head, Sabine. It's a shame."

What was? That she couldn't read, and her parents would never support her learning from Ambrose, even unofficially? Or that she was a girl, a poor girl at that, and therefore not someone he could take on as a proper apprentice? Sabine left, a sour feeling dampening her earlier rush. Maybe her mother had it right after all, collecting secrets and wielding them against people. When you had no power, you had to seize some yourself.

ELLIS

All Ellis had been able to think about was the fight in the church. Even the next morning, it still didn't seem very real. Caleb hadn't been able to tell him much more than Stephen had, and of course it was yet another thing his parents wouldn't talk about. Instead they had come down hard on him for lying about being sick, which Ellis resented.

"To go into the forest, of all places!" his father had raged. "If your arm was hurting, you should have told us and we would have arranged something. I never had you down as such a hot-head. You need to start thinking about your actions, Ellis!"

The whinny of horses brought Ellis back to the moment, and to the window from where he was sweeping corn from the mill floor.

"It's Lord Josiah," he said, surprised. "What does he want?"

"What?" Mr Miller elbowed him from the window. His lordship's carriage pulled up just outside the mill, a footman leaping down to open the door. Out climbed Josiah, and behind him, Katherine, in a flowing gown of deep purple far too fine for here. Ellis glanced at his father. A deep crease sat between his eyebrows.

"Carry on as you are," he called to the mill hands. "I won't be gone long."

Ellis watched his father stride out. He felt Caleb at his shoulder.

"They're here again?"

"What do you mean, again?" asked Ellis.

"Father and Lord Josiah met last week. That was business. So I don't know what this is. Especially as they were hardly friendly yesterday."

Ellis was frowning too, now. Was this something to do with that comment Mr Baker had made about his parents having Lord Josiah in their pockets? Why would that matter today, when surely the priority was settling Aramor down, and deciding what to do about the wolf?

"You've been here all along," said Caleb. Ellis blinked.

"What?"

"If you want to go and eavesdrop, that's what I'll tell Father."

"Caleb, you need to stop knowing what I'm thinking before I've even thought it."

"Else what, I'll be accused of having arcane powers?"

The way things were going, Ellis wouldn't have put it past the townsfolk to accuse a twelve-year-old boy. Caleb hesitated, then said, "If you don't listen in, I will. They're keeping something big from us, El. And Mother isn't happy. She hides how she feels well but she has been cold with Father a few months now. I've heard her say he betrayed her more than once."

"In what way?"

Caleb shrugged. Ellis could not imagine his father ever betraying his mother. Their marriage had always seemed so solid.

"Do you think this is to do with the wolf?" he asked.

"No," said Caleb, after a long pause. "I think it is to do with you."

Ellis thought back to what he'd confessed to Red, about feeling like he didn't belong. His heart began to race. Caleb could be wrong. There were many reasons their mother could be upset, all kinds of possible secrets.

But whatever it was, he had to know.

Whispering to Caleb that he'd be back soon, Ellis tiptoed down the mill staircase, dipping down to avoid banging his head on the door frame, and into the cottage. He traced voices to the parlour, the nicest room in the house.

"...people are saying..." That was Lord Josiah, and even muffled Ellis could tell he was irate. They'd closed the door, but when he squatted by the keyhole Ellis could see well enough. His father stood by the window, arms folded, facing Lord Josiah. Opposite Lady Katherine sat his mother, hands folded on her lap. Her moss-coloured tunic brought out the green in her eyes. She threaded her fingers together, squeezed, then relaxed them.

"Fear is not a bad thing." Lord Josiah was saying. "Fear draws people together. Fear appeals to people's better natures. If people were merely afraid, I would do nothing." He paused. "A fact for you. Five years ago, wolf aside, was Aramor's most harmonious winter to date. The prisons were empty. Only a few cases of theft. Very little for the guards to do. A prosperous winter, too." Another pause. "Fear keeps everything in check."

Heat rose within Ellis. There was something disgusting about this well-fed, indolent nobleman daring to say that people cowering in their homes and children crying suited him! No wonder people had been so angry yesterday.

He waited for his father to smartly tell his lordship that these were people's lives, not chess pieces to move into convenient places. Instead, Mr Miller glanced at his feet.

"I agree that there was a certain . . . sense of togetherness."

"One solution might be to impose a curfew," said Josiah. "It may not really make a difference, but it will make people feel safer. And that is more important than whether they are safe or not."

"If you are asking my opinion –" Mr Miller's voice was cold – "I have none to give. But this is not why you are here. You want to discuss our arrangement."

Lord Josiah cleared his throat. All of a sudden he did not appear so composed. "It is almost time."

Mistress Miller got to her feet. "He isn't fifteen for another month."

Ellis stiffened. Him. They were talking about him. So Caleb was right.

"We do need to discuss this, my love," his father said softly, reaching for her hand. "I know you do not like it, but a month will pass quickly. And now there's been a third attack." *What?* Ellis swallowed an exclamation. "It might even be for the best if we moved more quickly—"

"No." Mistress Miller pulled away her hand. "I won't hear of it."

Lord Josiah and Ellis's father both opened their mouths, but Lady Katherine got there first.

"Of course we won't rush this." Her voice was hushed. "That would not be fair. An agreement is an agreement, after all."

Mistress Miller sniffed, hugging herself. Then she stalked out. Ellis leapt up but the door was open before he could hide.

His mother looked at him. Tears glistened in her eyes. Instead of telling him off, she hugged him. Ellis tentatively returned it, aware that the other three adults in the parlour were watching. His mother let go. Ellis called after her, but she waved him away and vanished upstairs.

"Ellis, come here." His father's voice was neutral. "His lordship and her ladyship want to see how you are after the attack."

Mr Miller clearly didn't realize Ellis had been listening – the angle of the door had hidden him. Reluctantly, Ellis stepped inside. Both Josiah and Katherine were looking at him in a way that felt somehow . . . intense. He'd met both before, but only in passing, and although Katherine had greeted him warmly, Josiah had paid Ellis no attention. Not sure what he should do – did you bow to a lord in your own home? – he clasped his hands in front of him, and waited.

But no one spoke. Lady Katherine kept glancing at Ellis's father, but his eyes were on the floor. Lord Josiah crossed his arms, expression impassive. Did he make them awkward, Ellis wondered, or was there something he was missing here?

Josiah broke the silence. "Well, your colour is healthy enough. Are Ambrose's medicines doing their job?"

"Yes, your lordship."

"And the arm?"

Ellis wasn't going to mention he'd had it looked at by Red's grandmother just a few days ago. Before he could speak, his father did. "It's healing, but it's slow progress. Isn't that right, Ellis?"

"It must be difficult not being able to join in activities with your friends," said Lady Katherine. She was still smiling. "I often see the boys practising with bows, or playing at sword fights. Do you have other interests you can distract yourself with, at least until it heals? Reading, perhaps? We have many fine books we would be happy to—"

"Katherine," Josiah snapped. "The lad is fine. But no foolish going outside after dark until either the wolf is gone or winter is over. No going into the forest, either. Do you understand?"

Lord Josiah knew he'd sneaked away yesterday? And, come to that, Katherine was aware he could read. How much else did they know? Ellis didn't see why he should promise this man anything, so he stayed silent. Josiah pursed his lips, then shook himself and turned away. "Katherine, go back to the carriage and let Miller and me discuss things alone."

"Very well. Goodbye, Osmund, I am sure we will speak soon." Her ladyship nodded at Mr Miller as she rose. As she passed Ellis she brushed his hand. "Escort me outside, will you, Ellis?"

Ellis would rather have eavesdropped again, but he didn't see how he could refuse. He showed Katherine to the end of the hallway, and opened the door for her. The waiting footman stood to attention but Katherine lingered. Softly, she said, "I know this must be very confusing for you, but it will make sense soon. Don't be afraid. Please call into the manor the next time you're delivering flour, Ellis. I think Doctor Ambrose ought to check on your arm again, just in case. If you did want to see the library. . ."

Ellis rubbed the side of his neck, not liking the directness of her gaze. He couldn't think of anything to say. Katherine looked a little disappointed, as though he had failed some kind of test. She drew her cloak around herself more tightly, tilting her face upwards.

"It looks like more snow is coming, don't you think? Perhaps people won't mind a curfew too much if it's this bitter. Are your clothes warm enough for winter? Your brothers', too?"

He cleared his throat. "I should get back."

He could feel her eyes on him as he strode away. They made his back feel like it was burning.

RED

All day, Red ached. She had woken up feeling terrible. It wasn't just a muscle ache, either, the kind she had grown accustomed to since picking up Martha's workload at the bakery. This was deeper, like it was eating her up from the inside.

Was she ill? Red couldn't remember the last time she'd even had a sniffle. Mother always said she was just like Granny. "Never once can I remember her taking to her bed. If only I was the same!"

Maybe she'd had a nightmare and fallen out of bed again, Red thought as she shaped currant buns and lined them up for the oven.

It couldn't be all the walking she'd done with Ellis yesterday – that wasn't out of the ordinary. Perhaps it was all the worrying, knowing that wherever she stepped, accusing eyes would follow. . .

As Red was cleaning up at the end of the day, wanting nothing more than to crawl home and sleep, there was a rap on the door. It was Ellis, looking pale.

"Red? Can I talk to you? Not here. How about a walk?"

Red forgot her aches. Somehow she'd got it into her head that Ellis would steer clear of her for a few days. Many times she'd replayed yesterday's conversation in her head – the way he'd said she was different like it could be a good thing. She was trying not to get too hopeful, or excited. He was frustrated and going through a strange time. It was quite possible he would come to his senses.

All the same, she did feel excited as she hung up her apron and donned her cape. Five minutes later they were outside town, following the path of the frozen-over river south, the opposite direction to the forest.

"There's been a third attack," Ellis said, and Red gasped.

"Oh no! I've been so busy all day I haven't gone outside. Who was it? What happened?"

"All I know is what Lord Josiah said to my parents." And Ellis told her Vincent had been set upon in the forest. Red shivered, drawing her cape around her more tightly. Despite herself, she pictured Vincent in his smart regalia flailing through the trees, shouting for the wolf to face him like a man. A sudden force catapulted him on to his back, and Vincent was writhing and flailing and screaming. . .

"Horrible," she said. "Three attacks. There'll be more, won't there?"

"Seems likely."

"Are you scared?"

"Yes and no," said Ellis. "Mostly I worry about other people. Stephen's house isn't very secure. I am not sure if he's my friend any more but I don't want anything to happen to his family. Your cottage would be easy to break into too. Are you scared?"

Did he really care for her safety? "This isn't what you wanted to talk about, is it?"

He bit his lip, then met her eyes. "I don't know if my parents are really my parents."

Red gave a start. "What makes you say that? You don't look that much like them, but that isn't so very strange."

"That's what Sabine's mother said weeks ago when she accidentally-on-purpose bumped into me. She knows. She must do."

Ellis dug his hands deeper into his jerkin pockets. He described Lord Josiah and Lady Katherine's visit to the mill, and what he'd overheard. Red wanted to ask questions but made herself listen instead. "...so I cannot help but feel that either he's my father, or she's my mother. It makes so much sense I can't believe I never thought it before. My being taught to read, my being tended to by Doctor Ambrose, my parents being so cautious over my safety..."

"So you think either your father had a relationship with Lady Katherine, or your mother with Lord Josiah? They can't both be your parents or you would have grown up as their son without any pretending."

Ellis skimmed a pebble over the ice. "Either is possible. My mother was a servant at the manor before I was born. And my father would have delivered flour there. I cannot picture either of them betraying the other, but I don't know them, do I? If this is true, they've lied to me my whole life." He looked up. "And something is going to happen when I turn fifteen."

Red felt a chill settle on her. "Have you asked your parents to tell you the truth?"

"Not yet." He swallowed. "I am afraid. I don't know what I even want to be true."

Red wondered who else knew about this. It was possible

from the things Martha's father has said that he had guessed. That explained his resentment of the Millers. "Don't ask unless you're ready, then. It is a lot to take in. Especially with everything else."

Ellis nodded. "Thanks for listening. I needed to speak to someone." He paused. "Do you want to know another thing that seems ridiculous? All the time I spent with Martha. I could never have had a conversation with her about something like this. She wouldn't have cared. It is so clear now that she didn't really like me."

"I think she'd have liked you a lot more if she knew you might be a lord or lady's son." The words were out of Red's mouth before she could stop them. Ellis looked startled, then laughed.

"You are very wise, Red."

Wise was one thing Red was certain she was not, but she liked that he thought that.

"So. . ." Ellis let the word hang. "We have maybe an hour before it gets dark. Shall we forget about everything and have a little fun?"

Red tucked her hair behind her ears, immediately feeling awkward. "How do you mean?"

He held out a hand. Red took it. His skin was in places hard, a working hand, with a curiously shaped thumb, but she liked how secure it felt to hold – and the warmth it sent through her. Ellis guided her down the riverbank and stepped on to the frozen river. Red pulled back.

"I have terrible balance. I'll fall."

"Don't worry. I won't let go."

Red's legs startled to wobble. But she decided to trust him. Taking his hand again, she took a deep breath and nudged one foot, then two, on to the ice. Ellis edged backwards, smiling encouragingly.

"Not so bad, see?"

Red experimented sliding her left foot forwards – and yelped as it shot out from under her. She tumbled over, pulling Ellis with her.

"I thought you weren't going to let go!" she gasped.

"I haven't. I didn't promise to stop you falling!"

They both laughed, and Red felt light inside. They clambered up. After a little while, Red gained confidence. It was actually fun to feel her body moving so freely – a little like dancing, only with no one watching and giggling at her ungainly limbs. There was plenty more falling over – no doubt come tomorrow they would both bear ugly bruises – but Red didn't care.

"I love this!" she called, sliding past Ellis. He beamed at her.

"It is a good way to forget yourself, isn't it? We are starting to lose light, though, so we should probably leave."

Red hadn't noticed. If only they had longer! To feel such joy and freedom, after so long watching others have all the fun... She almost wanted to cry. "Can we come back?"

"Of course. Less falling next time, though." He winked, and she giggled, letting him help her up the bank. But, as they neared Aramor, the light mood shifted. Red felt heaviness settle across her shoulders. With every step, it felt more and more loaded.

With darkness came the wolf. When would there be a fourth attack?

$\mathcal{S}$ABINE

As darkness crept in, Sabine's mood turned blacker and blacker. She had been closeted in the manor all day, despite Lady Katherine being out for most of the morning. With every hour that passed, she grew more twitchy. She needed to see Martha. One of the servants had been to the market and had heard that Martha was feeling much better, though she swiftly became hysterical if asked about the attack. Sabine couldn't rely on that continuing. She needed to make certain.

And in the afternoon, everything became blacker still, because her little brother arrived bearing a message from her mother.

She wanted to meet – to talk about Martha.

Did she know? How could she? Her mother didn't have eyes everywhere. She might suspect, but that was as far as it went. Or was it?

Sabine felt worn, sorely tempted to send her brother packing with the message, "Haven't you heard there's a murderous wolf on the rampage?", but she knew that was not really an option. Her mother only met secretly with her when it was significant.

And this was.

The evening dragged. Considering that Vincent lay recovering in his room, and the disturbance at the church loomed large from the day before, it had been an eerily mellow evening. Lord Josiah and Lady Katherine seemed to be in a wistful kind of mood after returning from their trip, and Sabine had even seen them clasp hands as they walked in to dinner. Katherine ate little, gazing out of the window although there was nothing to see.

Sabine retired to bed early. She opened her narrow window and breathed in the fresh air. Her nerves were worse now, so she rubbed some dry herbs she had cut weeks ago between her fingers and inhaled them. The bitter aroma was calming, but only slightly.

Gradually the manor went to sleep. Servants doused candles,

doors closed, the kitchen dog quietened. Sabine pulled her hood over her head and slipped out of a side door. The gusty wind of the morning had settled, and although there was ice everywhere, no more snow had fallen. Sabine trudged along, listening out for footsteps or hooves from anyone else disobeying the curfew Lord Josiah had decided to impose only hours ago. She could not afford to be caught. Or explain why, in one hand, she was clutching a wooden wolf.

After what seemed like a longer walk than usual, Sabine reached the north bridge. She had met her mother here twice before in the dark, both times to talk over gossip from the manor. Sabine was able to tell from some distance that Mistress Forrester had not yet arrived – no candle. That was a little strange. Sabine had purposely left late, telling herself it served her mother right to stand around in the cold waiting if she was going to insist on these meetings. And Mistress Forrester was never late.

Perhaps her mother was playing with Sabine by keeping her waiting. The thought made Sabine laugh – it would prove just how alike they were. She paced along the bridge, hugging herself.

This really was very late now. Surely her mother wouldn't do this to prove some kind of point. Sabine stamped warmth back into her feet, then decided to move. If she carried on walking down the path she'd meet her mother sooner or later. As long as no one else was around it hardly mattered where they spoke.

Lost in thought, Sabine carried onwards, pressing the wooden wolf deep into her palm – then stopped. The bridge her mother would normally cross further down the river had vanished. Splinters of wood clung to the banks.

Must have collapsed in the ice, Sabine thought. She debated what her mother was likely to have done. It was not impossible she had turned back, but more probably she had cut north across the grassland, to cross the river close to the forest. Heading south instead would add a good half hour to the walk, so Sabine was confident her mother would not have considered it an option.

And yet... Would her mother really have taken the path by the forest? It would be a foolish thing to do, especially so soon after the attack on Vincent, and Mistress Forrester was no fool. However, she was determined...

Sabine passed the wooden wolf from one hand to the other, counting to ten. Then she turned north.

Blood pounded in her ears as she neared the turn that would take her right up to the forest perimeter. Tonight was even blacker than it had been when she and Martha... No, she must not think about Martha, about that. It had not happened. If she thought that enough, perhaps she could fool herself, like she had managed to fool everyone into blaming Red for that door. The blood pounded louder. Perhaps her heart would pop out of her chest. The wolf would smell her blood and come running... Wouldn't it be funny if the wolf did get her, after all the time she spent thinking about it! It mightn't be the worst end. Quick. And at least people would remember. Even if probably no one missed her.

You are being ridiculous, thought Sabine, then stopped. Crunch. She whipped round, far too aware the only weapon she had was the small knife she always took out with her. An evergreen bush rippled. She raised the knife, ready to use it – but it was only the breeze. Sabine's nerve snapped. She ran. Her breath rattled, chest tugging as she put distance between herself and the spidery trees, heading for Aramor.

"Open up!" Sabine hammered on the door to the Forresters' cottage. After what seemed for ever, it inched open.

"Sabine?" Her father sounded drowsy. Sabine pushed inside. Only now did she realize she was shaking.

"Where is Mother? We were supposed to meet. She hasn't shown up."

The Woodcutter rubbed sleep from his eyes, stifling a yawn. Impatient, Sabine grasped his arm.

"The middle bridge has fallen into the river. Either she headed south, which is unlikely, or she took the forest path. I assume she isn't snoring in bed. You do know that we meet after dark sometimes?"

Finally her words sank in, and her father became alert. "I told her not to go. A curfew is a curfew. She swore she wouldn't, but the bed is empty."

Sabine pursed her lips, furious at her mother for lying. All this could have waited! "We need to gather a search party. Something has happened."

"Perhaps we should wait to see if she returns."

"I tell you, she went near the forest. If she has been attacked, she will need help – urgently. And I cannot very well form my own search party, can I?"

Sabine put her hands on her hips, hoping she sounded authoritative. Her father gazed at her a second. He looked utterly ground down – no doubt picturing his warm bed, and the long day's work that would start in a few hours. But without a word he shuffled off, presumably to get dressed. Sabine paced the kitchen, trying to keep herself calm.

It took fifteen minutes for her father to round up a group of the neighbours, mostly woodsmen like himself. They stood in the mud with flaming torches and axes as her father explained the situation. Sabine watched from the door frame. Part of her desperately hoped that her mother would breeze home any moment, but the fact that she hadn't already cemented Sabine's gut feeling that Mistress Forrester was in trouble.

Three men set off to the south, just in case Mistress Forrester had taken that route, but the larger party – including her father – marched towards the forest. Sabine watched their back views grow smaller and smaller, feeling little and helpless and hating it. What if this time none of them came back? Something snapped inside her. She dived inside, grabbed her father's lightest axe, and caught the men up.

"Sabine, go home. This is no place for girls." Her father looked ashen, and his voice shook. Was he remembering the doomed hunt five years ago, and his dead friends? Sabine squeezed his arm.

"I don't want you to have to do this alone. Without someone who loves you here, I mean."

Her father made a frustrated, growling kind of noise. "I would be happier if you were safely at home."

"And I am happier with you."

"Why must you be so stubborn? So be it. There is no time for an argument. Stay behind me."

Shutters opened as the men marched through the town, trembling voices asking if the wolf had struck again. A night guard stopped them, demanding to know why they were breaking curfew. The Woodcutter explained and the guard allowed them to pass. If Sabine had made a mistake about this, soon everyone would know it. She realized she was still clutching the wooden wolf, so slipped it into her pouch.

"Which part of the forest would she have passed by?" one of the woodsmen asked. Sabine told him. Another wanted to know when they had been supposed to meet. Two other men ran from a cottage and joined them. Sabine heard the words *Martha* and *Vincent* and *kill it once and for all.*

Soon the group were at the edges of Aramor, the track to the forest in sight. The footfalls of heavy boots suddenly sounded very loud. Without anyone saying anything the men circled Sabine, axes raised. Someone handed her a flaming torch. She strained her ears, but heard nothing apart from low scuffling. Rabbits? A wolf would make more noise, surely. Though it hadn't when it had seized Martha. . .

Her father swung his torch, illuminating the edges of the trees. He gestured to the left, mouthing "the path", and the men nodded.

Sabine kept a steady grip on both torch and axe, glancing over her shoulder as they drew closer. The trees opened up, revealing the path. Her father gave a start. A low groan rolled out of him, like an animal in pain. And then, lit by dancing flames, she saw it too.

A thick trail of blood, leading into the forest.

And, hanging off a holly bush, her mother's cape.

At dawn, after a few hours of fitful sleep, the men returned to the forest. Sabine stayed at home this time, sipping nettle tea that had long since gone cold and provided scarce comfort. She knew they wouldn't find her mother. She and the men had followed the bloody trail immediately after happening upon the cape. It thinned after two minutes' march, then ended in an enormous pool of crimson. No one needed to tell Sabine that it was highly unlikely anyone could have survived such a vicious attack. Venturing into the heart of the forest in the darkness was pointless as well as dangerous. So back to Aramor they went.

She had stumbled home in a numb haze the men took for shock. They had been kind, reassuring her that her mother couldn't have suffered, that the wolf killed swiftly and cleanly. After seeing how it had mauled Martha and Vincent and to a lesser extent Ellis, Sabine knew they were lying and nearly said so. The only thing that stopped her was the knowledge that, sooner or later, someone would ask exactly why she had been sneaking off to meet her mother in the dark, especially with the curfew. Had Sabine been less panicked she would have anticipated that before urging her father to gather the search party.

My only option, Sabine thought, *is to convince everyone I am completely distraught, and then perhaps they will not ask awkward questions.* In their eyes, after all, she was just an emotional girl.

Her entire body felt as though it was drooping like a wilted flower. Exhaustion, probably. She did not feel very sad, not in the way her elder sisters did. Their eyes were red and raw, cheeks puffy from tears. She could hear them talking now, mostly working out how to look after the family, and cursing Sabine for being lucky enough to occupy a good position no one could rightfully demand she leave.

"It's Sabine's fault." Her eldest sister's voice was vicious. "Mother was meeting her. We still don't know why. It would be just like Sabine to insist on some remote spot in the darkness, for no reason other than she could, deliberately defying a curfew! She's so. . ."

"So what?" asked Sabine's second sister.

"Strange." The word cut like a knife. "She always has been. She doesn't look it, and she doesn't act it, but she is. Do you remember the horrible stories about gargoyles and other awful creatures she used to tell the twins when they were tiny? For weeks they woke up in the night screaming! I think she enjoyed scaring them."

"She doesn't care about anyone apart from herself and Father. Not a single tear for Mother, did you notice?"

"I'm glad she lives at the manor now and we don't have to see her so often. Little freak."

Sabine hurled the tea across the room. The tankard bounced against the floorboard and rolled under a stool. How dare they sneer at her like that! *Strange.* She would *not* be called strange again, by anyone. Her sisters would have tears and wailing and misery if that was what they expected, by the bucketload, and she would lie through her teeth until everyone believed she was just like them.

Her sisters were right about one thing, though. Before laying into Sabine, they had bemoaned what an ill-fitting end this seemed for their careful, discreet mother, who always mapped every move before she made it, subtly ferreting information and shelving every titbit in her mind's library until needed. Mistress Forrester's judgement was what saw meals on the table in difficult months, and new shoes, and clothes. Blackmail paid more than honest woodcutting.

If someone had taken an axe to her, Sabine would not have been too surprised. Plenty of people had reason to hate her.

But not the wolf. It was a dumb animal. Unless it really was a phantom witched up by someone who desired chaos in Aramor. Sabine had dismissed that up until now, but she was starting to wonder. . . The wolf had never gone for Red, had it? She wandered in the forest all the time, even after dark. Easy pickings. And then there was the oh-so-odd attack on Ellis. . .

Sabine kicked her feet against her chair leg, scowling. Then shouts came from outside.

The men were back.

Sabine slipped out, pushing ahead of her sisters. Her father looked like a wild man, twigs clinging to his torn jerkin, and lower legs streaked with mud. His eyes glistened as they found hers.

"I'm sorry."

He looked as though he wanted to walk into the house, keel on to his bed and not wake up – exactly as she remembered from five years ago, after the failed hunt. Sabine felt a stab of panic. He was going to withdraw from them all again, she knew it. The man who had once bounced Sabine on his knee singing nonsense songs and carved her a wooden menagerie was retreating further and further.

She could *not* let that happen a second time.

"Father." She took his great bear paw hands in hers. "You know what you must do, don't you? You must lead a hunt. Not like the last one. Bigger, with everyone who can swing an axe. Lord Josiah won't protect us. We must do it ourselves. You know the woods. You know the wolf. You loved Mother. It must be you."

Her father hesitated, glancing round. The men looked as worn as he did, and almost as lost.

"Everyone needs this," Sabine said softly. "It's what Mother would have wanted. Maybe the wolf is some kind of phantom. But what if it isn't? You could end this. Avenge your friends."

Her father opened his mouth. She was sure it would be to say no. But then he turned. And his voice rang out, loud and clear. "The town square. Gather as many people as you can. This can't continue. Not here. Not our wives, and sons, and daughters. Not our houses. Never mind Lord Josiah. Aramor is our town. And it is time we took control!"

RED

How could so much change in one night? thought Red, as she shuffled towards the town square. She had never seen a crowd like this. Was everyone in Aramor here? Inside she felt numb, struggling to wrap her head around what had happened during the night. She had been in such a deep sleep that her mother had had to shake her awake, her brain so groggy that at first she had been sure Mistress Forrester's death was part of her dream. Then of course her imagination had fired up, and...

Ugh. Red needed to get a grip on herself. Ahead of Red were

Mr and Mistress Baker. He had his arm around her waist. The head of the boy who'd banged on the door to tell them to assemble in the town square bobbed further up the crowd. Anticipation crackled. Red did not like feeling so penned in, like a chicken. If only she could fight her way out of the crowd, somewhere she could breathe! It was becoming harder and harder, and Red felt panic rising. She couldn't faint, not here! People would trample over her.

Be calm, Red tried to reassure herself. If a hunt was going to be announced, that wouldn't affect her. It was a perfectly sensible thing to do. These attacks couldn't go on. The last thing Red wanted was for more people to be hurt. So why did she feel so anxious? Because the wolf had never harmed her? Because Granny didn't believe it was worth fearing? Because the forest was her special place, and it felt as though it was about to be violated?

"Red!" Ellis elbowed his way to her side, Caleb beside him. Red was so grateful to see someone she trusted that she grabbed his hand without a second thought and squeezed it. He squeezed back, and Red had no time to wonder at that, because the crowds fell silent.

"Despite our differences we can agree on one thing." The deep, booming voice belonged to the Woodcutter. Red could just about see him over the top of heads, standing on a crate someone had pushed by the fountain. *Just like last time*, she thought. In one hand he carried an axe twice as large as any she had seen before. Its sharp edge glinted, and maybe it was just a reflection from somewhere, but to Red it looked crimson. "The wolf has terrorized us long enough."

No one stirred. The only sounds were distant coughing, and the even more distant yapping of a dog.

"This is not something a curfew will fix. We are getting no guidance from Lord Josiah. If we do nothing it could be your family next. I do not want anyone else to suffer."

Nodding from the crowd. Red had never noticed how big the Woodcutter was before – or perhaps it was just that for the first time in ages he was stranding tall again.

"I propose a hunt." The word sent murmurs rippling through the crowd. "And this time we won't leave until the animal is dead. It is older and weaker than it was. Until last night its attacks were unsuccessful. We will not live in fear any more!"

These last words were shouted. The Woodcutter thrust his axe into the air as though it was feather light. Cheers erupted from the crowd. Red could feel their relief, and for a second she was carried along with it. Finally, someone was taking control, taking the fight to the forest, and it was one of them, someone everyone trusted and wished well.

The Woodcutter shouted for silence.

"I know some of you do not believe the attacks are committed by a real wolf. I do not dismiss your beliefs, even if I disagree with them. I only ask that until we are sure you put aside such dangerous talk. The hunt will depart at sundown. As many able-bodied men as wish to join us are welcome. Make yourself known now, or later at the inn. Everyone else –" he paused – "stay home. With luck, by tomorrow this will be over."

This time the cheering was deafening. People turned and hugged each other. The Woodcutter leapt down from the crate. Red caught sight of a slight figure leaning on tiptoes to whisper in his ear: Sabine. Sudden fear stabbed at her. What did Sabine have to do with this?

Someone spoke her name. Red focused on Ellis.

"Sorry, you said something?"

"What do you think of that?" To her dismay his eyes were bright. He too stood straighter. When had he let go of her hand? "Finally something is happening."

Red tried to collect her scattered thoughts. The crowd was dispersing, some joining neighbours, chattering excitedly, others to return to shops and homes. There was already a large throng of men and boys amassing by the fountain.

"I don't know," she said. "It seems a bit. . ."

"A bit what?"

"Too much."

Ellis pulled back, a line between his eyebrows. "Mistress Forrester was killed."

"I know, and that is terrible, of course it is, but. . ."

"You think there shouldn't be a hunt?"

Red didn't know what she thought or why she was – yet again – being awkward.

"Red." Ellis was looking at her strangely now, and Red's heart sank. "One of the people it attacked was me. Have you forgotten? What about Martha? Her life will never be the same again. Vincent's neither, probably."

"I know all that!"

"Then you do understand." Ellis's attention moved to the fountain. The men there smacked each other on the backs, as though they were already a team. Someone had brought out a whetstone and was sharpening axe blades. With them were several lads Ellis and Red's age. They swaggered about with easy belonging, jabbing the air with hunting knives. One of the boys' fathers smacked his son on the back and said something that made everyone laugh. Red spotted Bart, counting arrows. It looked as though he was whistling. Had she ever seen him this happy before?

Then Ellis said the words she was dreading. "I'm going too."

"That's madness," said Red immediately. "You only have one arm. It's not even your strong one. The Woodcutter said he needed able-bodied men—" She choked on the words, but too late. Ellis scowled.

"I won't go home and let boys like Bart risk their lives. I'll hold a torch if they won't let me take an axe. I should be there, and I will be there. You have no idea what the last few weeks have been like without my friends."

"You had me." Her smile felt shaky, and Red was conscious of everything, the gap between her teeth, and how wide her mouth was, and the shoulders Sabine had once called boyish. "We had fun on the ice yesterday, didn't we?"

His eyes were on the men. She felt like she wasn't there. "I've been distracting myself. Sneaking off, and wandering through the forest – none of that is real. This is. Being part of things. Belonging. I am *not* an outsider."

"And I am?"

"I wasn't talking about you, Red."

"You were, though." She pulled away from him. Inside, it felt like part of her was breaking. "The time we spent together isn't 'real'. That's what you said, in those words. Were you just using me because I was there when other people weren't?"

His eyes widened, and she knew her words had sunk in. She willed him to say something to prove her wrong: we are friends; I would never use you. Instead he was silent. Was he torn, or trying to avoid hurting her feelings?

Red couldn't bear it. "Don't go on the hunt, Ellis. You don't need to prove yourself to people who turned their backs on you. Just like you don't need to try so hard to please your parents. Can't you just be yourself?"

He hesitated. Then his hand adjusted the sling, and she knew she had lost. "This is me, Red. I need to do this."

She turned her back. She wanted to cry. Not just because she had been so wrong about Ellis and she felt a fool, but because she couldn't even voice the reason she knew this hunt was so very wrong.

ELLIS

Ellis felt a little sick as he closed the gap between himself and the group by the fountain. Weeks ago he would have been the first to volunteer, and they'd be happy to have him. Now...

They might reject him. Laugh. They really might. Either it would be done kindly, or they would cross their fingers as though he was tainted.

His mouth felt dry. He tried to project confidence. "I want to join the hunt."

The men turned. The expressions on their faces changed,

some to sympathetic, others to annoyed. Ellis struggled to keep eye contact.

"I'll carry a torch if that is most helpful. Nobody needs to protect me."

The Woodcutter strode over. His eyes, at least, were kind. "Ellis, we have many volunteers already, and although your willingness is appreciated—"

"I think Ellis should go." Ellis gave a start. He hadn't noticed Sabine.

One of the men snorted. "I don't think so. At the present moment, he is a liability."

"For more than one reason," muttered Bart, unsmiling.

"He should go because the wolf spared him once." Sabine didn't seem at all intimidated challenging the men. In fact, she acted like she was one of them, even though the other women and children had left. "And I think you want a chance to redeem yourself, don't you, Ellis?"

Her eyes turned on him and Ellis almost took a step backwards. Could she see inside his head, or was he that easy to read? Since when was Sabine in control, anyway? Not trusting himself to speak, Ellis said nothing. The men looked at the Woodcutter. He waved a hand as though it was unimportant.

"We don't have time to stand around talking. If young Miller wants to come, he can."

Ellis released a deep breath, feeling his body relax. Sabine gave him a small smile. Ellis turned his back. He didn't trust her. The men moved to make space for him. Bart and a couple of other boys glared as though he had no place, but no one challenged him. For now, anyway. Perhaps, Ellis thought, he could somehow win them over, remind them he was one of them really.

Someone at his shoulder cleared their throat: Caleb.

"Do you want me to take the cart home?"

"If you are able to." Ellis felt bad for dropping his brother, but this was more important than flour. "We were nearly done anyway."

Caleb dropped his voice. "El. . . Red is right, you know. You don't have to do this. It's dangerous. I don't trust this lot to have your back. I think Bart would quite happily accidentally-on-purpose stick an arrow in you given the chance. "

"I have my own back, thanks." Ellis knew he sounded stubborn and childish. Sure enough, Caleb rolled his eyes.

"Why is it so important what other people think of you? I think you would be happier if you cared less."

"We live in a town, Caleb. Of course what people think matters. Is it so bad I miss being part of things? Being somebody?"

"Being part of things is only worthwhile if the people are worthwhile. And I see people who dropped you the moment you really needed friends. Like Red pointed out. And then you dropped her."

He felt heat rising inside him now. "I did not."

Caleb just looked at him. Ellis kicked his heel against the cobbles, hard. He refused to lose his temper with his little brother, not here, even though Caleb was being infuriating. "Can you tell Mother and Father where I am? They won't like this, but I don't care what they think any more."

Caleb glanced over his shoulder. He knew all about Ellis's suspicions – Ellis had filled him in the first chance he'd got. "I don't think we should talk about that here."

Right now, Ellis didn't care who overheard them, but Caleb was probably right. "The last two sacks of flour are for the Weavers and then the low farmhouse. Can you manage that?"

Caleb nodded. He pressed his lips together. Something about it reminded Ellis of Caleb as a little boy, and how he'd been so anxious to act Ellis's age that he'd always suck in pain rather than cry and be called a baby. Ellis softened. He leaned in and gave Caleb a quick hug.

"Sorry. I don't want to argue with you. Don't worry. I won't get eaten."

"You'd better not. You're the only person that sulky horse doesn't hate." Ellis stifled a laugh; it was true, even from over where they had left the cart across the square, Dorothy's expression was disdainful. Caleb lowered his voice. "Be careful."

That made him think of Red, and what Granny had said. Ellis glanced round, but Red had gone. He felt a stab of guilt. He shouldn't have spoken to her like that, fired up or not. He hoped he hadn't hurt her. She was unexpected and smart and intuitive but this time, he was sure she was wrong. Perhaps she'd see that when they came home having killed the wolf, and then they could put that disagreement behind them – as well as the whispers of witchcraft.

Someone smacked him on the back. "What do you think – will ten arrows be enough? Or should I wrangle a larger quiver from somewhere?"

Bart sounded cheery – too cheery, perhaps. He pulled back his bowstring, miming shooting. Ellis could not help but feel it was being done on purpose. He hadn't been able to bear watching the archery tournament in the end, but he'd heard from Stephen that Bart had been victorious.

"It is up to you." Ellis tried to keep his voice friendly. "You know as much about archery as I do."

"Suppose so. Stand close to me with your torch, Ellis, I'll need good aim. It must feel good to finally do something useful after weeks of kicking your heels?"

"I have not been kicking my heels," Ellis snapped.

Bart smiled, but it was not a nice smile. "No, you've been messing about with the girl who let in the wolf that mauled my cousin. How very loyal of you. My uncle never liked you courting Martha. Seems he was right. I'd watch out tonight if I were you. Can't be too careful."

He laughed, but Ellis was under no illusions that Bart was joking.

Then the Woodcutter called the men to gather round, and Ellis forgot about Red.

In the end, some forty men and boys would be venturing into the forest. After gathering in the square they relocated to the inn. Axes were sharpened, maps pored over and meals eaten. Women bustled in and out, checking their husbands and sons were warmly turned out, without holes in their boots or cloaks.

Though he was determined not to show it, Ellis felt at a loose end. The other boys were not entirely ignoring him but neither were they friendly. Still, he thought, it was better to be part of this than not. Apparently one boy had dared Stephen to step forward, but Stephen had not budged. Now they were laughing over his cowardice, Bart suggesting that they duck him in the river to teach him a lesson, ice or no ice. Ellis wanted to point out that joining the hunt was voluntary, and as an only child with four ageing grandparents and a sick father to support, Stephen had other loyalties, and hunting was hardly a strength of his anyway. In the end he said nothing. Speaking up would only make them turn on him. And only that morning Stephen had scurried down an alleyway to avoid Ellis, just as Ellis had feared. So much for years of friendship.

Everything will be better when this is over, Ellis told himself, and busied himself handing round drinks.

Just as lunch was being cleared away, a slender figure in a fur-lined coat appeared: Lady Katherine, accompanied by two of her dogs and one of the manor guards. She held up a hand as the room went quiet.

"Please don't stop on my account. I come only to offer support. Heel."

The dogs immediately obeyed. Lady Katherine looked at the Woodcutter.

"My dogs are trained bloodhounds. If they are able to pick up the wolf's scent they may be of great assistance. You are welcome to borrow them for the night. My guard here is adept at controlling them."

The Woodcutter looked awkward, as though uncertain of how to speak to such a grand lady.

"That is a generous offer, my lady," he said, eventually. "Thank you."

"It is the least I can do. I will not interrupt you longer." She gave the room a quick smile, then turned to instruct her guard, signalling that everyone should get back to what they were doing. Ellis watched, wondering what Aramor would be like were Lady Katherine in charge. She was less meek than he had always assumed, with natural authority but also a warmth he could see people responding to. Lady Katherine noticed him watching her. She joined him.

"I won't stay long. I can see I am making these men uncomfortable. Are you part of this?"

He nodded. "I am not sure what use they will find for me yet."

Lady Katherine pursed her lips, and he got the distinct impression she would like to tell him to stay at home. But all she said was, "Please stay safe, Ellis. I would not want to see you hurt again."

And to his surprise she laid her hand on his good shoulder,

giving it the gentlest of squeezes. Then she was gone, only pausing to exchange a few words with Sabine. Ellis glanced round in case anyone had seen, but they were all occupied.

ℒABINE

After clearing the plates from lunch, Sabine sat on a stool, observing preparations but most closely her father. *I knew it,* she thought. She'd always clung to the belief that his old self was buried in there somewhere. But even she was taken aback by his sudden energy. Already he seemed younger. Was this a way of distracting himself from thinking about her mother? Or was it determination, for this hunt to achieve what the first had not?

And all it had taken were a few small words of encouragement! If Sabine had known, she would have found a way of getting him back years ago. A voice at the back of her mind whispered that maybe it wasn't a coincidence that he had become so alive on the very day her mother had become so very dead, but she pushed it away. Messy emotions – unhelpful as ever.

Deciding to return closer to sundown, Sabine slipped away to visit Martha. Her friend was on her feet but still had not left her room. She was clutching a blanket round her shoulders like a grandmother, nose pressed to the grubby bedroom window which overlooked the town square. Her lighter cuts had closed up now, but the worst two were raised and puffy, the skin around bright pink. Still, it looked nowhere near as bad as Sabine had expected.

"It might do you good to get some fresh air on your face," she said, passing Martha the herb tea she had quickly made downstairs.

"I don't think so," Martha muttered.

"You can't stay inside for ever. You are not only a pretty face, you know. Show people that."

"Easy for you to say. You don't know what it's like."

And I'm glad of it, Sabine thought. People acted like pretty girls were the winners, but Sabine thought it a greater advantage to be ordinary. You had much more control over how people saw you that way, and you did not have to deal with unwanted attention either. It was a mistake to stake who you were on any one thing, like Martha, or even Ellis, though he at least wasn't sitting around moping.

Sabine told Martha about preparations for the hunt, describing the anticipation and almost jubilant mood, and how, for many, this was the chance to exorcise bad memories from the past.

"They are doing this for you, too," she finished. "Not only Bart, but everyone. They're outraged that it could dare attack you in your own home. It has spurred them to action."

Her friend laughed shortly. Sabine tensed. Martha turned and looked at Sabine – a long, hard, bitter look so totally unlike her that Sabine took an involuntary step backwards. In a distant-sounding voice, Martha said, "We have been talking for thirty minutes now. Do you know what I think is curious?"

"Tell me."

"You have not once mentioned your mother. You don't care, do you?"

She hadn't? Sabine considered lying, but Martha knew her better than that.

"My mother was not a nice woman," she said softly. "I didn't like reporting what went on in the manor so she could gather secrets." She hesitated. "I know she must have something Lady Katherine or Lord Josiah do not want becoming common knowledge. How else did she get me my position? People think bullies jeer or hit others, but there are quieter ways of making lives unpleasant. So no. I don't think I do care."

"At least that's one thing you're not lying about."

Sabine bowed her head. "Martha. I'm sorry. You know how sorry I am. But you understand, don't you, why it had to be this way?"

"Go away, Sabine."

"Tell me you understand."

"I said go away."

The tops of Sabine's ears burned. She was desperate to push it, get Martha to swear that her lips were sealed, but the last thing she wanted was to annoy her. So for once Sabine did as she was told and backed out, closing the bedroom door behind her and tiptoeing downstairs. Her intention had been to return to the inn, but, once in the bakery yard, she stopped, feet rooted to the spot. Half under the shelter was the cart Martha's parents took decorative breads and biscuits to the city in once a month. Had it even been used since Martha had been attacked?

Maybe it was the cart, or maybe it was how biting Martha had been, but her mind slipped back to that night, and this time Sabine was unable to stop it. . .

*

235

The only sound was the clip-clop of the horse's hooves as Sabine and Martha navigated the small bakery cart to the edge of the forest. To Sabine, everything was heightened – the earthy smell of wet mud, the fresh tang in the air, the hoot of owls and chatter of small animals. The moon cast a dreamy sheen over the naked branches, and the icy puddles gleamed.

I am almost like a wolf myself, Sabine thought. She imagined it stalking through the dead leaves, senses alive to the tiniest sound and smell. A delicious shiver crept up her spine. She felt so alive. Why hadn't she sneaked here under darkness before?

Beside her, Martha was rigid, like ice that wouldn't thaw.

"You said this would be thrilling," she whispered.

"It is."

"It isn't. It is such a bad idea! We shouldn't be here. If our parents found out—"

"Our parents will not find out. They're asleep." Sabine felt her lips push into a big, open smile. "Doesn't it feel wonderful? Just being free? When was the last time you did something you weren't supposed to?"

"Never, and it feels terrifying. Can we leave, please? We've seen the forest, we don't need to linger. The wolf might be here. What if it can smell us?"

"I just want to see it."

"You said you just wanted to pass by! Why are you so obsessed with the wolf, Sabine? Is it because of your father? I don't think he'd be happy if he knew about this."

"Then he won't find out. Will he?"

Martha bristled at her sharp tone. "I don't know why I listen to you. Sometimes I think the way you get people to do what you want is uncanny. Sabine, please, let's go back home. It's a monster. You saw what it did to Ellis."

Sabine pulled the reins from Martha's grasp, holding them out of reach. "Are you going to fight me for them?"

"Sabine! Stop it. This isn't funny."

Martha made a grab, but Sabine easily evaded her. She spurred the old bakery nag on, closer to the trees. Red had seen the wolf, walked away without a hair on her head touched. Red! What made her so special? "Are you afraid?"

Martha's eyes were huge in the moonlight. "Right now what I'm afraid of is you."

"Then leave me here." Sabine tossed her the reins, leaping down. "I am going closer. Maybe I'll pick a few herbs. There is a yellow-green root I have seen here before which seems to alleviate headaches, and Doctor Ambrose's book had a picture of St John's wort. If I am lucky I might find some."

"You and your herbs! Sabine, no. Come back. *Please.*"

It almost made her laugh, how pathetic Martha sounded. Sabine hummed to herself, going right up to the edge of the trees. She closed her eyes. Her skin prickled, and she shivered in anticipation. This was so delicious. No wonder Red ran in the forest as though she were a wild animal herself. There was something elusive and almost magical about the forest of Aramor, like the whisper of a secret. . .

A piercing scream filled the air.

Sabine spun around. Something had launched itself on to the cart. Martha's arms and legs flailed hopelessly like a rag doll's. The horse whined and teetered on to its hind legs, then bolted. Martha and the beast rolled off into the grass. Sabine threw herself out of the horse's way, then grabbed a heavy branch and dashed towards the snarling and screaming. Blindly she struck out – but the wolf was gone. Only Martha lay there, blood dripping down her face, and screaming, screaming, screaming.

Even now, that scream echoed in her head. Sabine leaned against the bakery door – the very door she had told that awful lie about. She pressed her palm to her forehead.

Right now, what I'm afraid of is you.

The horse hadn't fled far. The cart had got caught by a low-hanging branch, and the horse was whining so loudly that Sabine found it easily. With difficulty she calmed the animal, then led it to Martha. She had to half pull, half push Martha into the cart – her friend didn't seem to be able to muster any power to her arms and legs, though none were broken. She shook all over and Sabine was afraid she would faint. Sabine urged the horse into fast canter, mind whirling. One thought cut through the others: *no one can know.*

She had been lucky. They didn't meet a soul on the journey back, even one of the night guard, and no one had heard Sabine drawing the cart into the bakery yard. Inside, she unlocked the door and helped Martha into a chair. It took three attempts to light a candle. She was trembling too, now. She dug around for a clean cloth to press to Martha's cuts.

"Listen," Sabine said, in a harsh voice that didn't sound like hers. "We were never at the forest. Do you understand? You were attacked here."

Martha was sobbing so hard Sabine worried she'd wake the Bakers. She clutched her friend's shoulders, leaning in close.

"Martha. You will be fine. You are not going to die. Listen. It will be much better for both of us if they never find out where we really were. You will have no sympathy if people think you brought the attack on yourself. But if you are a poor victim, you will. It's not a bad thing to be pitied." *Especially not with a ruined face*, she thought, but kept that to herself. "And I don't want to lose my position, or be accused of possessing unnatural interests. Say it, go on."

"I was attacked here."

Martha was only half-conscious, almost delirious. Good. She might not even remember that Sabine had left her, or how she'd begged to go home.

Quickly Sabine set the scene – chairs on their sides, scattered pans and tools. Her heart thumped so loudly she could barely hear Martha groaning. That no one heard was a miracle. When she was done, Sabine whispered to Martha that she'd be back, then overturned the table with a tremendous thud. The moment she heard movement above, Sabine fled, leaving the back door ajar.

"Sabine?"

Mistress Baker was peering at her. When had she walked into the yard? Sabine snapped back to the present. She squeezed her eyes shut, and managed to summon a few weak tears. Martha's mother dumped her basket on the doorstep and gathered Sabine into her arms. She smelled of jam and her tender touch felt strange.

No one ever held Sabine like that. "Oh, Sabine. I'm so sorry. Your poor, poor mother. It is too much to bear, isn't it?"

Sabine sniffed, leaning her chin on Mistress Baker's shoulder. "Martha—"

"She doesn't have it in her to comfort anyone else right now. But, listen, Sabine, you are not alone. You have been a good friend to my girl. If you ever need advice, I will gladly give it. A girl shouldn't be without womanly guidance, especially not at your age. I know I am not your own mother, but I'm here. Martha will support you too, given time."

Sabine almost wanted to scream at her: *Why are you being so kind? If it wasn't for me, Martha would never have been hurt!* She found she couldn't speak, so she sniffed instead. Then she realized she and Mistress Baker were not alone. Red stood at the bakery gate, basket looped over her arm and face scrunched in anger. Her eyes were intense, as though they could see right through Sabine. Slowly, deliberately, she raised her hands.

And made the sign of evil.

ELLIS

As it had the last time he had ventured into the forest, Ellis's heart began to beat the second he glimpsed branches clawing the sky. He should feel safer in the company of armed men than he had with Red, even at night, but he didn't – and that wasn't only because this time he was unarmed, it having been decided he'd be of more use bearing a torch. There was something so reassuring about Red. Again he wished they hadn't argued.

The Woodcutter raised a finger to his mouth, and beckoned a group of sturdy farmhands forwards. He gestured them left where the path forked, and within seconds they were swallowed by darkness, accompanied by Lady Katherine's guard and bloodhounds.

"Everyone else, with me," he murmured. "And keep your voices down."

An owl hooted. Everyone jumped, several even raising their axes. When the group realized it was a false alarm, they relaxed. Someone even released a shaky laugh.

The forest was different in the darkness. Noisier. Ellis hadn't expected that, especially on such a still night. Apart from the crunch and shuffle of feet, there was squeaking, perhaps of mice or smaller hunting animals, and flapping that had to be bats. The torch did little to pierce the blackness enveloping them.

Brave was the very last thing Ellis felt. Were the others as tense and on edge? Were they too now wishing they'd stayed at home? The Woodcutter strode ahead, stance strong and determined. Ellis wanted to believe in him, yet he could not help but be very aware that only days ago this man had been a figure of pity. Could they really trust the Woodcutter to lead them? He had never explained exactly what had happened on the first hunt which only he had survived. . .

Ellis glanced over his shoulder. The entrance to the path was long gone. How long had they been creeping along now? Ten minutes? More?

"This isn't right." Bart's voice broke the silence. "Where are the animals?"

A farmhand gestured for him to be quiet. Bart scowled. But then the Woodcutter said, "He is right. This forest used to be full of life. Yet all we've encountered was the owl, and perhaps mice."

"Red said over the last year the animals have been thinning out." Ellis spoke up. "There's nothing left for the wolf to hunt."

A man at the front stumbled. Another caught him before he could fall. Ellis swung his torch. It picked out the carcass of an animal, and a big one, too.

"Speaking of wolves," murmured Bart. Ellis inspected the body, searching for signs of how the wolf came by its end, but it had died too long ago. It must be one of the shy grey ones Red had mentioned. Had the wolf turned on its own kind? The beast Martha had described was bigger than this animal looked to have been. He was pretty certain that whatever had bowled him over was, too.

Could it be a phantom? Ellis reminded himself that he did not believe in witchcraft, but in the darkness, the almost full moon huge in the sky, he suddenly felt he could believe anything. If the wolf was unnatural, it would explain a lot. Including why the forest was so very silent...

RED

Red had tailed the smaller group at first but swiftly realized their route would take them around the forest perimeter. The maybe thirty remaining men and boys marched into the heart of the forest, keeping two or three abreast rather than fanning out, even though the forest floor was even and easy to walk on. Why were people so afraid of straying even inches from the path? Did they really believe the muddy track protected them? She spotted Ellis near the front and hardened her heart; they weren't friends, not any more. Red slipped into the trees, easily keeping hidden.

She didn't fully know why she felt the need to do this. She hadn't intended to, but she could not bear the prospect of another silent evening with her mother. Was her unease partly because she couldn't shake off the feeling that the hunt was somehow Sabine's doing, and she didn't trust her? Sabine wasn't here – safely ensconced in the inn, waiting for news – but Red had watched her going round offering the men refreshment, all demure and obedient like the perfect daughter. Red wasn't fooled. She wasn't fooled by the tears Sabine had shed on Mistress Baker's shoulder, either. Maybe it had been dramatic to make the sign of evil at her, dangerous even, but she hadn't been able to help herself. . .

Granny's cottage loomed out of the darkness. The candle Granny kept by the window to light the way for Red if she happened to visit had been extinguished. Granny must already be in bed. Red stiffened, ready to burst from cover if the hunt dared venture closer and disturb her. Instead they walked straight past. Red let out a shaky breath. Ellis had all but admitted he'd once believed Granny a witch. What if everyone else thought the same? They might get nasty. Would Red be able to protect her?

Someone tripped. The men stopped. Red crouched behind an ivy bush, wishing she was close enough to overhear. There was gesturing now. A disagreement? When would they give up and go home? The men's feet must be frozen by now – hers were. Or would they keep going, determined to get a result – even if there wasn't one to be found?

Suddenly the hairs on her nape stood up. A funny feeling crept over her. Cold and stinging and prickly. The feeling of being watched. . .

And not by the men.

Almost in slow motion, Red turned.

There, just feet away, shrouded by the same bush, was a wolf.

Its bright eyes fixed on her. Red knew instinctively that this was *the* wolf. It was bigger than the corpses she occasionally stumbled upon, and darker, almost black, the kind of creature Martha could easily mistake for a demon. The pricked-up ears were large and pointed, and the teeth. . .

The teeth were sharp. Very sharp.

Red knew better than to move. The wolf tilted its head to one side, surveying her. Patches of its muzzle were white. Its hind legs were bowed. Skin hung off its bones.

Still it did not strike.

Red's heartbeat raced. Had the wolf even blinked? Its eyes sucked Red in like a whirlpool. There was something hypnotic about those eyes. . . A faint voice in the back of her head screamed at her to run. But it had not attacked her yet. That gave Red courage. With an arm that shook, she extended her hand, as though to a dog. The wolf bared its teeth. Red recoiled, ready to spring backwards.

Out of the corner of her eye she spotted the men, inching apart. Archers crept forwards, taking aim.

Red didn't think. She plunged forwards, waving her arms.

"Run! Now!"

The wolf streaked into the darkness. An arrow embedded itself into the ground where it had stood. Red's hands flew to her mouth. What had she done! *Saving the wolf's life?*

Hands grabbed her shoulders.

ELLIS

With a sickening crunch Ellis realized the girl Bart had seized wore a crimson cape. Red's eyes were big and scared. She didn't attempt to pull away or resist. She had frozen. The Woodcutter bellowed for the archers to track the wolf. Their running footsteps thudded into the blackness. Ellis knew they would be too late. The wolf had not been fast – had it limped? – but it had a head start, and the forest was its domain.

"My arrow almost had it!" Bart roared. "How dare you? First you let it attack my cousin, and then you save it. Traitor!"

He flung Red against a tree. She tried to move but the bottom of her skirt caught on a branch. The Woodcutter moved to Red's side before Bart could do anything else.

"Stop it, Bart. She is just a girl."

"She'll be the reason more people die!" Bart kicked the tree just inches from Red, face red and furious. Red's eyes took on the stubborn look that like everyone else Ellis had once taken for stupidity. Before he knew it the voice shouting was his.

"Why did you do that? That wolf had killed people! It attacked me. I thought we were friends, Red! And you wonder why people think you're strange!"

Her chin jutted. "It isn't the wolf you're looking for. It's old. Didn't you see? It couldn't have done the attacks."

"Thanks to you we didn't get a decent look at it!"

"I did, and it was exactly as the Baker girl described," growled a burly farmer. "It had burning eyes. It is the wolf all right."

Agreement passed between the men. The Woodcutter placed a hand on Red's shoulder. Suddenly he sounded weary.

"Unless our archers find it, we will not kill it tonight. Come. We must return to Aramor and plan our next move."

Bart spat on the ground by Red's foot, growling a name that made Ellis flinch. He stalked off ahead of everyone else.

The drag back to the town was silent but an ugly, mutinous atmosphere hung in the air. Ellis pretended not to notice that Red kept looking his way, imploring him to understand. As though he was the one who had betrayed her, rather than Red betraying the whole town.

There wasn't space in his head to worry about Red, anyway. Ellis was far more worried about what was going to happen in Aramor.

$\mathcal{S}$ABINE

Sabine flung open the inn door the moment she heard the march of heavy feet. She had barely slept since her mother's death and felt heady, almost as though she was floating, but there was no way she could nod off in a chair like the scattered other women awaiting news.

"They are here! And they have—"

The rest of the sentence died. Even from a distance it was obvious that her father was not bearing the corpse of the wolf. Instead, he escorted a girl wearing a red hood.

Fury swelled inside her. Red! Why did she always appear at the wrong moments? If she had somehow sabotaged Sabine's father's moment of glory by being her usual stupid self—

Sabine needed to compose herself. She'd get nowhere by losing her temper – though she dearly wanted to. Instead she paced as the other women stirred, fingers wrapped around her wooden wolf and cursing under her breath. For once she didn't care who heard her.

Men and boys filled the room, weary, smelling of moss and mud and sweat. It didn't look as though any were injured. The innkeeper roused himself and got to work pouring ale without being asked.

"Well?" She could wait no longer.

Her father sank into the nearest chair. Flakes of snow nestled in his hair and the shoulders of his jerkin. "We found it."

"And?"

"It escaped."

Someone thumped a table. "It did not escape!" Bart was shaking he was so incensed. "Why is no one as angry about this as I am? This ... *creature* sent it packing."

Red hunched over, saying nothing. For a moment Sabine was speechless. "By accident? Or on purpose?"

That set the other men off, all shouting at the same time,

no one making full sense. Sabine looked from her father to the others, jaw dropping as she pieced together what had happened. Red was almost hunched double now. Something about the way she bowed her head – as though she knew exactly what she'd done, and had done it anyway, just to spite everyone, no, spite *Sabine* and her family. . . How dare Red make the sign of evil at her! Unable to control herself, Sabine stomped over and gave Red a sharp push. Red stumbled, catching the back of a chair to keep herself upright.

"You have done some horrible things, but this is the worst!" Sabine cried. "Leaving the door open was careless. But this . . . you are dangerous."

"I didn't leave that door—"

"Be quiet, Red! No one cares!" Sabine so badly wanted to push Red again that she did, and it felt good, though this time Red kept her balance. "Bart is right when he calls you a traitor. You don't deserve to live in this town after this. You should be hounded out."

"At least I'm not pleased my mother's dead," Red spat. Sabine froze.

"What?"

"Your tears are crocodile ones. You have no goodness in your heart. Not a shred of emotion. The hunt isn't about avenging her death, or helping Martha. It's about you feeling powerful. You like this."

"What is this?"

Red flung out her arms. "The hysteria! The drama! I can see it in your eyes. You persuade others to do your bidding and think nobody notices, but I do. You know a lot more about these attacks than you have been letting on, too." She was suddenly standing at her full height, a whole head taller than Sabine. The expression in her eyes was fierce, almost wild. "The wolf and the forest have always sucked you in. I've seen you there at night, collecting herbs, and Martha's told me how precious that wolf charm you think no one knows about is to you—"

"How dare you." Sabine shook with rage. "How *dare* you."

"Oh, I dare. It's time someone did."

"What precisely are you accusing me of, Red? Because I would watch yourself. You are the one who is strange, who actually scared a dangerous predator off the moment it was about to be killed! And whose beloved granny hides in the forest because she can't bear the company of normal folk?" She pulled herself straight. "If you dare dirty my name it won't end well for you. I'm warning you, Red."

The Woodcutter stepped between the girls. "That is enough, Sabine. You say too much. Know your place."

Sabine glared at him. "You're going to let her get away with what she did?"

"I did not say that—" The door creaked, and her father stopped. A second group of men filed in, cheeks flushed with cold. Her father hastened over, as though Sabine was suddenly unimportant.

"Well?"

One of the men leaned forward, murmuring in the Woodcutter's ear. His expression changed.

"What's happened?" demanded Sabine. Her father waved her away without even looking round and vanished outside with the newcomers. Sabine stood fuming, wanting to scream at how unfair it all was. She was the one person who had never given up on her father and he had the gall to order her to keep quiet like a meek child!

People were watching her. Was it her imagination, or was there a wariness that had not been there ten minutes ago?

Her rage cooled a touch. *All right, Father,* she thought. *I will go home as you wish, and mind my place for now. But this is not over.*

And she gave Red a look that said just that.

RED

Red did not remember leaving the inn or walking through Aramor's silent streets until she reached home. The adrenaline of shouting at Sabine had worn off almost immediately, to be replaced by horror.

What had she done?

Granny had always impressed on Red that there was nothing wrong with being different. But there was definitely a lot wrong with everything she had done tonight. Following the hunt. Scaring the wolf away. Accusing Sabine. Thinking back, Red couldn't believe it was her. It all seemed so glaringly, obviously foolish. Why hadn't she stayed home like everyone else?

Almost the worst thing was that Red still couldn't explain any of her actions, and that really did scare her. Instinct wasn't a good enough reason. Animals did things on instinct. Not fourteen-year-old girls who should know better, especially after those horribly vivid dreams.

Somehow Red made it to her bedroom and sat on the bed, still in her clothes. There didn't seem any point getting undressed. She wouldn't sleep, would she? She'd lie there fretting. When people stole, they were fined, or sat in the stocks, or, in the worst cases, flogged. More severe crimes had more serious, even gruesome punishments: banishment. Loss of limbs. Even death. Everything was written down in the Book of Law Lord Josiah kept in the manor. But there wouldn't be anything there on how to punish Red – unless they decided her actions amounted to treason. And that was very serious indeed.

Red gulped. She could taste bile rising at the back of her throat. No one whose voice mattered would speak in her favour, would they? Mother would be appalled and nobody would pay attention to Granny. Ellis might have stuck up for her once, but he'd picked his side today and it wasn't hers.

As soon as possible, Red had to find out what awaited her. Most things, she felt she could brave, but the unknown was the worst. Her best hope, she decided, was that they banished her. She didn't belong in Aramor, never had. And tonight had proved that without a doubt.

$\mathcal{S}$ABINE

The creak of the door opening jerked Sabine awake. For a moment, she was disorientated before remembering she was in her parents' house and she had fallen asleep in the rocking chair by the dead fire.

Her father crept inside in the clothes he had worn for the hunt. Seeing her rise, he placed a finger to his lips.

How long had Sabine slept? A couple of hours, if the early dawn light was anything to go by. Her father must have been up all night. He pulled a stool up beside the rocking chair. Sabine rubbed the sleep from her eyes.

"So what happened?" she asked. "Did the other group find something?"

The Woodcutter sighed. Sabine pulled the old shawl she'd draped over herself tighter.

"Tell me. Please, Father."

"So like your mother. Always wanting to know things."

That stung. "Why shouldn't I want to know things?"

"Because this does not concern you. You're fourteen, Sabby, and a girl." She flinched at the unexpected use of her childhood pet name. "Sometimes I think you forget that. Playing at doctoring and the hunt... I half-expected you to seize an axe and insist on joining us."

This was clearly supposed to be a joke, but Sabine did not smile. "I don't play."

"Of course not, Sabby."

"You are belittling me. If I had not put the idea into your head there wouldn't even have been a hunt, and you would not have led it." Sabine paused, then added, "Don't tell me it didn't feel good to have people look at you with respect and remember who you used to be. I always knew you'd come back to us, even if Mother couldn't see it. She used to call you useless."

"I don't want you speaking of her like that."

"Why not? She wasn't nice to either of us. I don't see you mourning either."

"You need to watch your tongue." Her father's voice sharpened. "This is what I mean when I say you don't know your place. I blame myself. You were headstrong even as a little girl. I should have paid you more attention, given more fatherly guidance." The Woodcutter leaned forwards, serious now. "I need you to be honest now, Sabine. Was there any truth in what that girl accused you of in the inn?"

"None at all." Sabine hoped he could not tell that her heart had started to race. "I don't know what she is talking about."

"So you have never been to the edge of the forest, and never collected herbs, and never possessed any charms?"

"Never. The only part that is true is my owning a wooden wolf, but you carved me that, and it is a toy, not something sinister. Red made everything up, Father. She doesn't like me."

"So that is all it is? Lies?"

"Lies."

"It had better be," said her father. He paused. "There is nothing else you need to tell me?"

Sabine didn't like the distance she sensed opening between

them. "As my father, or as the wolf hunter general?"

His eyes narrowed, and she thought for a second he might tell her off. Instead he left. A few seconds later she heard his bedroom door close.

Sabine stayed in the chair, rocking herself. For the first time, she felt a little afraid of what she had started.

ELLIS

Caleb shook Ellis awake just after noon, with a bowl of soup and news.

"They are having a meeting to decide what to do about the wolf and they want me there? Why?" Ellis was still groggy after arriving back at the mill in the middle of night and falling asleep fully clothed. "Surely we know what to do. Gather another hunting party and kill it."

Caleb perched on the edge of Ellis's bed. "I think they want to question you about what happened when you were attacked."

"There is nothing to tell."

His brother shrugged, picking at his nails. Immediately Ellis felt apprehensive. He couldn't help remembering how the Woodcutter had hastened off in the inn. Had something else happened?

He swallowed a spoonful of the soup, although he no longer felt very hungry. "Maybe I'll stay here."

"I don't think you have a choice," said Caleb. "Father has been asked to attend, and he promised to make sure you do too."

"Don't they trust me to turn up?"

"Seems not."

The worry inside Ellis doubled.

His parents said little when he dressed and went downstairs. Neither told him off for joining the hunt without asking their permission, just ate their own lunch silently. Ellis almost wished they were angry, so then he could get angry back. He watched both closely as they chewed and swallowed and sipped. Which one was his real parent, and which wasn't? Or were neither? Had he always known instinctively that he didn't fully belong here?

But the time for dwelling on this wasn't now. He trekked along with his father towards Aramor, neither speaking. Fresh snow dusted the fields and trees and sloping roofs, and it would have been pretty if he was in the mood to take it in.

The meeting was being held in the inn. Ellis's father instructed him to wait outside until he was called. Ellis stamped his feet to keep them warm and watched people file in. Most were men who were prominent figures about Aramor like his father, but a few were farmhands or woodsmen who'd been on the hunt. The last arrival was Doctor Ambrose, looking distinctly ill at ease. He nodded to Ellis as he passed, but did not stop to ask how he was healing up.

The heavy wooden door closed.

Ellis walked to the end of the lane, then back again, wondering how long he was expected to hang around. Even though he didn't think he had anything to fear, he found he couldn't keep still. Why would no one say what was going on?

By the time the door opened Ellis had wandered up and down the lane at least ten times. The men sat around a long table, tankards of ale in front of them and a large fire burning at the hearth. At the head sat the Woodcutter. It crossed Ellis's mind to wonder who had decided he had the authority to speak for the townsfolk. No one seemed inclined to challenge him, not even outspoken men like Martha's father.

There weren't any spare seats so Ellis stood, clutching his cap in his hands, very conscious of the eyes boring into him. The snow on his boots started to melt, forming small puddles around his feet.

"Ellis," the Woodcutter said. "Could you describe what happened the night you were attacked?"

"I cannot remember much." To his relief, his voice sounded strong enough. "Clucking woke me. I thought someone was stealing our chickens. So I went outside to stop them."

"And there the wolf attacked?"

Ellis opened his mouth to say yes, then stopped. Was that strictly true?

"Ellis?" the Woodcutter prompted. Ellis cleared his throat.

"I never actually saw the wolf. I blacked out."

"You don't remember being clawed? You were clawed, were you not?" The Woodcutter glanced at Doctor Ambrose, who gave a small nod. Even though he hadn't said anything wrong or untrue, Ellis felt like he had.

"Maybe that happened after I was out, I don't know."

"What did you hear?"

"Chickens squawking, mostly."

The Woodcutter got up and started to pace. Mr Miller had always said the Woodcutter was an intelligent man, the kind of person who if he were wealthier could have influence. He asked a few more questions. Ellis described how the previous coop of chickens vanished, and his parents' theories about neighbours being responsible. That caused a stir, with a few heads turning to look at Mr Miller, who wore the usual impassive expression Ellis was coming to resent. After asking him once more if he saw anything, the Woodcutter let Ellis go, and there he was, out in the snow again.

There didn't seem anything else to do but go home. Ellis got to the end of the lane before sudden frustration stopped him. He was fed up with secrets. This meeting concerned him, didn't it? This animal might have altered the entire course of his life. Forget being the dutiful son who did as he said – this was too important to walk away from.

Ellis returned to the inn, circling the building until he found the trapdoor which led to the cellars. To his surprise, it was open. He was about to swing himself down when, without warning, a crimson-cloaked figure appeared. Red looked as surprised to see him as she did her.

"What are you doing here?" Ellis broke the silence first.

"Same as you, from the looks of things," said Red. Ellis couldn't exactly deny anything so he scowled instead.

"If you hadn't scared the wolf off this would all be over. Why did you do it?"

Red bit her lower lip. "I can't explain."

"You could try."

"Why should I? You don't care about me. Now are we going to listen in or not, because this is wasting time?"

Ellis turned his back on Red and climbed down the ladder into the cellar, which was a little tricky wearing a sling. He wished he had a candle. It was next to pitch black in here, and cold, reeking of stale ale. Water – or more likely melting snow – dripped. Almost bending double to avoid banging his head, he crept in the direction of voices, hearing Red follow.

"Martha is too distraught to speak to us, and Vincent remembers nothing." The Woodcutter's voice sounded clearly from above. They must be directly under the table here. Ellis settled down on a sack. Red sat across from him, not meeting his eyes.

"Absolutely nothing?" someone asked.

"He was blind drunk when he was attacked." That was Doctor Ambrose. "My guess is he was initially struck from behind, possibly knocked unconscious, but we won't be getting any useful information from him."

"So our only description is from Martha Baker," said Ellis's father. "And Martha describes a phantom creature with red eyes and unnatural size that sprang from nowhere. A beast of evil." Another pause. "Do we really believe that?"

"The wolf we saw last night had reddish-brown eyes," said the Woodcutter, and a couple of others murmured in agreement. Ellis could just picture the men making the sign of evil.

"Speaking as a medical man." Ambrose's voice was quiet and level. "The injuries of all three surviving victims are consistent with wolf attacks, and with each other. In other words, it is believable that the same creature attacked each one."

"The beast of evil," said Ellis's father, with sarcasm.

"I do not like to speculate."

"There was nothing otherworldly about the wounds?" asked the Woodcutter.

"The wounds and bites could have been caused by any large animal."

"Do you think the wounds and bites *were* caused by a large animal?" pressed the Woodcutter.

Ambrose sighed. "It is not impossible. A large hunting dog, perhaps. I would not stake my reputation on it. But if this is the wolf, then it is acting strangely. Especially in the case of young Miller. With him, it had a golden opportunity for a lovely meal. Your daughter's assessment, not mine."

"Sabine?" The Woodcutter sounded puzzled. "When did she say that?"

"We've discussed the attacks several times. Clever girl, your daughter. Very clever, in fact. I do find it very curious that the wolf ventured into town the second time."

There was scuffling to Ellis's right. Mice, probably. At least in the darkness Ellis couldn't see the spiders he felt sure must be lurking here too.

There were sounds from above of benches and stools being drawn back. For a moment Ellis thought the meeting was over, before realizing they were filling their tankards.

"The more they say, the less this makes sense," he muttered. "Don't you think they're missing something?"

Red opened her mouth, then closed it as Ellis's father's voice echoed down.

"Are you going to disclose exactly why we are here? I thought you had new information."

The Woodcutter's reply was drowned out by a thudding; someone knocking a chair over, perhaps. So Ellis was right. Something had changed. He was about to say something to Red when the scuffling came again.

This time he was sure it wasn't mice.

RED

Ellis suddenly leapt up, startling Red.

"Who's there?" he demanded. "Show yourself."

"It's only a mouse," Red whispered. "Don't make so much noise. They'll hear us."

Ellis ducked down deeper into the cellar. Red had almost lost sight of him when someone cried out – a girl.

"Sabine?" Ellis exclaimed. "What are you doing here?"

"Be quiet and listen!" Sabine's voice hissed from behind a

couple of stacked barrels. "If you didn't see me, I haven't seen you. All right?"

Red's head spun. Sabine, creeping into a cobwebby cellar to eavesdrop? Yesterday Red had got the impression Sabine was as much part of the hunt as it was possible for a girl to be, and had the ear of her father, too. Red often saw them walking round the market together, Sabine's arm in her father's. Were they not close, then? The Woodcutter had sounded so puzzled when the doctor had called Sabine clever. As though he didn't see her at all.

Ellis muttered something, but he settled into a comfortable position and quietened. Judging from the movement above, the men had finished collecting their ale, and were sitting back down again.

The Woodcutter cleared his throat. "So, the real reason we are here. Yesterday's hunt."

Red's knees started to knock, and not just because of the cold. If she had eaten today, she felt sure she would have been sick by now.

Banishment, she told herself, and hugged her knees tight to her chest. She had to cling on to hope it would be nothing worse.

"The wolf escaped. We would have had it, but the beast was scared off by a girl who'd followed us."

Red closed her eyes. Here it came.

"But that isn't important." What? Her eyes flew open. "From the girl's description, I am coming around to thinking that it was not the wolf we are looking for."

"Why do you listen to this girl?" That was Mr Baker. Red hadn't realized he was present. She was astonished he had managed to contain himself this long. "Red does not know her left from right half the time. Need I remind everyone that it was her carelessness that led to Martha being attacked?"

"Baker, it was old. It limped off. Now." The Woodcutter's voice deepened. "As we entered the forest, we split into two groups. And the group who did not encounter the wolf returned with news. Lady Katherine's bloodhounds traced the wolf back to town."

What? Red's eyes went to Ellis. He looked as baffled as she felt.

"What do you mean?" Mr Baker sounded suspicious. "We know the wolf has been in town. That is where it attacked my daughter."

"You misunderstand. The wolf comes from the town."

"But we've had wolves in the forest for years. There are whole packs of them."

"Not any more." Red could just imagine the Woodcutter leaning forward, an intense expression on his face. "The old beast we encountered is probably a lone survivor, of little risk to us." He

275

cleared his throat. "The bloodhounds picked up the wolf's scent from clothing Vincent wore the night he was attacked. They took the second group straight back to Aramor, to an abandoned out-building that belonged to the old tavern, right at the edge of town. There is ... evidence there we cannot ignore." He paused. "Old blood. Chicken feathers and carcasses. Clumps of dark fur."

Red knew where he meant. The old tavern had been boarded up years, since the owner's death. It was shot through with rot, and would probably soon collapse. She felt her jaw drop as his words sank in.

"You are saying that the wolf may not be a wolf at all." It was Mr Miller who spoke. "The wolf ... is one of us."

"It could be. We didn't find any weapons, but... Doctor Ambrose, in your opinion, could the wounds on the victims have been caused by knives, instead of claws?"

"It is possible." The doctor sounded reluctant. "It is ... distinctly possible."

The wolf is one of us. Red suddenly found it hard to breathe.

"So I was right all along!" cried Mr Miller. "It was a neighbour who stole our chickens and attacked our son. They've been hiding behind the legend of the wolf to cover themselves!"

"No. You're wrong. You're all wrong!" Mr Baker's voice was

a roar. "My daughter saw the animal! She describes it clearly, still has nightmares. To say the attacks are by anything other than a wolf is preposterous—"

"Your daughter is hysterical and overimaginative and no doubt enjoying the attention," snapped Mr Miller. "Neither my son nor the guard saw anything."

"How do you explain Mistress Forrester's death?" Mr Baker shot back. "She was dragged into the forest – exactly like the wolf's victims five years ago."

"I think we are all aware that Mistress Forrester had enemies," said Mr Miller.

"Including you? You know all about enemies!"

Thud. Footfalls and shouting, as though several men were leaping up at the same time. Was Martha's father attacking Mr Miller, in front of everyone? Mr Baker's shouts rose above the scuffle.

"You don't want to admit that what we are really dealing with here is witchcraft! There *is* a wolf. It's a phantom wolf, no doubt summoned from the abandoned building. The signs are everywhere. You all choose to ignore them. You admitted yourself you found wolf fur. Where does that come from if the attacker has two legs? I know what your game is, Woodcutter. You are scared your daughter is responsible—"

"Throw him out," the Woodcutter ordered. Mr Baker's shouts grew louder, then were silenced by the slamming of a door. He pounded on it from outside, yelling as though possessed himself.

"Ignore him. He will tire," said the Woodcutter. Red marvelled at how composed he sounded. "It is true, we did find fur, but that could quite possibly come from an item of dark clothing, which may be what Martha Baker saw." He lowered his voice. "I do not know if evil spirits and witches really exist, but as I said yesterday, I am not keen for a fear of witchcraft to properly grip the town. It is destructive. The fire at the church was bad enough."

"I know what Baker would say to that," Mr Miller said, and there was a silence. Red's heart was racing, and she was sure Sabine's must be too.

"My daughter is a good girl who would never dream of engaging with the supernatural." The Woodcutter sounded defensive. "Those accusations yesterday were nothing. Just girls sparring. But—" A thump, as though he'd banged his tankard on the table. "We will stop at nothing to weed out whoever is behind this. And if I am wrong, and the wolf is the work of a malicious witch, then no accusation will be ignored. Whoever's door it takes us to. That I swear on my wife's name."

"What now?" someone asked.

"We find out who the wolf is, of course," said the Woodcutter. "Tomorrow we turn the town upside down."

Neither Red, Ellis nor Sabine moved as the meeting broke up. Red had cramp in her foot but she didn't dare shake it out. There was a nasty taste in her mouth that she realized was blood from biting her lip, hard.

Sabine rose first. She went straight to Red, crouching so she could look her right in the eyes.

"You withdraw your accusations against me and I will never trouble you again," she said. "I cannot have anyone suggesting I might be some kind of witch. Do you understand?"

"Why are you so worried?" asked Red. "If you've done nothing wrong you have nothing to fear."

Sabine laughed, a harsh, nervous sound. "Do you really believe that? A rumour is enough to ruin anyone when witchcraft is concerned. What if they find nothing on the search tomorrow? Of course they'll believe it is witchcraft then."

"Your father will protect you despite what he said, surely?" said Ellis.

Sabine turned her back on him. "You need to be careful too, Red. Every strange thing you have ever done or said, however innocent, will be remembered and held against you. We must make out that we are two silly, feuding girls who don't get along and speak without thinking. That is the kind of thing these men will believe."

Red opened her mouth to do the sensible thing and agree. Instead what came out was: "I'll say I made a mistake about you if you admit you were wrong about my leaving the bakery door open."

Sabine went rigid. Red could almost hear her brain whirring. Then: "No."

"Why not? It's a fair bargain. Mistress Baker will believe you if you are clever about it. Maybe even Mr Baker, too. You're persuasive."

"I said no."

"Why not?"

"Forget about the bakery door! It isn't important. What matters is you accused me of being a witch, and you need to withdraw it. Immediately."

Sabine's bony shoulders had started to shake. Why was she being so stubborn – and stupid, too? She clearly realized what danger she was in.

Slowly, Red said, "Why is the bakery door so important to you, Sabine? Would you really rather have people whisper that you're a witch than go back on what you said?"

Sabine tilted her chin. It came across as defensive rather than defiant. "I don't have to explain myself to a freak like you."

"What are you hiding? Do you have something to do with this, Sabine?"

"If you won't agree then I am leaving." Sabine got up, then jumped as Ellis stepped forwards. In a funny kind of voice, he said, "The bakery cart was out of place the morning after Martha was attacked."

"So?" Sabine shot back.

"Martha's parents never use it on that day. It should have been shut away. That struck me as odd at the time, but I couldn't think why. And when I went to see Martha she screamed something about trees."

Red's mind raced. The bakery. The wolf – or the attacker – sneaking into the heart of town. That was the attack that had really struck fear into everyone, and changed everything.

Even though it made no sense...

"It's a lie!" she cried. "Martha wasn't attacked in the bakery at all."

Sabine's face went tight. "Of course she was. You are being ridiculous, as usual."

Suddenly Red wasn't in the cellar. She was at the forest edge, in the darkness, watching Sabine stare into the trees, as she had so many times. Only this time it was dark, and Martha was nearby in the cart, waiting. She could picture it perfectly.

"You took her to the forest," she said. "It is your fault she was hurt. You lied about it and you kept lying, even when people were scared."

Sabine pushed past Red. She dug her foot into the first rung of the ladder and paused. Then she swung round.

"You're not the only person who needs to watch herself, Red." Her voice trembled with emotion. Anger? Or was it fear? "If talk turns to witches, I know exactly whose door they will knock on first, even before mine."

Red went cold.

"Your precious granny is everything people think witches are. She was even a midwife, wasn't she? Strange things happen in childbirth. Healthy babies being lost and sickly ones surviving. It won't take much for people to turn on her."

To Red's horror every word of this rang true. "No. Granny hasn't done anything wrong. She would never hurt anyone."

"So you say. And who believes you?"

"Sabine, please. Don't make trouble for Granny. She is the person I love most in the world. I would do anything to protect her."

"Anything?" Sabine said, pointedly, and Red flushed. In her head, she heard Granny's voice. She knew what Granny would want her to do – and that was not protecting Sabine and her lies.

"Think about it," Sabine said when Red didn't reply. And she disappeared up the ladder.

Red gulped. "Granny."

"Red. . ." said Ellis.

"Leave me alone." Red was frightened she was going to cry. She swung herself up and out into the open. More snow had fallen. Its gleam was almost dazzling after the black of the cellar. She shielded her eyes and stumbled forwards, not caring where she was heading. All she could think about was Granny, Granny, Granny. . .

"Look who it is."

Red jerked upright. Barring her path were Bart and two other boys. Bart stepped forwards, arms folded.

"Traitor."

Red swallowed. "Let me pass."

"So you can help the wolf kill us all? You should leave. You aren't welcome here."

"The wolf isn't a wolf. It's a person. I've just heard them talking about it—"

"I don't believe you. Traitor."

A hand settled on Red's arm – a familiar hand, with a flat, broad thumb. "Let Red go home, Bart," said Ellis. "You're better than this."

One of the other boys grabbed Ellis's bad shoulder. Ellis yelped in pain and let go of Red.

"Better?" Bart sneered. "I thought you were better than to keep such bad company."

"Preferable than keeping your company." If Ellis was scared, he was hiding it well. "Bullying Red isn't really about avenging Martha, or protecting the town, Bart, is it? You just want people's admiration, to make your mark. Or maybe you want to hurt people because you never got to be a soldier. Go home. Things aren't as you think."

"We do what you say, do we? I don't think so, Ellis Miller. Not any more." Bart took a step towards Ellis. "You're not best any everything now. You're nothing."

He lunged forwards. Ellis might only have one arm but his reactions were lightning-quick. He sidestepped, extending a leg. Bart toppled into the snow with a yelp. The other two boys were in his face now, red and furious. One threw a punch Ellis only just dodged. Red snapped to life and hurled herself in between the closest boy and Ellis.

"Get back, freak," snarled the boy.

"Don't call her that," Ellis shouted.

"Ellis, stop it!" cried Red. "You're only making yourself unpopular."

"I don't care. What kind of place is Aramor if we bully people who are different? This has to – ouch."

Bart's fist buried itself in Ellis's nose. Ellis staggered backwards. Starting to panic, Red looked right, then left. Two more boys had appeared from nowhere. If they joined in Ellis was going to get worse than a broken arm.

"If you lay another hand on him I'll turn you all into mice!" she shrieked. That stopped them. Red dragged Ellis away, round the side of the inn. Then they ran, through the lanes and alleys towards Red's house. Red unlatched the door.

"Inside. Come on."

Ellis didn't protest. Red called, "Mother?" but there was no response. Just as well. Red did not feel up to explaining why her gown was so filthy, or why she had Ellis Miller in here with blood trickling from his nose. She lit a candle, then strode to the main room and closed the window shutters. Ellis pressed the end of his sleeve to his nose, hovering in the door frame.

"You shouldn't have threatened them like that, Red," he said. "That was really dangerous."

"I should have let Bart beat you to a pulp, should I?"

"Yes. I would have been fine."

Why did boys always say things like that? And Red had thought she was stubborn. He was right, though. She had done herself no favours. Suddenly the afternoon caught up with Red. She started to tremble and sank down on the closest stool, feeling sick.

Granny.

ELLIS

Ellis peered through the gap in the shutters, doing his best to ignore the stabbing pain from his shoulder. Outside looked clear, but he wouldn't put it past Bart and his followers to show up, if they really were angry... The light was dying, at least, bringing the curfew with it. He should be safe enough to sneak off then.

"Can I say here for a bit?" he asked. Red gestured towards the table. She looked grey, and not just with dust. Ellis settled on a high-backed chair, pressing the end of his sleeve to his nose again.

It didn't feel broken, at least, or even hurt very much, though the punch had been a forceful one.

"Not very long ago those boys were my friends, you know," he said, quietly. "Even Bart. He used to laugh about how one day he'd best me at archery, and I laughed back, but now I think back, he didn't say it like a joke. This situation is dredging up everyone's worst natures."

"Not everyone's." Red looked at him. Ellis wetted his lips, feeling suddenly like he took up a lot of space in this cramped room.

"I'm sorry." The words came out in a rush. "I said things to you that were hurtful and I didn't mean. With the hunt ... I just wanted to belong. I should have stuck up for you with Sabine, too. I do think a lot of you, Red. I don't really believe the time we've spent together isn't real."

Red drew her heels on to the edge of her chair and hugged her knees to her chest. Something about the position made her look vulnerable. "Granny always says that actions speak louder than words. But I wish you had not stepped in just now. It wasn't a very clever thing to do. They will turn on you."

"They were already."

"Not like this."

"Too late to change that now. And I'm not sorry."

A dog howled from outside, followed by something that sounded like smashing. Red paled. Ellis pulled his chair next to hers.

"Your granny will be all right tonight, Red. Bart and the others didn't even mention her. They don't know what we overheard yet."

He extended his good arm. Red hesitated, then nodded, and Ellis drew her against him.

"By tomorrow they will," she muttered. "How long before this becomes a witch hunt? The Bakers are already convinced."

"I don't think people are going to listen to Mr Baker, not if the Woodcutter and the other men insist they are looking for a person." That was what Ellis hoped, anyway. "There is time to make plans."

"Not if Sabine starts spreading rumours about Granny. Do you think she will, Ellis? Be honest."

Was this the first time she had used his name? It made him feel a little funny. Not in a bad way. But definitely funny. Especially as this close he could smell the dust of the cellar on her, and feel her tangled hair brush his cheek.

"Sabine is scared," he said. "If people find out she led Martha to the forest and lied about it, she's in even worse trouble than she already is, much worse than us. But I don't care about Sabine.

Listen, Red, is there anywhere Granny and maybe you could go until this is over?"

Red shook her head. "Granny sometimes says she wants to leave Aramor for ever. She talks of the forest of Lulmor. It's completely wild there, twice the size of Aramor. She's always felt at home among the trees." Red sighed. "It's just a dream really. If she left I would have to go too and I am not sure Mother would be happy about that." She paused. "I really thought I was going to be punished for what I did yesterday. I got it into my head they were going to banish me. I was so scared. And now here we are, talking of Granny leaving."

"At least somewhere else you would both be safe."

"I don't know if Granny is strong enough to travel even if we did have somewhere to go. She sleeps a lot in the day now, and seems much older than she did even a year back."

A few months ago Ellis would have promised to protect Red and Granny and thought that enough, but he was no longer that naive. "Who do you think is behind the attacks? If we could work that out, this would all be over."

"I can't see this ever being over," murmured Red. "Rumours and accusations always linger, like Sabine said. You don't believe your life will go back to the way it was, do you?"

Ellis glanced downwards. Then he shook his head. "Maybe one

day soon we can both get away from Aramor." The words came out of nowhere. "We're almost fifteen. If we managed to put some money aside we could travel. See places."

Red's eyes were big. "You and me? Together?"

"Why not? We could live in a nice town close to a forest, and find jobs. Something that isn't a mill or a bakery. Maybe even by the sea. I've never seen the sea and I'd like to."

Red giggled. "Ellis Miller, you need to stop, or I'll think you're asking me to marry you. Because that's the only way the two of us will ever wind up in a nice little house in some faraway daydream."

Ellis coloured up. He couldn't think what had possessed him to say something so stupid! Just for a moment, the thought had been so tempting. Feeling sheepish, he said, "At least I made you laugh."

Red smiled, rather shyly. Then her smile vanished. "Why would someone do this? Why?"

"No one seems very sorry that Mistress Forrester is dead." He hesitated, remembering the morning by the water pump. "If she knew about me, how many other secrets might she have found out?"

Red shifted under his arm. "Maybe blackmail is how she was able to get Sabine her position. I assume Lord Josiah or Lady

Katherine don't want the truth getting out, if you're right about this."

"If someone wanted Mistress Forrester out of the way they wouldn't attack other people pretending to be the wolf. It's . . . well. Silly."

"So why do it?"

They sat in thought a while. Then, slowly, Ellis said, "When Lord Josiah was at the mill . . . he said something about the power of fear. How it makes people behave. This whole situation suits him."

"He wouldn't attack you, though, surely?" asked Red.

Maybe it would suit Josiah better if Ellis wasn't there. Or maybe he didn't care. Lady Katherine was the one who had been friendly.

Lady Katherine, with her big, well-trained, wolf-like dogs. . .

"I don't like this, Red," he said. "Throwing names about makes me feel grubby."

"I don't like it either. Someone's behind this, though. Someone we know." Red's voice became tiny. "Ellis, I . . . I don't want to say this, but. . . Your parents have reason to want Mistress Forrester kept quiet too."

Even feeling the way he did, the words were a smack to the face. "They wouldn't pretend to be the wolf! What possible reason would they have for causing chaos? And they wouldn't harm me.

Never. They—" He swallowed the words *love me*, because he wasn't so sure about that. Red rubbed her nose, eyes flickering downwards.

"I shouldn't even have said it. Sorry. Maybe someone really was taking the chickens and you interrupted. Mr Baker's a strong man. He hates your parents."

"How do you then explain the attack on Martha? My parents, seeking revenge? Then what about Vincent?"

"Well, could it be the Woodcutter, then?" Red spoke over Ellis's objection. "I know he seems the last person to pose as the wolf who killed his friends, or hurt his wife, but in the space of two days he's practically running the town. According to Mother, Mistress Forrester lost patience with him years ago, so maybe he's fallen out of love with her."

"Do you think Sabine is helping him?"

Red hesitated, then shook her head. "No."

"But you are not sure."

She sighed. "When we were younger, the other girls would go silent when I passed by, as though I wasn't there. Sometimes they'd even throw sticks. Once, I asked why. And do you know what the girl said? 'Sabine told me to do it'. And this is who I've angered! That was stupid. Why didn't I just agree?"

The enormity of what they were facing was finally sinking in. Ellis felt both helpless and hopeless. There was something neither he nor Red had mentioned, too. The person behind the wolf had killed once. And now they were being well and truly hunted. What would they do next?

From outside a bell pealed – the night guard, announcing the curfew. Seconds later came the click of the latch on the main door.

"Grace?" called Red's mother.

Red and Ellis hurriedly broke apart. Red's mother's eyebrows shot upwards when she walked in and saw them sitting awkwardly side by side.

"Oh," she said. "Hello, Ellis."

Ellis couldn't think of what to say, so he mumbled that he had to get home. Red went with him to the door. He didn't like leaving her. He wanted to say something strong and comforting, something she could cling on to when it was dark and she was trying to fall asleep, but he couldn't think of what. So he settled for, "Please look after yourself, Red."

Red nodded. "You too," she whispered.

SABINE

Sabine slammed the door to her bedroom at the manor, breath rasping from running up two flights of stairs. The noise made her jump. Cursing her recklessness, she stood still, listening, but there were no footsteps, and no one called her name. Sabine allowed herself to relax – but only a touch. She eyed up her bed, wondering how easy it would be to tug it across the door, but that would only make more noise. Why didn't this silly door have a lock?

She'd simply have to hope no one disturbed her. Both Lord

Josiah and Lady Katherine were ordinarily in the library around this time, so she should be safe for a little while. Pushing cobwebby hair behind her ears – when had she last brushed it? – Sabine slipped her hand under her mattress. Everything was there, as it should be: her herb collection and her charms. The wooden wolf was in the pouch she carried, as usual.

Why hadn't her father warned her the wolf had been traced to town? It was ridiculous being forced to crawl into that horrible, damp cellar to find out things he should have confided in the comfort of their own home. Sabine felt hurt and betrayed and humiliated, and for once she found herself unable to block these messy emotions out. The way he had sounded so surprised when Doctor Ambrose had called her clever! Worse, his defence when her name had come up – so half-hearted...

He is saving face, trying to keep people happy, she told herself, but she didn't fully believe that. Sabine wished she'd handled bargaining with Red better. Threatening her grandmother, too! Sabine didn't much care about Granny, but she knew what it was like to love family fiercely. Even if they didn't love you back in the same way...

It was Red's fault, Sabine thought. She was the one who'd brought that stupid bakery door into it again. That was the worst lie of all. Why had she tried to be smart and scapegoat Red? People might have been sympathetic if she had turned on the tears and made out she and Martha were silly girls whose innocent curiosity had them in the wrong place at the same time.

Now Red knew the truth, and so did Ellis. Would they tell people? Red might be too afraid but Sabine was less sure about Ellis. He was one of those naive kinds of boys who had a very strong sense of right and wrong, and that made him a threat. He might even feel he owed it to Martha, though he seemed to have moved on from her.

The one thing Sabine did know was that she needed to protect herself and she needed to do it now. She could not rely on maybes and could bes, and even though it pained her to admit it, she could not rely on her father either. Sabine stuffed her herbs and charms into a spare pouch. She hesitated over the wooden wolf. All those years, the happy memories... What could be more innocent than a child's toy? But she knew others wouldn't see it that way.

Goodbye, she thought, and with a lump in her throat dropped the wolf into the pouch.

Now what to do? Her plan had been simply to dispose of everything, maybe hide the pouch somewhere she could collect it when this all died down. . . Would that be enough, though? Was there something more she could do to protect herself?

Sabine could see her reflection in the grubby glass of her narrow window, illuminated by the candle on her cabinet. She stared into her own eyes. When had they become so sharp, her cheekbones jutting, cheeks so pinched?

She didn't want to be this person who dealt in threats and lies and secrets.

Too late, Sabine thought, and hardened her heart. She grabbed the candle and left.

Aramor was silent when she arrived. Sabine had to pinch herself to keep alert; her body was drooping with exhaustion now, though it was hardly late. Most families were probably eating their evening meal, cosy in front of their glowing hearths. As she passed under the main gate she heard clinking, and ducked into an alley just in time to evade a night guard. Once he had gone she wove her way to the bakery. Light from above told her that Martha and her parents were upstairs. The back door – the door of her worst nightmares – was locked, but the storeroom window to one side was loose, and just about big enough for someone Sabine's size to wriggle through without causing too great a disturbance.

Inside, Sabine quickly found what she was looking for. She hesitated a moment. Once she did this there was no going back. She didn't want to. But it no longer felt like she had much choice.

With a leaden feeling, she did what she had come to do.

RED

The moment Red woke the next morning, everything came back to her. *Granny.* Red tumbled out of bed, dressed quickly and raced downstairs. In the hallway she collided with her mother.

"You're early, Grace."

"I need to see Granny."

Mother immediately looked exasperated. "That will make you late for work."

"I don't care. This is more important."

Mother stepped in front of the door, folding her arms. "You are lucky to have kept that job. The Bakers won't tolerate any further mistakes. What will you do if they dismiss you?"

"Something. I don't know."

"Grace ... please don't do this." Her mother's tone turned pleading. "I know that Aramor is a frightening place at the moment. I am frightened myself, and I dare say Granny is as well even if she claims not to be. She wouldn't want you to lose your job because you were worried about her. You can wait to see her until after work, can't you? Think of me, too. We had a nice evening for a change, didn't we?"

Her tone was inviting, and Red felt a little sick. Last night all Mother had talked of was what a nice young man Ellis was, clearly under the impression that something was going on between them. She had been so delighted that finally Red was doing something she considered normal that Red couldn't bear to correct her. At least it had been a distraction from fretting.

"The more you keep me the later I'll be," she said. Mother looked at her a second, then raised her hands in a gesture of helplessness that somehow made Red feel worse than if she'd shouted.

Outside, Red raced towards the forest. Two men stepped into her path.

"Where are you going so quickly?" one barked. For a moment, Red thought they were guards – but both were woodsmen. Since when did townsfolk patrol the streets?

"Only to work," she said meekly.

The man grunted and let her go. Red took a diversion down a narrow lane that led in the direction of the bakery, then doubled back to the forest path. The moment the trees closed around her she felt as though she could breathe again.

"Granny!" Red hammered on the front door, out of breath from vaulting over tree trunks and tearing through bushes – today she'd taken the quickest route, which skipped the path entirely. "Granny, open up! It's important."

Why was she taking so long? Red was about to move to the windows when the door swung open. Red hurled herself at Granny and enveloped her in a crushing hug. To her embarrassment, she burst into tears. Granny patted her shoulder.

"Red, what's this about? Here. Let me hold you."

Everything Red heard yesterday came tumbling out. "...and then Sabine will tell everyone you're responsible and they'll search your cottage," she finished. "If there's anything they might be suspicious of you have to destroy it."

"So this is what it has come to," said Granny. They were sitting down now, Granny stroking Red's hair.

"I'm so scared you'll be blamed." Red did her best to control the sobs. Granny sighed. Her bones creaked as she leaned back.

"Don't worry about me, Red. They will not find anything here."

"Are you sure? Nothing from your time as a midwife? No, I don't know, funny charms or whatever else witches keep?"

"Red, you are panicking, and I want you to calm yourself." Granny's voice was firm. "The only thing they will find will be a sweet and doddery old lady who likes her own company. It's you I am worried about, my love."

"I never wanted to make enemies. Sabine has hated me all our lives. I don't know why."

"I could hazard a guess. And it is not because the two of you are so different."

"What do you mean?"

"I think you and Sabine are much more alike than Sabine can bear to admit. But never mind that. Red... Aramor has always been my home. I've been happy here, in the forest I love. I had always seen myself dying in Aramor, and being laid to rest at that copse by the stream." She closed her eyes a second. "Now, though... Your friend Ellis is right. It is too dangerous here for us."

Fear shot through Red. "Do you really mean that?"

Granny nodded. "There is something I need to explain to you, Red. Something that may help you understand just how dangerous this is."

"What is it? You sound so serious."

"I am serious. When we have more time, very soon, I will tell you everything."

Granny was scaring Red a little herself now. "What if whoever is doing this is caught?" she asked. "That would mean we could stay, wouldn't it?"

"I don't think so, my love. Trust me when I say your life is only going to get more difficult the longer you stay here. I have misjudged this. It was different for me when I was first. . ."

"First what, Granny?"

Granny raised a finger to her lips. Red waited, but all she could hear was birdsong.

"What is it?"

"Voices."

"Granny, you're imagining things. I have good hearing, and—"

Granny shook her head. Perplexed, Red went to the door and tilted it ajar. Granny was right – down by the stream there was a flash of colour and movement. Men. Woodsmen, from the looks of things, though they were still quite far away.

So they were coming to speak to Granny. Red fervently hoped Granny had been telling the truth when she said they'd find nothing. At least the Woodcutter seemed to want to be honest, not the kind of man who would find someone innocent guilty just to appease everyone else.

Then Red froze. Granny's cottage wouldn't be the only place they'd be searching today, would it? Sabine might not have as much influence over her father as she might like. But she still had his ear. And Sabine was not as honest as he was.

Seconds later Red was flying out Granny's back door and streaking through the trees, ducking down and keeping herself hidden.

She hoped she wasn't already too late.

There were men outside her house. Red cursed, crouching behind a barrel on the other side of the road. The men had their backs to her but her mother was gesticulating, in the way she did when she was worked up. From the untidy state of her dress Red guessed she had been dragged outside while getting ready.

What to do? Red couldn't exactly march up and demand to be let in. They wouldn't trust her not to hide something, and they wouldn't believe her if she told them she suspected suspicious items had been planted in her room. If it had. Red might be wrong. She hoped so. What would they even do if they did find something? Throw her into prison in the guard house? Duck her in the river like they had in the witch trials from decades back? Worse?

Two more men strode out of Red's cottage, empty-handed. They had a few words with her mother, bowed their heads and then retreated down the lane. Red leapt up and ran to Mother.

"Did they search the house?"

Her mother's hand flew to her chest. "Grace! You startled me."

"Did they find anything?"

Mother shook her head. She looked scared. "They said they were looking for the wolf. I don't understand. They want to ask you some questions. I told them to go to the bakery."

Of course! Red was gone before her mother could call after her. She'd been silly! If Sabine was going to play this game she wouldn't go to Red's house, with Red's mother there the whole time.

Red put on speed, skidding down the lane and darting out of the way of a cart at the bottom. If she cut down the alleyways, she might just get there first, assuming the men were not also hurrying. And they might be. There was an entire town to search, after all.

The bakery gates were open. The yard was empty apart from the tabby cat tossing a dead mouse from paw to paw. Red leaned her hands on her thighs, gulping in air. Had she ever done so much running? She burst in through the back door. Mistress Baker looked up from where she was moulding a pie.

"You are late."

Red threw open the door to the storeroom. At the bottom shelf next to the rye flour was the basket where she kept her spare coifs and aprons. Red reached inside – and out came a little pouch she didn't recognize. She sucked in a breath when she saw the contents. Dried herbs in small glass bottles, peculiar-looking charms and trinkets, even a wooden wolf...

It screamed *witch* – the kind of things people in Aramor considered witchy, anyway. Red was a little thrown. This was quite the collection. Even though Red did not believe in witches, the sight of all these bits and pieces frightened her a little.

But it would frighten the men more. As Sabine well knew.

Red didn't have time to reflect on why Sabine was so interested in such things. She slipped the pouch under her cape and rushed out, stealing round the other side of the bakery and climbing over the wall to avoid bumping into the men.

For once she knew exactly what she was going to do.

ELLIS

Today was not a delivery day, but there was no way Ellis was staying at the mill. He was pulling his sturdiest boots on when Mr Miller demanded, "Where are you going?"

"Aramor," Ellis said shortly.

"And the mill floor is going to sweep itself?"

Ellis glared at his father. "Until I broke my arm Caleb did the sweeping. He only let me take over because I was desperate to help. Don't pretend you really need me."

Mr Miller looked taken aback, but only for a moment. "I forbid you to go to town."

"Why?"

"Don't question me, Ellis. You are safer here. And you will not argue. I don't like this recent hot-headedness. One of the mill hands told me you got into a fight yesterday. I've told you before that trouble is best avoided."

"So I shouldn't defend my friends?"

"You should not have got involved."

"What would you have me do instead? Hide in the mill and hope everything bad goes away like you do?"

Finally, Ellis got the reaction he wanted. His father drew himself straight.

"I don't know why you are deliberately being rude, but you are most certainly not going into town. Go to your room and stay there."

"No. I won't." Ellis could feel himself getting hot inside. Hoping he wasn't going to lose his temper, he stood. He was taller than his father now, and that gave him confidence. "I heard everything that was said at the meeting yesterday and I'm not staying here. And yes, I eavesdropped. It's the only way I find out anything."

Ellis's mother came in. Her hair had not yet been pinned up, and she looked as though she had slept badly.

"What is going on?"

"Ellis is refusing to obey me," said Mr Miller. "Worse, he's admitted to dishonesty. I thought better of you, son."

Mistress Miller rubbed her forehead. "Please let's not have an argument. Ellis, your father has your best interests at heart, even if you can't see it. Do as he says."

Something in Ellis snapped. "Why? I don't even know if he is my father."

Both his parents paled. His mother found her voice first.

"What makes you say such a thing?"

"Because it's true, isn't it? Or are you not my mother?" Realizing he was almost shouting, Ellis lowered his voice. He had a horrible sense that he might be close to tears. "I know you have an agreement with Lord Josiah and Lady Katherine. I am some sort of deal you've struck to – to – I don't know, gain favour. Please don't lie and say it isn't true because I have never belonged here and now I at least know why. And if you don't tell me the truth I'll go to the manor, and demand answers there."

Neither Mr or Mistress Miller moved. Ellis glared at them.

"Fine, then. I'll go."

He turned.

"Ellis, wait," said his father.

Ellis glanced over his shoulder. His parents – or, at least, the man and woman he'd always thought of as his parents – were holding hands. Both of them looked sad.

"I suppose it is time," Mr Miller said. "That is, if you are ready, Tamasin?"

Mistress Miller swallowed. "The truth was going to come out soon enough. Sit down, please, Ellis. This isn't a short story."

~SABINE

Sabine watched the men striding in and out of houses from a distance. She would have preferred to have been closer, but she didn't like the way people had been looking at her. After another night of barely existent sleep she felt wrecked, and somehow all her gowns were filthy, though she had at least tidied her hair. News of Red's outburst in the inn had clearly spread. Before, she had been able to go as she pleased, and no one had thought anything. Now there were whispers. Looks. Silences.

As though they think I'm some kind of other, thought Sabine, and burned with anger. She dismissed the thought that this was how it must feel to be Red.

It was midday now and she had no idea if they had searched the bakery yet. Earlier she had tried to subtly encourage her father to consider that maybe he should go there as a priority but he had only told her to stop meddling. Sabine suddenly wished her mother was there. Mistress Forrester would probably have figured out who the wolf was already, or at least known the right questions to ask to the right people, or produced some obscure kernel of information which made everything slide into place. Her skills would be of far more use than the Woodcutter's, who seemed to think turning the town upside down was the right way to unearth answers.

"Sabine. You look lost." The voice belonged to Mistress Baker. She had a basket covered by a towel on one arm. "I have made meat pies for the men. Still warm. Feeding them seemed the least Amos and I could do. I doubt anyone will get much done today. Even if we had the customers." She moved a little closer to Sabine, lowering her voice. "Barely anyone has entered the shop all morning. It's as though people are scared to eat our bread. If this carries on. . ."

"Have they searched the bakery yet, then?" Sabine kept her voice light. "They've not found anything, I suppose?"

"No. Why would they? We have nothing to hide." Mistress Baker sounded genuinely surprised – and a little affronted. Sabine felt a twinge of guilt. Martha's mother was a nice woman who went out of her way to be kind to Sabine. She didn't deserve any further hardship. Would the Bakers be ruined by this, tainted by employing Red?

"Where is Red?" Sabine asked. "I am surprised she's not helping you."

"I don't know. She ran in then straight out again. That was hours ago. She hasn't returned." Sabine frowned, immediately suspicious. Mistress Baker continued, "We are going to have to let her go. My husband thinks I have been a fool for keeping her in a job. I probably am. Maybe it is safest to keep the shop within the family."

"Mmm." Sabine had stopped listening. Her eyes were on the alleyway which led from the square to the part of town where her family lived. Her sisters had just emerged, younger siblings in tow. Midday was an odd time for an excursion. Normally they ate around now. Her mother had always been particular about doing things at certain times, and her daughters had inherited that fussiness.

"Excuse me," Sabine said to Martha's mother, and crossed the square. Her eldest sister gave her a dirty look.

"Where were you earlier? We could have done with your help. Or are you pretending to be one of the men again this morning?"

Sabine ignored the jibe. "Why aren't you at home?"

"Too noisy. I suppose they have to search everywhere, but I was surprised they are bothering with us. Father was probably keen for his family to be ruled out sooner rather than later, so he does not lose respect – Sabine?"

But Sabine was gone, hurrying down the alleyway her sisters had come from. *I am worrying unnecessarily*, she told herself. There was nothing at her parents' house to be found. Sabine barely kept anything there these days. The search was a formality, nothing more. When the men there heard what their friends had found in the bakery they wouldn't even bother to finish the search. They would have found their witch, and Sabine would have time to properly work out what to do next—

She rounded the corner and skidded to a halt. Her father stood outside the house with two others. In his hand was something she recognized.

The pouch she had planted on Red.

The Woodcutter looked up. Their eyes met. He held the bag aloft.

"Sabine. What is this?"

Sabine sat on one side of a table in the guard house. On the other were her father and two guards. It was a dark, poky little room with a tilting window that looked like it was scowling. A rotten smell crept up from below them.

Everything was laid out on the table. The herbs she had painstakingly mixed, with the little pictures she had drawn on parchment stolen from Lady Katherine to remind herself what they were for. The charms, clearly well worn. And, worst of all, her wolf, lying forlornly on its side.

They looked so sinister all together. If her father recognized the toy he had carved himself, he was keeping that very quiet. Most likely, he had forgotten. The things that made such an impression on her did not for him, it seemed.

That hurt. But Sabine could not dwell on that now. "These aren't mine."

"They were in the room that used to be yours."

"That doesn't mean they belong to me. The twins sleep there now."

"The twins are seven. Are you saying these ... things are theirs?"

"No." Sabine was not ruthless enough to drop her innocent brother and sister into this. Her older sisters she felt no loyalty to, but her father would never believe they could be responsible for anything of this nature. "Where did you find these things?"

"Hidden under the floorboards."

"Anyone could have put that there. It is obvious that floorboard is loose the moment you step in."

The Woodcutter didn't look convinced. Neither did the two guards sitting either side of him. Sabine leaned forwards, hoped she came across as the right mix of outraged and confused.

"Father, you don't believe this, do you? I'm not a witch. These aren't mine."

"Whose are they then?"

"Red's, of course! I told you, we have a feud. She wants you to believe I am guilty, because she's scared you will come for her. Everyone knows how odd she is. Even as a child she would never join us to swim in the river, and she'd scream if anyone splashed her. Aren't witches afraid of water? And if you had only—" She stopped. She couldn't very well say if they'd got to the bakery sooner Red would be sitting here rather than her! How Red had worked out what Sabine had done she had no idea, but this couldn't be anyone else's handiwork.

Sabine took a deep breath, then another. "Father. This is a misunderstanding. You know me. I have no reason to want to hurt or scare people. Martha is my best friend. And Mother—"

"I cannot overlook this because you are my daughter, Sabine."

The Woodcutter sounded sickeningly reasonable. "We all face the consequences of our actions. You see why I had to allow your possessions to be searched. There is no reason to believe anything wrong of Red. There was nothing in her house."

"Or the bakery?" Sabine couldn't help herself.

"Or the bakery. And, my love. . ." His tone deepened. "In all conscience, there are other things I can't overlook too."

"What?" cried Sabine.

"Your unmaidenly interest in the victims and their wounds. The knowledge I hear you have of ailments and the body, far beyond what would be normal for a girl of your age. Your keenness to engage in bloody surgery—"

"Because I want to know more about healing!" shouted Sabine. "Doctor Ambrose asked me to help him and I did."

"It is unmaidenly," her father repeated. "When I saw you standing there, your dress doused with blood, I was shocked."

"Then you are narrow-minded," Sabine snapped. Instantly she knew this was a mistake. The guards drew back, as though defending herself was more proof of how unmaidenly and therefore unnatural she was.

I need to stop talking, Sabine realized. *I need to . . . think, and work out what I can possibly do or say to save myself.*

318

One last time, though, she had to try. "You really believe I am the attacker. That I summoned a phantom wolf and knowingly hurt people."

"We have to consider it."

"Will you carry on searching? Because the person truly responsible is out there."

"I am not discussing this."

"What happens now, then?" Her eyes felt wet. Not crocodile tears this time.

One of the guards spoke up. "We have no choice but to keep you imprisoned until we finish conducting further investigations."

"What?" Sabine's eyes went big. "You cannot mean that."

Her father rose to his full height. Gently, almost regretfully, he said, "Everyone is relying on me to get to the bottom of this, Sabby. I would be doing Aramor a disservice if I was not thorough. If you have done nothing wrong you have nothing to worry about."

"Do you expect me to believe that?" whispered Sabine. "Even if you do find who is really responsible there will always be doubts about me."

"I must do my duty. To your mother. And my dead friends."

"You didn't even like her!" Could he not see how twisted this was? "Father. I don't know what's going on, or who is attacking people, but—"

Her father walked out. Sabine gaped at him. A guard took her arm. Sabine shook him off.

"How dare you touch me like I've done something wrong. Father!"

She shouted and shouted. She didn't care about being dignified. The guard watched. When she finally gave up, he said, "Are you going to come with me?"

The cell wasn't quite as dingy as she'd feared, but it was dark and grimy, more somewhere you would keep an animal than a human. Sabine held her head in her hands and wept.

How could things have come to this?

It was all sinking in now. Even if she was released, her life as she knew it was over. She would never, ever be able to experiment with herbs again, or visit the forest, or somehow persuade Ambrose to teach her what she knew. She would probably be dismissed from the manor and sent home to her uncaring sisters and the father she no longer understood and expected to work in some lowly, tedious job before marrying someone suitable. For others maybe that would make them happy. Not for Sabine. *If I am even lucky enough for a boy to look my way,* she thought. No one would want a girl known to be strange.

And she *was* strange. Sabine cried harder. *I hide it, but I am, I know I am,* she thought. *I am like Red, not Martha and the other girls I look down on because they seek ordinary lives. Why am I like this? Why do I always want more?*

Even if there was another attack tonight, that wouldn't prove her innocence. If people believed she had conjured a phantom wolf four times already, they'd believe she could do it again from inside a cell, even without her charms. If anything, they'd take it as proof of her guilt.

And the real culprit would walk free. More people would be hurt. And Sabine didn't want that.

Her father had to wake up and realize he was drunk with power and doing things he'd later regret, he had to. It was thin hope, but Sabine clung to it.

Perhaps her friends would help her. She'd never been the kindest person, but people did like her, didn't they? Martha wouldn't want Sabine to be accused. Martha didn't like Red any more than Sabine did. Martha would realize what Sabine had been trying to do, and—

What was she thinking? Martha hadn't left her room in days.

She was in no position to fight for Sabine. More than that, Martha was a threat. She was the one screaming about phantom wolves. If her father interrogated Martha, she'd crumble. Everything she told them would back up what they suspected – especially the truth about the night she'd been mauled.

It was all so unfair. Maybe if the townsfolk had been just the tiniest bit more open-minded, Sabine would not have become infatuated with the danger of the forest. Maybe she would be a kinder, better person, who did not hurt others because she was afraid of herself, and did not need to lie. Maybe she could even have used her cleverness for something worthwhile.

Maybe, of course, was no use to her now. Neither was getting angry, or being sorry. And she was sorry – deeply, bitterly sorry, and not just because she had been caught.

Sabine slumped against the wall and closed her eyes and tried to think of nothing.

RED

Red had watched from a distance as Sabine was marched from her cottage to the guard house. Sabine looked defiant but also, Red thought, scared. It was going to be hard for her to lie and cry out of this one.

Inside, Red felt peculiar. For once, she had got what she wanted. Sabine deserved this. If their positions were reversed, Sabine would be gloating. So why wasn't Red? Was it because she kept thinking about what Granny had said – that they were more alike than different?

All I ever wanted was to be left alone, Red thought. To dance in the forest and pick pretty flowers I don't know the names of and sniff the dew off the leaves.

Who was the wolf? None of the names she and Ellis had floated last night really made any sense. She supposed she could see what Lord Josiah might have to gain, but equally, she could not see his lordship lurking in the shadows and attacking people.

Red's stomach growled. The long, fraught morning hanging around town waiting for things to happen had drained her. Maybe after eating she could find Ellis. It felt strange for so much to have happened without speaking to him. She'd hoped she might have seen him by now. Last night, it had felt like they were close. What he'd said about getting away from Aramor and a little house... She'd teased him to hide her awkwardness but her heart had beat that bit faster, too. He really did seem to want her safe. He didn't care about all odd things about her she'd assumed he would in the days she'd watched him flirting with Martha. And she didn't think he'd forget her once this was over, either.

Walking out to the mill might help calm her, assuming Ellis was there. The need to tell someone about the trick Sabine had so almost succeeded in pulling was eating her up.

Then Red remembered. The bakery! How had she forgotten the

job she couldn't afford to lose? For the second time that day, Red rushed over. Mr and Mistress Baker were in the kitchen, talking in low voices. The oven was fired up and the aroma of meat pies made her mouth water. But before Red could speak Mr Baker said, "You are dismissed."

Dread gripped Red. "Please don't. I'll make up the time I wasn't here today or you can not pay me. I'm sorry. With everything going on, I—"

"I don't want to hear it. Go." Mr Baker turned his back. Mistress Baker cleared her throat.

"We made a mistake to keep you on after Martha was hurt. We can't have someone here who we don't fully trust."

"But I need this job! My mother and Granny—"

"Are your responsibility, not ours. You will have to find another job, Red. I'm sorry."

Red's head spun. She couldn't think of anywhere that would have her. It was already widely known in town that she was careless, and unreliable, and jobs were thin on the ground in winter.

"Please." Her voice shook. "Mistress Baker, you always said you owed my granny—"

"You are dismissed!" snapped Mr Baker. "Stop attempting to appeal to my wife's softness. Now take your things, and leave."

With a lump in her throat, Red did as she was bid. Outside she stood in the yard, staring at the untidy outbuildings for what was probably the last time. The tabby cat leapt down from the shed roof and rubbed up against her legs, mewing. Would anyone lay out a saucer of milk for him now Red was gone?

Mother won't be able to look at me ever again, thought Red. *I let her down. Keeping this job was the one thing she needed me to do. And I failed.*

She walked. Not, for once, to the forest, but south, towards the river where she and Ellis had passed that golden hour on the ice that almost felt a dream. She didn't care where she ended up. She just wanted to put distance between herself and Aramor.

What kind of future could she expect now?

ELLIS

Dorothy had not been saddled and ridden for years, and every moment of the canter to the manor it felt to Ellis like she was letting him know just how unhappy about it she was. With lots of coaxing, he finally reached the manor gates, dismounting and leading her up the path. For perhaps the first time, he took everything in front of him in – really took it in. The tidy gardens, with their little herb beds, the hedge maze that everyone in town agreed was frivolous, the canopy of vines that on summer days would be cool to walk under. And beyond, the manor, by far the grandest building Ellis had ever seen, all decorative arches and tall windows and oak border frame.

It didn't feel like somewhere he should be. A few feet up the path Ellis lost his nerve and swerved round to the track which led towards the servants' entrance.

He had been feeling nauseous when he left the mill and he felt even more nauseous now, the conversation with his parents going round and round his head.

This is a bad idea, Ellis thought. *I should be in town. Anything could be happening there and I wouldn't know. Red might need me.*

But instead he was here, about to confront who he really was. The servants' entrance was right next to the stable, and he found a somewhat confused groom to take Dorothy. He was working himself up to enter when a large dog bounded over, barking excitedly. Overwhelmed by the sudden noise, Ellis backed off, bumping the stable door.

"Heel!" Lady Katherine's voice rang out, sharp and authoritative. Immediately the dogs quietened. Her ladyship strode over, eyebrows raised. Her smart coat and boots indicated she was dressed to ride. Ellis opened his mouth and suddenly didn't know what he wanted to say. Katherine's expression switched to one of knowing.

"They've told you," she said. "Here. Come inside. Josiah is not here. But I think it better you speak to me alone."

The room Katherine took him to was richly carpeted, with glorious tapestries hanging down the dark-panelled walls and blocking out the draughts. The full log fire immediately made Ellis too hot, and yet he didn't feel comfortable enough to take off his jerkin. Katherine perched on the edge of a cushioned chair, gesturing for him to sit.

"Poor boy," she said. "Was it a total surprise?"

He found his voice. "I got it wrong. I thought. . ."

"That I was your mother?" She smiled sadly. "It is a natural enough assumption. We do look a little alike. More so than you and Josiah, really. It wouldn't have been hard to pretend that you were my son too." A pause. She folded her hands in her lap. "I would have liked that, in case you are wondering. Children were always something I wanted. This is a lonely house. The dogs are wonderful companions, but not the same."

Ellis's cheeks flooded with colour. He didn't know if he could have this conversation. It had been bad enough with his parents. Or rather, his mother, and the man who it turned out wasn't his father.

Mistress Miller had done most of the talking. She described

herself as a young woman, newly married and thrilled to be working in a house as grand as the manor. Her intention had been to
stay there until Mr Miller inherited the mill from his uncle. What
had she had not expected was for her good looks to catch the eye
of Lord Josiah. At first, the Millers had been amused by the lord's
attention. Both could see how easy it would be to turn this to their
advantage. Pretty trinkets and rich gifts from his lordship could
be sold. Before too long, they would be able to purchase the new
waterwheel the mill badly needed, as well as everyday things like
clothes and new boots.

"It seemed worth it at the time," Mistress Miller had said. She
did not look at Ellis. "You are lucky. You have never known what
it is to be poor, and hungry, with shoes that leak and clothes that
have been repaired again and again."

Then Mistress Miller had fallen pregnant and there could be
no doubt as to who the baby's father was. Somewhat to the Millers'
surprise, Lord Josiah had appeared keen to provide for the baby,
especially when it turned out to be a boy. Ellis could not imagine
this, but then he could also not imagine a man as seemingly joyless
as Lord Josiah being seized by a passion for his mother.

"A man like him is under pressure for an heir," Mistress Miller
had said. "He and Lady Katherine had lost several babies, and he

has no other family any more. An illegitimate child is better than nothing."

There had been talk of giving Ellis to Josiah and Katherine, to pass off as their own. But Mr Miller had seen more potential in raising Ellis themselves, in exchange for favours from Josiah.

Ellis had got angry at this point, accusing Mr Miller of being mercenary. Mr Miller did not deny it.

"Your mother views it as a betrayal now too, but we had to survive," he'd said in a low voice. His words were almost identical to those Granny had used, and Mistress Miller before her. "Thanks to that choice, we have all led comfortable lives. That would not have happened if we had given you up. Lord Josiah wouldn't have gifted us a single coin."

"But we always agreed that you would go to Josiah once you were fifteen," said Mistress Miller. "You'll have a better life with him than you ever could hope for here. You can already read and write, and you're as educated as you can be without raising suspicion. Lord Josiah has other grand houses, Lady Katherine too. You have said before that you would like to travel."

"And that makes using me as a bargaining tool better?"

"I never saw you that way." His mother sounded hurt. "We do love you, Ellis."

"Both of us," added Mr Miller, rather gruffly, but Ellis was not sure he believed him.

"Ellis?" He gave a start. Katherine knelt in front of him, holding his hands. Ashamed of his rough skin, Ellis pulled them away.

"Is your husband even interested in getting to know me? He wasn't friendly when he came to the mill a few days ago."

Katherine sighed. "Josiah has become quite solitary the last few years. In time, he will show an interest."

"My mother said you were the one who sent us gifts and insisted on my having a tutor."

"I would have done more. Like have more of a relationship with you. But it wasn't my place to insist."

Ellis's nausea returned. Surely this was some kind of dream and he would soon wake up. His voice sounded thick. "Where am I even supposed to sleep tonight? The mill? That doesn't feel like home, not any more. I don't even want to speak to . . . them. Or am I expected to live here now? No one told me anything. This is my life!"

"You can do whatever you choose. We cannot control you and I certainly would not want to even try. There is a third option. One that will give you time and space for this to sink in." She rose. "I have some of my own money set aside for you. Money enough for you to seek your own fortune for a while, well away from everyone. You may have it today if you wish."

Leave Aramor? Only yesterday Ellis had pictured doing just that. But that had been before his world had been turned upside down – again. "Why would you do that for me?"

"Because you are the closest thing I will have to a son. I am not resentful of your mother and Josiah, but I did resent the decisions they made as to how you were to be raised. I think you are old enough to make your own decisions now."

Ellis felt about five, not almost fifteen. Yet the pull of leaving all this behind, at least for a while, was strong. He wasn't cut out to be some grand lord's heir. But neither did he feel much like a miller's son any more. That would mean forgiving his parents and pretending none of this had happened. How could he?

He could leave. Actually leave Aramor. Forget the wolf, the friends that hated him, everything. Red could come, Granny too, maybe.

Ellis looked at Katherine. Her smile was a nervous one, as though he was an animal that might bite.

"I would only ask one thing," she said. "Please let me know you are safe."

That thought that Katherine – someone he had always seen as so far removed – would worry about him... Ellis wished he knew her better, that they had gone riding together or played chess or whatever else Katherine would have done with a son. She crossed the room, and opened a cabinet. Out came a large bag of coins. Ellis shook his head.

"I cannot take this."

Katherine tossed the bag at him. On instinct Ellis caught it. "You already have." There was something impish in her smile this time, and it instantly made her look younger. Ellis surprised himself by giving her a hug. An awkward, one-armed hug that didn't feel right, but, from the way she hugged him back, clearly felt right to her.

Ellis left the manor weighed down with gold but feeling lighter in himself. Leaving Aramor. He could hardly believe it. Simply riding off was not something he was prepared to do – if he really did this he would need clothes and supplies, not to mention say goodbye to Caleb and his little brothers. Dorothy wasn't his to take, either.

Before he did any of this, though, it was time to brave town.

*

Ellis could tell it was not a normal day immediately. The streets were teeming, and the shops were open but empty. Spying the butcher's wife, Ellis leapt off Dorothy.

"What is going on?"

He gasped when he heard about Sabine. "She is actually in the guard house? Her father let that happen?"

"If she summoned the wolf she's no daughter of his." The butcher's wife made the sign of evil. Ellis wondered if the woman knew how mad that sounded. Did she really believe a few herbs and a wooden toy could give a fourteen-year-old girl that kind of power?

On a normal day Red would be at the bakery mid-afternoon, so first Ellis went there. His knock at the back door went unanswered and when he went round to the front the shop was shuttered. Either Red had been turned away or she had never made it to work. The sense of vague unease that had been with him ever since arriving at town sharpened. Leading Dorothy by the reins, he went to Red's house. There he found her mother, standing outside being comforted by the tailor. When she saw him she stopped.

"Are you looking for Grace?"

Whenever he heard Red's real name it threw him. Ellis nodded.

Red's mother came closer. "I am worried for her."

"She hasn't been accused of anything?"

"No. But our house has been searched. Twice. And those boys have been here over an hour now."

Over the road, leaning against the wall of someone's house, were Bart and his friends. Catching Ellis looking, Bart embedded the knife he'd been playing with in the soil.

Ellis knew he was being taunted. Even so, it did not feel like an empty threat. He turned his back, feeling their eyes bore into him. "When did you last see Red?"

"Ten minutes ago, round the back of the house. I don't think the boys saw her. She seemed . . . strange. Said she'd been walking and thinking. Then she left. I don't know where to."

Ellis glanced upwards. Already light was dying. Very soon it would be dark. "Did she say anything about going to her grandmother?"

"She's already seen Granny today. Normally that's the first place I'd think of." And Red's mother started to cry. The tailor put his arms round her, stroking her hair and murmuring her name. Red's mother clearly cared a lot more than Red realized. When Ellis asked if she thought Red was in danger, the reply was a shrug.

There was nothing more to be gained here. "I will find her and make sure she's safe," Ellis said. "That I promise."

"Thank you." Red's mother was sobbing harder now. Ellis left her with the tailor. Bart and the boys had vanished but Dorothy was pacing about glowering. Ellis stroked her nose, thinking.

It took over an hour to search the town. Thanks to delivering flour, Ellis knew the streets and alleyways thoroughly. Everyone vanished once curfew set in so Ellis had to go around knocking on doors, hiding whenever a guard approached. No one he spoke to had seen Red. It was possible she was on the move and he'd simply missed her, but Ellis had a growing certainty that Red was no longer in town. Perhaps she had gone to see Granny again, after all. Dorothy was plodding now and Ellis was weighing up whether to take her back to the mill or carry on when he heard voices. They were coming from the fountain – and he recognized them.

"...blaming everything on Sabine." So this was where Bart and his gang had slunk off to. Ellis was surprised a guard hadn't already sent them on their way – they were hardly being subtle about defying the curfew. "It's wrong. A filthy lie. They've got so caught up with her that they're missing what's right under their noses. How much clearer does it need to be? She's old and she's strange and she doesn't even like people!"

Granny. Ellis edged as close as he could without revealing himself, rubbing Dorothy's side and hoping she didn't give them away.

Bart was still speaking. "I don't believe the wolf comes from the town. I think that's what they want us to believe, to keep us scared."

One of the others kicked a pile of snow. "On the hunt, we were men. Today, we're children. Expected to go home and let them do everything."

"Maybe we should take control ourselves," Bart said slowly. "We could pay the old woman a visit. See what she'll confess to when there's a little pressure."

Ellis cursed, hoisting Dorothy around and disappearing the way he'd come. Forget finding Red. Granny needed help – urgently. If he hurried, really hurried, he'd make it to her cottage well before the boys. He thought he remembered the way.

But he wouldn't be doing it on horseback. Dorothy needed resting. But where? There was no time to take her to the mill.

Then Ellis saw Stephen, scurrying towards him, head bent.

"Hey!" he called.

Stephen looked up. He hovered where he was a moment, then turned and doubled back on himself. Ellis scooped snow off the top of a barrel and rolled a snowball. It exploded on the back of Stephen's head. Stephen yelped and stopped, and Ellis caught him up.

"I need a favour."

Stephen didn't meet his eyes. "I'm not supposed to talk to you any more. I have to get home. Shouldn't even be out."

Ellis thrust Dorothy's reins in his hand. "I need you to look after Dorothy. Call it a last act of friendship. I won't ask anything of you again or even speak to you if that's what you want."

"Ellis, it isn't like that," murmured Stephen. "I never wanted to cut you out, but it was either you or me—"

"I don't care. I have something I need to do, and I need to do it now. Will you take her?"

Gingerly, his old friend took the reins. Once upon a time Stephen would have offered to help but Ellis wasn't surprised that he didn't. Just another person who wasn't who Ellis had thought he was.

"You rest up," he whispered in Dorothy's ear. Then he ran towards the forest.

RED

She was aware of everything. The soft hush of the breeze. Snowflakes drifting lazily. The light movement of mice and other small animals. Something that smelled like rotting meat, cutting through the otherwise fresh air. The blackness enveloping her was impenetrable. Red had walked the forest heaps of times in the dark. She knew the way to Granny's in her sleep. Yet today she felt stifled, even trapped.

I should have come earlier, Red thought. *Why did I waste all that time wandering by the river?*

Her toe nudged something solid. Red crashed over. Something sharp dug into her shin. Red's feet cycled round as she tried to free herself from its grip. Then suddenly she was rolling downwards, stones digging into her side and twigs catching in her hair. She came to a halt at the bottom of the slope and sat winded for a moment, breathing heavily.

Then it came. Nearby. A low, unmistakable howl.

Red was on her feet in a shot and running, tearing through long grass and bushes and leaping over logs. She fought her way to higher ground. Underfoot it became smoother and Red knew she'd found the path her mother was always imploring her to stick to. As though the wolf cared about such things! Right as the thought raced through her head the howl sounded again – this time closer.

Red spun, expecting a huge monster to hurtle from the bushes and bowl her down. Her cape caught on a branch and tore. Red pulled free and ran as she'd never run before. Granny's cottage took her by surprise and with a final burst of speed Red made it to the door and near fell inside. With her boot she kicked it shut.

Red lay where she was for a moment, disorientated and gasping for breath. Never before had she felt the forest was her enemy. She was going mad. Or maybe she was finally seeing things the way everyone else did.

She clambered up, ignoring the stitch in her side. Her palm was wet, but Red couldn't tell where she was bleeding from, or even if the cut was a bad one. She stepped forwards, and almost slipped. A puddle. What was a puddle doing on Granny's floor? Melted snow, probably. Granny must have gone out and returned recently. There was faint light in the gap under the curtain which separated her bedroom from the parlour.

"Granny?" called Red. "It's me. Are you all right?"

No reply. Had Granny fallen asleep? Her eyes growing accustomed to the gloom, Red pushed the curtain back. The light came from a candle on the windowsill. Granny lay hunched under the quilt, almost hidden apart from her bed cap. Red was about to call out again when she spotted another puddle. Only this one she could actually make out. And it was dark. She dipped her finger in it and sniffed.

Blood.

The wetness on her hand hadn't been from a cut at all.

And neither had the puddle she had almost slipped in been melted snow.

Something else was on the floor too, a trail leading to Granny's bed. Clumps of fur. Dark fur. It smelled different in here, too. More ... earthy. The stool by Granny's bed was overturned. Her boots lay on their sides, at opposite ends of the room. And was the bed at a funny angle?

Granny stirred and grunted. Red snapped to life.

"Granny! Are you hurt?" She was at the bedside in an instant. Granny made a growling noise, turning round. She muttered something. Red couldn't make out the words, but Granny's voice ... it was deep. Too deep. Granny's eyes peeked out from under the quilt, gleaming big in the half-light. Too big. She shifted again. Hands snaked out from beneath the quilt, but they did not look like Granny's. Too large. Then Granny moved, and the quilt rolled away, exposing cheeks that were not skin but fur, and Granny's smile was teeth, all teeth.

ELLIS

A scream pierced the air. Ellis froze. *Red.* He ran. He had no plan and no weapons. And he wasn't close. The scream had been distant, from deep within the forest. He prayed he wasn't too late.

The torch he'd grabbed from Stephen's house picked out the path. His chest rattled. His fingertips were ice. He was more afraid than he'd ever been but also more determined.

Red, he thought. *Red, Red, Red.*

He reached Granny's cottage. Had the scream come from there? Ellis crashed through the open door, shouting Red's and Granny's names. Immediately he saw blood, and fur. In the bedroom it was worse. Signs of a struggle were everywhere.

The bed was empty. And on it lay Red's cape.

Almost torn in half.

"Red! Granny! Where are you?"

No one answered. Had they fled – was that why the front door was open? Ellis searched for something to arm himself with, then decided there was no point. Whatever was out there – a wolf, a phantom or a human attacker – he'd be on the ground before even having the chance to strike.

He left the cottage and plunged into the trees, leaving the path.

"Red! Granny!"

A howl answered him. Ellis cursed. That had been no human. There really was a wolf!

And it would hunt him down in no time. . .

Ellis opened his mouth to shout for Red and Granny again. Then he felt it. A presence. He stared ahead, at the stream in front of him, reflecting the full moon. Then, slowly, he turned.

Not ten feet away stood the old wolf. It was bleeding, a couple of chunks of fur missing from its side. Up close its reddish eyes were more of a chestnut brown, and huge. Even huger were its sharp, hungry jaws.

Their eyes locked. Even injured, Ellis knew the wolf would overpower him. *I'm sorry, Red,* he thought. He waited for it to pounce. But the wolf stayed put. Then, deliberately, it glanced backwards.

A second wolf slunk through the trees. In an instant Ellis could tell this one was young and fit and powerful. Its fur was thick and midnight black. But its eyes were not red.

They were deep hazel, flecked with gold.

Red's eyes.

RED

The forest was loud. And it smelled. So strong. Nothing had colour, but Red did not need colour to guide her any more. She was all instinct. Red the girl was distant, someone she sensed, but could not touch. She bounded after Granny-wolf in her new, lithe body. A scent drew her. Prey. She thrust her head back and howled.

Granny stopped ahead. Her ears – one bitten almost in half – twitched. Red's hunger was burning now, a magnetism that could not be resisted. Her prey would not escape this time. Especially not with Granny-wolf injured and weak. She would hunt it down and sink her teeth into flesh and she and Granny would feast.

Then she saw it. This prey was bigger than the last one she had snared. A human boy, holding fire. Red snarled, and would have pounced, but Granny stopped her with a warning growl.

No. Her voice echoed in Red's head.

I am hungry, Red answered. *You are hungry. Let me kill it.*

No.

The human boy stood rooted still. He should be running if he wanted to live. Stupid human boy.

I must kill it!

No.

The boy crouched down. He lay the fire on the grass, then extended a shaking hand.

"Red?"

The word was an arrow piercing her heart. She knew this word. It meant something. The human boy meant something. There was a pull deep inside her, a warm feeling of belonging. . .

"It's you." The boy's voice wobbled. "Red. You're a. . . Is that Granny? Are you both. . ."

Memories. She was outside a building she somehow knew was named a mill. There were chickens. She had gobbled them down once before. Carried several into the trees for Granny. They had not sated her hunger, but they were easy pickings so she had returned. Then the human boy appeared. This human boy. Prey. She had dived for the kill, slamming him into the wall. Her jaws shot open, poised to deliver the death blow. . .

Then a voice had shrieked in her head. Not Granny-wolf but girl-Red.

No. I can't hurt him. I won't hurt him. Ellis.

Her hunger was immense. Every fibre of her being screamed for her to devour the unconscious human boy. But girl-Red overpowered wolf-Red. She seized the chickens instead, and ran.

The next time she had encountered the girls, the stupid ones who went to the edge of the trees. She had watched from a bush, determining which was easier prey. One was closer; the other sat in a horse-drawn contraption. Something she did not understand warned her not to go for the standing girl. So she pounced upon the other. She would have killed her had the standing girl not run at her, wielding some kind of weapon.

Next had been the man. He had not taken much hunting because he was making so much noise. But other men had been near, forcing her to flee again. By this time she had been feeling weak she was so ravenous. Granny-wolf was even weaker, unable now to hunt at all.

So the fourth time, when prey presented itself, she had not failed. The woman had been dispatched quickly. She and Granny-wolf had fed well that night.

The boy said that word again. "Red."

The wolf in Red faded. Her mind was once again human, within her four-legged body. She wanted to say Ellis's name but all that came out was a howl. Ellis flinched, and hopped back.

Granny's voice spoke in her head.

Red. You are doing well. I know you can control yourself. Remember what I've taught you.

It all came back to Red – the nights she had been a wolf, Granny had taught her how to hunt, and move with stealth. Red had been frightened the first time she had transformed, but the wolf she'd sensed was Granny had explained everything.

It will take some time before you remember who you are and what you can do. It was the same for me, when my grandmother instructed me in the ways of the wolf. You may recall snatches but believe them to be dreams, or you may wake up feeling unusually tired. Once your wolf-self is awoken, it takes time to fully adjust...

I don't want to attack people! Red had sobbed. *I don't want to be a monster!*

You are not a monster, Red. It is who you are, and who I am, and as natural as breathing. For a long time I have been able to feed myself from the forest, but not any more. If you and I do not seek new prey, we cannot survive.

All those times Red had pictured the attacks were not her imagination; they were memories. And all those times she had woken up scratched and achy were not fitful sleep; they were from bounding through the forest and its sharp brambles.

I am the wolf, thought Red. *Not a phantom. Not a vengeful human. Me.*

ELLIS

Red – and it was Red, he knew it with utmost certainty – paced as
though in pain. The other wolf – Granny – stood still, watching.

Ellis's knees knocked. His heart had never hammered this fast.

"You're a ... werewolf. You're both werewolves." Or were
they? There was a full moon tonight but there hadn't been the night
of the other attacks. But there was no time to work that out now. He
glanced at Granny. "Were you the wolf five years ago?"

Granny bared her teeth. Ellis took another deep breath.

"You transform after dark. Red was ... using the room in the old tavern to ... transform back?" he guessed. "And you have no memory? Protecting Granny the night of the hunt was instinct, wasn't it? You sensed it was her. I know you cannot answer me, but ... you can understand, can't you?"

Granny inclined her head. Red was shaking and circling, full of nervous energy. Perhaps she couldn't properly control herself, if the transformation was new?

His mind raced forwards. "You'll attack again. You can't not. One day they will catch you. Find out what you really are." His breath was fog in front of him. "And then..."

Red made a whimpering noise. Granny bent her head, telling him she knew the risks, and why did he think she'd withdrawn from town to live in the forest? Ellis's head was still screaming *run*, not that he would get far on shaking legs. The wolves hadn't attacked him yet. But they must want to. He was not safe yet.

Although... "You could have killed me that night, Red. Yet you chose not to ... is that right?" She whimpered again. He tried to picture Red-the-girl in front of him, in her billowing cape. "I don't want anything bad to happen to you either. I think you know that you matter a lot to me. Everything I said last night about little cottages and running away was not entirely a joke. But you need to go more than I do. Both of you." He pulled the bag of gold Lady

Katherine had given him from where he had tied it to his belt. It had bounced against his thigh the whole run to Granny's cottage and he'd almost tossed it away. Now he was glad he hadn't.

"I want you to have this." His voice wobbled even more as he dangled the bag in front of the wolves. "Why I have it is a long story, but there is a lot of money inside. Enough for you to escape, and keep your secret."

Red whined. Ellis so badly wished she could speak. She moved in a circle, then closed the space between them. Ellis sucked in a breath, just about managing not to pull back. Red brushed her head against his side. Unexpected tears gathered in his eyes. Very tentatively, he put a hand on Red's neck.

"I mean it. Your life means more to me than money."

Red didn't move. Ellis dropped the bag and kicked it away from him.

"Go on. If you don't take it, I'll just leave it there."

Granny came over and gathered the bag in her jaws. She butted her granddaughter with her head. Ellis looked at Red.

"Goodbye, then. Live a good life, Red."

She looked back at him. Maybe it was his imagination – could wolves even cry? – but her eyes looked wet.

"Don't worry about your mother. I'll. . . I don't know what I'll say, but I will make it all right. She loves you more than you think. Someday I will come and find you. I'll repair your cape, bring it with me. You wouldn't be you without it." He tried a smile. "Little Red Riding Hood."

She pressed her face against him again. Then her ears pricked up. Granny was alert too, head turned to the direction of the path.

"Is that the boys?" Ellis whispered. "They are why I came here, to warn you. They're angry, and— Never mind. Go. Now. And quickly."

Red stayed where she was. Then she ran, Granny alongside her, vanishing into the night. Ellis's legs gave out, and he sank down in the snow, next to the dying light of his torch.

Everything in his head was tangled. But one important thing he did know, whatever happened next.

Red and Granny's secret was safe. And so, now, was Aramor.

SABINE

She did not know how long she had sat hugging her knees to her chest, face pressed against the by now fusty-smelling skirt of her gown. Night had passed – a very uncomfortable night, with Sabine curled up on a hard straw mattress trying to distract herself from how cold and miserable she felt by counting until she fell asleep. Now it must be sometime in the afternoon, although it was hard to tell without any natural light.

Food had been provided, but otherwise Sabine felt she'd been forgotten. She yearned to hear what was going on.

It was much later – perhaps evening – by the time keys clinked outside. A guard took her to the room she had been questioned in yesterday. Her father stood by the window, but he did not look as strident as he had before.

Sabine soon saw why. Lord Josiah was seated at the table. "Sit," he instructed

Sabine looked at him. There were so many things she was tempted to scream – that a man like him could never understand what it was like to be a girl like her, and maybe if he'd been a more attentive governor everyone wouldn't hate each other so much. But instead, she did as he said, keeping her head bowed.

Lord Josiah questioned her for some minutes, all the same things as she had been asked by her father and the guards. The Woodcutter only spoke when he was done.

"Red was seen entering our house yesterday shortly before it was searched."

Sabine waited.

"You say you dislike each other. Do you believe that feud would be enough for her to plant those things on you?"

Sabine's head shot up. He believed her now? Or was this some kind of trick? She stayed silent. Maybe there was a way to get out of this without blaming other people. She did not feel she could take any more lies.

Lord Josiah made an impatient noise. "This girl's grandmother has been killed by the wolf. Fur and blood were found in her cottage."

Sabine's first thought was how devastated Red would be. She adored her granny. Sabine's second thought was *I threatened this woman*. She hadn't for a moment imagined anything bad would really happen.

"What does Red say?" she asked in a low voice.

"Red has fled town," said her father. "No one has seen her since yesterday afternoon. Either that or she was attacked too. We did send a search party into the forest but there is no sign of her."

"Why would she run away?" Lord Josiah twisted the blocky gold ring on his forefinger round. "Her mother has no idea. And nobody else really knows her, so we have little insight into her motives."

Sabine found her voice. "You could try Ellis. They were friends."

His lordship's eyebrows drew upwards. "Ellis?"

"The miller's son. He was the first person attacked—"

"I know who Ellis Miller is, thank you," Josiah snapped, and Sabine wondered if she was missing something.

The door opened, and the captain of the guard joined them. More questions followed. Sabine realized that the men were having doubts about her. Now they seemed to suspect that Red had fled town after planting the charms and herbs on Sabine to buy herself time. Even though Sabine's heart leapt at the prospect of escape, she couldn't help but think how pitiful it was that they were desperate to believe such nonsense, just because Red fitted their idea of the kind of person who would do mad, unexplained things. Perhaps her brain had rotted after a day in the cell, but this made Sabine . . . angry.

Outside, there was a sudden commotion. A female voice, cross and commanding, and a quieter man. Lord Josiah broke off mid-sentence. The door opened. A harassed-looking guard appeared.

"Lord Josiah, Lady Katherine is here with Doctor Ambrose, and, begging your pardon, she is quite irate and requests to see you—"

"I believe the word I used was *demand*," snapped Lady Katherine. Lord Josiah's nose twitched, as though he was not sure quite how to deal with his wife in this mood. Sabine expected him to tell the guard he was busy, but instead he rose.

"We will reconvene another time."

Sabine caught a glimpse of Katherine as Lord Josiah walked

out. She stood tall, arms crossed, suddenly imposing, the kind of person others listened to. She gave Sabine a tiny nod before the door swung shut.

The guard who escorted Sabine back to the cell was more courteous than he had been the day before. Sabine settled on the mattress and thought about the last hour. She couldn't allow herself too much hope. But if by some miracle she was allowed to walk, she would, Sabine determined, live a better life.

What *better* meant she had to decide, but she had another long night to work that out. A second chance – if she got one – deserved to be taken properly. Even if it had been given to her, unintentionally, by the girl she had spent years hating.

EPILOGUE

Three years later

The river trickled gently over the soft sandy bed, clear enough for Red to see her toes. She dug them into the sand, watching as they vanished.

"I could do this all day." She sighed. The skies above her were bright and cloudless, the early summer sun warming her shoulders. Lush meadows stretched as far as she could see, mostly full of golden corn. The only sounds were the tweets of birds and hum from crickets.

Back at the cottage Granny would be sitting in her wicker chair, gazing out upon the forest which their little vegetable patch bordered. She spent a lot of her time watching the trees these days, though rarely alone – there were many older folk in Lulmor who kept each other company. It had taken three years but, Red thought, she and Granny were finally accepted. They had always been welcomed, but belonging was different. Red liked it. No one here knew exactly where they had come from or even cared. And Red had come to enjoy the work she did at the farm. The farmer had at first been sceptical of employing a girl as a hand, even one so tall and strong, but Red had won him over with her knack with the animals and love of the outdoors, even when the weather was at its worst. Tough Aramor winters made turning out on dark, chilly early mornings child's play.

Yes, thought Red, Lulmor suited both her and Granny. Especially the large, next-to-wild forest, which few townsfolk bothered to explore or even enter, except to fell trees or sometimes pick berries. At night, it hummed with life, and hunting was easy. Neither Red nor Granny had need to seek human prey.

Her mind drifted to Aramor. Her memory of fleeing town, or even how that had come about, was patchy. One moment she had been creeping into Granny's bedroom, almost blinded by fear. The next, she was awakening in an empty and unfamiliar barn, unable to recall much other than running, running, running. Granny had hugged her.

"Red, my love, I can explain everything. I didn't want to talk about this until you had greater control of yourself and could remember, but events have forced my hand."

Werewolf. Red smiled, watching the water swirled around her ankle. Such a scary word at first, much like *witch.* Her transformations were not strictly linked to the moon and its cycles, but there was not another name for what she and Granny were, so werewolf would have to do.

Adjusting had been tough. For what felt a long time she had been angry and resentful. Wrapping her head around everything was a real challenge – even little things, like hearing that Granny had often shadowed Red on her night-time walks through the forest in wolf form, mindful of her granddaughter's safety.

But now the ways of the wolf were as much part of her as kneading dough and shaping pies had once been. More, because it was natural. Who she was. And now that she could hunt without hurting humans, and control herself, she almost welcomed it. There was something very freeing about bounding through the trees, heightened senses tingling, caring only for the moment. Granny rarely joined her. She was wary after being attacked by what must have been the last of the grey wolves that final night in Aramor, so Red hunted for her too.

A voice called, "Grace?"

Red turned to see Agnes, a girl a few years older than her, who worked in the dairy.

"Come and paddle!" she called. "The water is so warm."

"I would love to, but I am meeting John for a walk."

"A walk?" Red raised her eyebrows, enjoying Agnes's blush. Once upon a time she could not imagine joking with a female friend like this.

"Yes, a walk," retorted Agnes. "Never mind that. Someone is asking around for you and I thought you should know."

Instantly Red was alert. "What kind of person?"

"Some kind of noble. Very finely dressed. His horse is fine too. Asked about your grandmother, too. He knows your name but also said you might call yourself Red."

Red stuffed her feet into her boots, grabbing her hat and apron from the bank. Panic filled her. The stranger could only have come from Aramor. But why would he be searching for her? And who could it be? The only man she could think of who could be described as noble was Lord Josiah, and surely it wasn't him.

Perhaps what Agnes considered to be finely dressed was not what she would. Lulmor villagers were simple folk.

"Thanks, Agnes."

Agnes followed as she hurried up the hill. "Do you want us to get him to leave? No one told him anything. If you need protection, speak up. We are all your friends here, Grace."

"I'll get a look at him first," replied Red. Agnes told her that the mystery man had taken a room at the inn, so, pulling her straw hat as low as she could, Red went there. It surprised her how nervous she felt, although she knew in all likelihood this man would not even recognize her. She spotted him immediately – the innkeeper had dragged benches outside, and several folk sat eating and drinking in the sunshine. Agnes had not been exaggerating when she said he looked fine – too fine for somewhere like this. Annoyingly, his hat shadowed his face.

Courage, she told herself. The stranger did not so much as look up when she approached. She gave him a furtive look as she passed. He was younger than she'd imagined from Agnes's description. Much younger. Her age, perhaps. His hands drew her attention. They did not quite fit with his clothing. Working hands. Broad, flat thumbs. . .

Red's chest went tight. "Ellis?"

The young man looked up. It was him, older, but otherwise unchanged. He stood, staring as though he couldn't believe his eyes.

"Red?"

"People know me as Grace here."

They looked at each other a moment more. Then they were hugging, and the strangeness melted away. Red pulled back, laughing.

"I didn't think I would ever see you again."

"It is not easy to find someone when the only clue you have as to her whereabouts is that she will probably live close to a forest." Ellis grinned. "I can't believe you're really here. Do you know how long I have been searching?"

"Please don't say three years."

"Not quite that, and not constantly, but I wasn't going to stop until I found you. I have your cape. I did promise to return it."

"I left Little Red Riding Hood in Aramor. She feels like a fairy tale now. But thank you." Red became aware that the other drinkers were watching with great curiosity. "Let's walk."

She took him down to the river. She couldn't get over how grand he looked! Red became very conscious of her plain gown, not entirely clean, and sun-brown, freckled skin.

"You feel familiar and unknown at the same time," she said. "I would never have recognized you. Especially without the sling!"

Ellis removed his hat. His hair stood up, and that made her feel a little better.

"I will probably be the lord of Aramor someday." He seemed embarrassed. "Fine clothes are something I have to get used to. It is a long story," he said, at Red's exclamation. "It was difficult at first. I was very angry with everyone. Things are better now. I've forgiven my parents. The Millers, that is. They did raise me. They do care. And my brothers are still my brothers. I can't turn my back on them. My father – Lord Josiah, that is – I don't see much of, but Katherine is like a mother to me. She has become a lot more involved with governing. People complain it is not her place, but I think secretly they are relieved that Aramor is not neglected any more." He sidled her a glance. "They believe you to be responsible for what happened. Not the truth, but they are convinced you are some kind of witch and the wolf was a phantom. The things Sabine said, you vanishing and the attacks abruptly stopping. . ."

"I *was* responsible." Red glanced down. "What I did is something I'll always be sorry for. Even if I couldn't help myself." She looked up again. "How is my mother?"

"Very well. She is married to the tailor now. She knows I've been looking for you and sends her love."

"What about Sabine?"

Ellis hesitated. "Sabine is . . . Sabine. But I did not come to talk about her."

They stopped walking. Ellis inhaled, taking in the view.

"You are happy here?"

"I am. So is Granny." She folded her hands in front of her, suddenly shy. "Granny tells me we owe this to you. So thanks. I don't remember that night. Ellis, I am so sorry I attacked you."

"You could have killed me, Red, but didn't. That's what matters most. My arm is fine now."

"All the same, I am sorry."

"I didn't come for an apology."

"Why did you come, then?"

"Because I think about you all the time," said Ellis softly.

"I used to think about you all the time too," Red blurted. "Before we knew each other, when you only had eyes for Martha. I thought you were so handsome. But I never imagined you'd even speak to me. I don't know why I'm saying this now. I think I'm nervous."

He took her hands lightly, letting her know she could pull away if she wanted to. Red didn't. Her heart was thumping. Only this time she liked how it felt.

Ellis leaned forwards. So did Red. Their noses brushed. For a moment they stayed where they were, gazing at each other. Then their lips met. The kiss was sweet and warming and made Red feel light inside.

"It doesn't put you off, knowing you are kissing a werewolf?" she asked, when they pulled apart.

"All I was thinking about was kissing *you*." His smile was shy. "Tell me about the last three years. We have a lot to catch up on."

". . .and from that day on, the wolf vanished, never to be seen again. Aramor lived happily ever after."

The feverish child's eyes were closed. At some point during the story – which had become much lengthier than the doctor had intended – he had fallen asleep. Good. The doctor rose, straightening her gown. She felt weary, having been on her feet since daybreak, but it was the right kind of tiredness. She went downstairs and exchanged a few words with the parents, reassuring them that the child's fever should break by morning.

"If it has not, I will return. Here is a healing draught. It will help him feel more comfortable."

The parents thanked her profusely. She was followed outside by the child's sister, a gangly girl of about twelve.

"I have never heard of a lady doctor before," she said.

"Lady doctor in training, to accurate," said Sabine archly. "And your brother had never heard of the wolf of Aramor before. I was obsessed with it when I was your age."

"Why?"

She paused by her horse. "I suppose because I was strange and I was drawn to other things that were strange."

"Are you still strange?"

"Most people believe a female physician is strange." The girl was still looking attentive, so Sabine added, "I was lucky. A very admirable lady helped me when I was at my lowest and her physician agreed to let me apprentice him. He always did have a soft spot for me."

"Your family let you?"

"Not exactly. That is another long story, but let's just say I do not have much to do with them any more."

The girl digested this. "It is a kind of magic, isn't it? Healing people?"

Sabine felt the sides of her mouth twitch. "You could say that."

The girl gave her a sudden grin, then ran inside. Sabine mounted her horse, and trotted back in the direction of Aramor, in no great rush for the five miles to pass. Her route took her by the forest edge. She had not been inside since events three years ago, but she often passed near. It felt like she owed everyone that, including herself.

Her patient today saw the wolf as a legend, not something that had ever been real. Sometimes it seemed that way to Sabine, too. Her father remained convinced that the wolf was one of the towns-folk, and every so often made attempts to find out who it was, but fewer and fewer people believed that now. The whispers of witch-craft surrounding Sabine would never die, but Red had carried the worst of those away with her.

Sabine did not believe the attacks had been a work of magic, and nor did she believe Red was the culprit, but she was too busy to chase the truth. She had a sneaking suspicion Ellis knew. There was something in the way he said the word *wolf* that betrayed it, on the few occasions they spoke.

She suspected that wherever she was, Red knew too.

Sabine thought about Red often. She wondered what she was doing, if she was alive, and what Red would make of her now, and whether they might even get along. Probably not. Sabine had not completely changed, though being occupied and challenged made a huge difference to how she felt about Aramor and herself.

Perhaps, Sabine thought, she would tell her next child patient about the wolf too. Those events had made her who she was, after all. Perhaps the boy today would pass the story down to his children, and then his children to theirs. It deserved to be remembered, even if the ending remained a mystery. The legend of the big bad wolf – and Little Red Riding Hood.

ACKNOWLEDGEMENTS

There are a number of people I'd like to thank for their help with this book, and support leading up to it.

Firstly, a huge thanks to my agent, Lydia Silver, for all her invaluable support and encouragement, and her flexibility in seeking out opportunities for me. No less of a big thanks go to my editors, Yasmin Morrissey, for entrusting me with bringing Red to life, and everything at the beginning of this project, and then to Ruth Bennett for picking up the mantle. Thanks also to everyone else at Scholastic whose hard work has brought this book to the shelves: Liam Drane for such an atmospheric front cover, Pete Matthews for a sharp proofread, and everyone whose contributions will come after I've penned this. Thank you!

Finally, thanks to everyone who may not have had direct input in this book, but whose support of my writing over the last few years and whose friendship have meant a lot. I know I get total tunnel vision with writing and this can get very boring very quickly, so thanks for putting up with me! In no particular order: my fellow denizens of the Next Circle, for sharing their knowledge and all the general chit-chat that has kept me sane. Grace, for all the writing chat and occasional vents. The Kalettes, Nina and Melanie, for all the WhatsApps and celebrating my wins with me. And then my family: my mum, Sheila, who is my biggest supporter, and my dad, David, and brother Luke for slightly less hands-on but no less appreciated cheerleading. My mother-in-law, Rosemary, for ensuring that the little people were in nursery, without which meeting my deadline would have been impossible. Said little people, for attending said nursery. Finally, my husband Hugh, for being there, and giving me space to write, with (for this book, anyway…) minimal interruptions.

Gushing is, alas, not one of my skills, but I really do appreciate everything. Thank you, everyone!

Have you read?

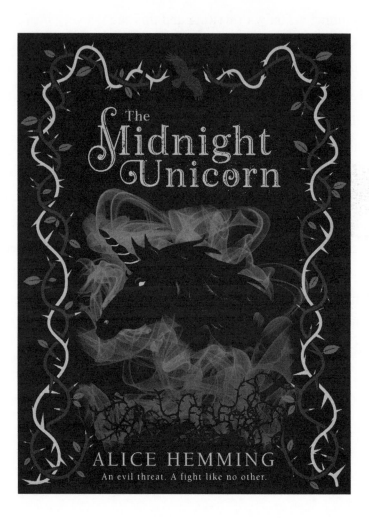

Have you read?

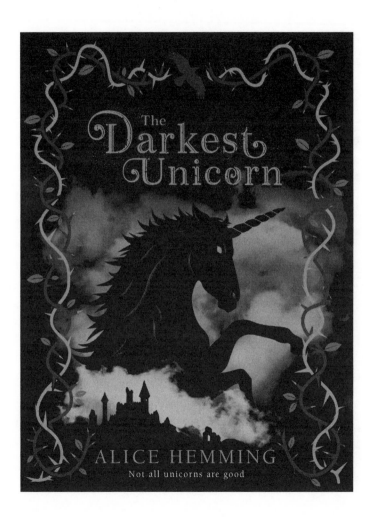

The Darkest Unicorn

ALICE HEMMING

Not all unicorns are good

Have you read?

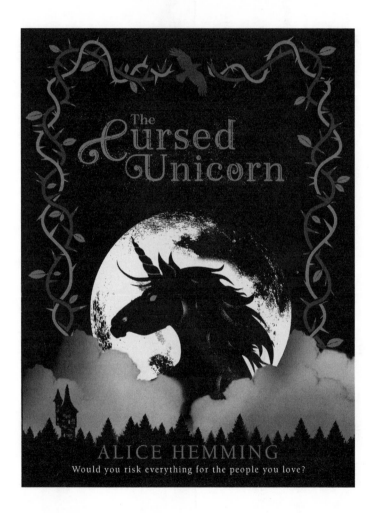